LAFITTE
LIVES

LAFITTE LIVES

CHRISTI KEATING SUMICH

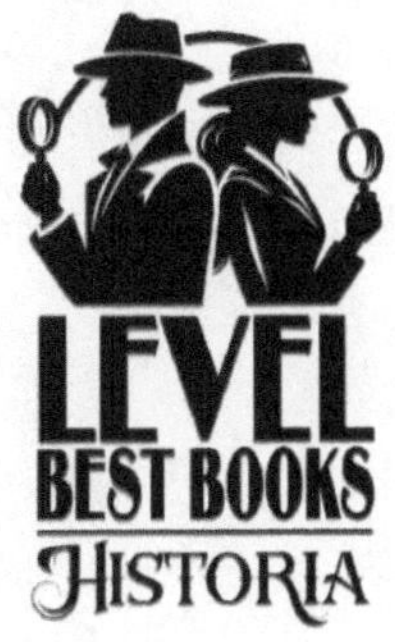

First published by Level Best Books/Historia 2026

This novel is entirely a work of fiction. The names, characters, and incidents portrayed in it are the work of the author's imagination. Any resemblance to actual persons, living or dead, events, or localities is entirely coincidental.

Christi Keating Sumich asserts the moral right to be identified as the author of this work.

First edition

ISBN: 979-8-89820-165-4

Cover art by Level Best Designs

This book was professionally typeset on Reedsy.
Find out more at reedsy.com

To Leni—you always believed I could.

"A short life and a merry one at that!"

—A pirate's motto,
attributed to Bartholomew Roberts,
a.k.a. Black Bart

Praise for Lafitte Lives

"Lafitte Lives is a ripping good pirate yarn surrounded by a touching story of family heartbreak and healing, all wrapped up in a tantalizing mystery. Steeped in rich period detail, it's a tale filled with secrets and surprises readers won't see coming. After all, never trust a pirate!"—**J.R. Sanders**, author of the Shamus Award-winning Nate Ross series

"Lafitte Lives is an incredible, unforgettable adventure from start to finish. Christi Keating Sumich brings history and mystery vividly to life in this expertly crafted novel. A true treasure for any reader."—**Nicole Beauchamp**, author of *Haunted French Quarter Hotels*

"In August 1831, Tobias Whitney, Sexton—caretaker—of St. Louis Cemetery No. 2 in New Orleans, makes a startling discovery. Hidden in a hollow space in a mausoleum is the diary of Dominique You—half-brother of Jean Lafitte. The diary offers a first-hand account of Lafitte's life after his reported death in 1823. As the title implies, *Lafitte Lives.* Find a comfortable seat, grab your favorite beverage, and let your imagination loose as Christi Keating Sumich delivers an engaging tale of the infamous pirate and patriot who may—or may not—have faded into the swamps and bayous of south Louisiana."—**Michael Rigg**, author of the New Orleans-based medicolegal thriller, *Voices of the Elysian Fields*

Chapter One

New Orleans

August 1831

The worst part of the job was the smell. A decaying human body releases an oddly distinct scent. It is a horrid mixture of rotten eggs and cabbage, mothballs, feces, and an off-putting garlic-like odor, depending upon the gases released at each stage of decomposition. Being an observant sort of chap, Tobias Whitney was well-versed in the stink of human decay. He could discern how far along a body was in the process of decomposition based on the particular aroma the tomb emitted. The hot, humid summer months were the worst. So much rotting flesh in one place combined to produce a nauseating medley of noxious aromas so foul that even Tobias, who spent his days in the cemetery, felt his stomach churn as he inhaled the soupy air.

Tobias had smelled foul odors before. Anyone who lived in New Orleans long enough had. At this time of year, the privy behind his cottage was the stuff of nightmares. But a body could get used to almost anything. Tobias had taught himself to focus instead on the delicate, honeyed scent of the flowering sweet olive bushes planted in the courtyards of homes all through the Vieux Carré, or the French Quarter as the Americans called it, for the express purpose of making the stench of so many privies in such close proximity more bearable.

Similar aforethought had gone into the landscaping at St. Louis Cemetery No. 2, where Tobias had been sexton for nearly three years. Unfortunately, the ethereal scent of fragrant flowering bushes and trees planted along the perimeter and throughout the cemetery grounds was far too subtle to mask the stink. It invaded his nose and marched its way down to his mouth. He let out a breath he'd been holding and put his sleeve against his nose as he inhaled. He spat to rid himself of the foul taste. Both actions proved futile. It was no wonder. The body interred within the tomb he was cleaning had been laid to rest less than a year before, and the tomb's inhabitant to his right was an even fresher burial.

As sexton, he was responsible for maintaining the cemetery. Some months were busier than others, and August was keeping him at sixes and sevens, between all the yellow fever burials and the rains making a mess of the cemetery pathways. The cemetery had flooded recently, causing the crushed oyster-shell gravel to flow in rivulets between the above-ground tombs and collect in the lowest spot. Unfortunately, the lowest spot was the site of a recently built tomb.

Above-ground burials were the custom here, in part because of French and Spanish colonists who settled in New Orleans, and for more practical reasons. Guthrie Toups, the octogenarian and retired sexton whom Tobias replaced, had explained the tomb burials most colorfully.

"These tombs are your bosom friend." He had waved his gnarled hand about, indicating the structures surrounding him, as he shuffled through the cemetery with Tobias on one of his final days on the job. "Smell like shite in summer but keep the floaters pinned down." When Tobias failed to comment, Guthrie explained.

"Used to be, I worked at St. Peter Street Cemetery. All those souls went right in the ground. Two times I recall the rainwaters floodin' the place somethin' fierce. Coffins poppin' up like gophers in springtime. Some washed down the street, right up to folks' houses. When the lids came off, now that was a sight!" A shudder wracked Guthrie's gaunt frame, rippling through his threadbare coat. "Took us weeks to round up the coffins. And then to find out who belonged where! Can't put a body back in a hole when you don't know who he is and which hole is his." Guthrie shook his head. "Damn shame. You think lookin' after these tombs is trouble until you gotta put coffins back whence they should never have been disturbed."

Guthrie, who insisted on being called by his Christian name, had been gone from the cemetery for three years and from the world for two. Technically, he had never actually left St. Louis No. 2. He was enjoying his eternal rest, only one row of tombs over from where Tobias was currently toiling. Tobias considered whether Guthrie's take on the tradeoff of floaters versus smell was valid. "Shite" seemed far too euphemistic a way to describe what was assailing his senses. Had the souls surrounding him been laid to rest underground, there would be no discernible odor, even in the August heat. However, in addition to being above ground, the vaults in St. Louis No. 2 were not airtight, a necessity since exposure to the elements ensured the bodies would decompose in a timely fashion. Following the bevy of recent rainstorms that Tobias's wife referred to as "gully washers," an additional component of stale, stagnant water added to the cemetery effluvium.

"God's teeth!" declared Tobias in frustration, blowing out a breath of putrid air as he gazed at the dispersed gravel and mud piled up along the front and sides of the low-lying tomb. He continued raking, attempting to redistribute the mud-soaked mess along the paths separating the tombs. It was slow going. The puddles of standing water made the task challenging, and ultimately futile, as the next drenching rain would produce a similar mess. It was the sort of mindless labor that allowed a person time to think, though Tobias, as of late, preferred not to indulge his brain in aimless wandering. It inevitably led back to dark and painful places, so instead, he replaced his internal monologue with the voices of others, imagining how they might describe what he was presently seeing. It engaged his mind and distanced him from his thoughts. He often remembered the tombs' description, construction, and proper care, as Guthrie had first explained them to him. Even now, he could so vividly recall the old man's gravelly voice, brittle as the oyster shells underfoot.

"Needed these tombs, the city did. So many coming to New Orleans after Jefferson bought her up, and so many dying here. Nowhere to put a cemetery unless you want to go digging graves in a swamp!" His guffaw had echoed off the tombs.

When Guthrie first began his tutelage, Tobias doubted that he could absorb any new information, so clogged was his brain with other thoughts. Still, the details distracted him. He yearned to learn all he could about the cemetery and the tombs where the bodies rested. He was fascinated, he feared morbidly so, by the amount of sadness this one place contained within its walls. Tobias could sense the pain and loss felt by the loved ones of St. Louis No. 2's inhabitants, the heaviness of their collective grief threatening to crush him at times. He felt the familiar weight bearing down on him as he looked to his left, at the open tomb whose faceplate had been removed in anticipation of its next occupant, a newly deceased young woman who would be interred there tomorrow.

He took a moment to wipe his brow and allowed himself to be transported back to the first time he had viewed an open tomb.

"'Nother good thing 'bout tombs is how many bodies you can stuff inside," Guthrie had explained.

Tobias had to bend his lanky frame nearly horizontal to match the smaller man's permanently hunched posture, but by doing so, he could peer into the yawning darkness of the tomb, the unnatural stillness of the space raising the hairs on the back of his neck.

"This one's a single vault," Guthrie said. "When the first one of the family dies, we put him in there, coffin an' all. When the next one goes, that first one gets taken out of the coffin, and what remains of him gets put down in the caveau." He motioned to the dark, far reaches of the tomb, beyond and below, where the coffin was to be placed. "And so it goes 'til all the family is holed up in their tomb together. Here's hopin' they get along, cuz that's some close quarters!" Guthrie punctuated this with a cackle and a bony elbow to Tobias's ribs.

Guthrie's litany of anecdotes and explanations encompassed nearly every inch of St. Louis No. 2, including the perimeter walls of the cemetery itself, which were composed of stacked tombs that Guthrie had told him were called ovens.

"Cuz they look like ovens put one atop the other, and they heat up the bodies faster than cookin' 'em. That's a good thing when you need to get a lot of bodies buried all at once."

Guthrie's mood had turned somber, the smile leaving his face. "I can remember stacking bodies up in '24 and '25 when Yellow Jack came for so many, and there was nary a place to put 'em. Brought 'em to the cemetery by the cartload and dumped 'em right outside the cemetery gates, they did. Left those poor souls rotting in the sun, spreading their miasma over the city like a damned blanket. Least these ovens do the trick!"

The thought of yellow fever victims drew an involuntary shiver from Tobias, even this day, in the summer heat. Guthrie's voice in Tobias's head was sometimes the only company he had, not that he was complaining. Tobias craved solitude and was thankful to have this job. It paid a decent wage, enough for his family to live simply but comfortably, and perhaps best of all, it allowed him time to read.

He looked wistfully at his favorite reading bench, positioned in a particularly serene spot deep within the cemetery. The only sounds were the cooing of doves and the whining buzz of cicadas, so incessant this time of year as to become background noise. He felt the book's weight in his pocket, ever-present and beckoning him to take a break. His vision blurred. He wiped the sweat from his forehead yet again to prevent more of it from dripping into his eyes. He yearned to lose himself, if only for an hour or so, in the all-absorbing action-adventure stories he loved to read. For the past few years, escaping from the world had become necessary for his survival. Strange, he often mused, that spending his days surrounded by the dead was the only way he could cope with the living. Strange, but understandable, given what happened to him three years ago.

With a stubborn shake of his head, he said aloud, though no one else was around, "Not 'til I put this tomb to rights." Most families who owned vaults cared for them or paid the cemetery to do so, which at the very least required replastering and whitewashing the brick from time to time. Even though the cemetery was relatively new, consecrated only eight years ago, he could already see the ravages the subtropical climate wreaked on those tombs without a caretaker to maintain them.

"Orphan tombs, these ones are," Guthrie had said of the tombs left to crumble. "Got no livin' kin to care for 'em." He had shaken his head, the wiry gray hairs swaying with the movement. "A whole family gone and no one to remember them."

Tobias considered Guthrie's words as he raked. He looked over his shoulder at one such orphan tomb and read aloud the inscriptions on the faceplate, "*Constance Bulwark, born 1770, died 1824. Faithful wife, loving mother. 'Blessed are the pure in heart, for they shall see God.' Jeremiah Longstreet, born 1758, died 1827. Honest in labor, kind in spirit. May his soul rest in peace.*" To preserve the dignity of the inhabitants within, he cleaned and made minor repairs to the orphan tombs, though this was technically beyond the purview of his duties. "You'll not be forgotten," he promised them before turning his attention to the task at hand.

The tomb before him was not an orphan, as the cemetery was contracted to maintain it, but it might as well have been. Its inhabitant had received no visitors since he was laid to rest. Still, this particular tomb had intrigued Tobias since its construction last November. Like most in St. Louis No. 2, it was brick. While not as extravagant as some tombs Tobias had seen, he found the elevated parapet facade aesthetically pleasing in a simple, elegant way. However, the feature that most fascinated him was the nameplate commemorating the occupant, Dominique You. You was a Freemason, and his tomb prominently displayed the square and compass symbol on the top of the marble nameplate. Below the name was an inscription in French. Tobias was Irish and could not discern the writing, but he knew from the accounts he had read in the papers that the inscription was from Voltaire's *La Henriade*:

Intrepid warrior on land and sea
in a hundred combats showed his valor.
This new Bayard without reproach or fear
Could have witnessed the ending of the world without trembling.

Dominique You was an infamous privateer and, some say, the half-brother of the notorious pirate Jean Lafitte. Tobias had read all about the adventures of the two buccaneer brothers in the weekly broadsheets he purchased. Lafitte had been killed in 1823, the same year St. Louis No. 2 opened. But while Lafitte's whereabouts in the years before his death remained a mystery, Dominique You had lived out his final years in New Orleans, keeping a tavern and serving on the city council. He may have been a privateer, but he was also a war hero, having served valiantly as a gunner in the Battle of New Orleans, warding off a British invasion of the city by commanding a company of artillery composed of fellow pirates.

Stories about Dominique You and Jean Lafitte were legendary around New Orleans and made the adventure novels Tobias read pale in comparison. Tobias vividly recalled his excitement when Dominique You was buried right in front of where he was now standing. Although You died in a state of penury, the people of New Orleans did not forget his heroism. He was given a lavish funeral at the Cathedral of St. Louis, with full military honors, the likes of which the city had seldom seen. Throngs of mourners had followed the coffin to the cemetery. As the sexton, Tobias had been there to witness it all.

Many brought flowers to lay on his tomb, chrysanthemums or early-blooming camellias. Others brought magnolia leaves fashioned into wreaths or dried herbs tied into bouquets with bits of ribbon or string. There were also rosaries, little vials of holy water, candles, and voodoo tokens left on You's tomb. The mourners were as varied as the offerings they brought, well-dressed gentlefolk alongside the more common sort. They were all here for the same reason—to pay their respects to the man who helped save the city from the British fifteen years before.

Tobias had caught snippets of conversations all around the tomb. One, in particular, stayed with him. A group of rough-looking men, ill at ease in their mourning attire, had gathered at You's tomb.

One of the men said, "Sailed with him, I did. No finer man you'd want at your side when things turned hairy. I'd trust him with my life."

"As would I," his mate agreed. "Fought beside him, too. Best cannoneer

I ever saw. That's why the general said he'd storm the gates of hell with Dominique as his lieutenant!"

Tobias had been particularly impressed by this, considering General Andrew Jackson was now president of the United States. He watched as they poured out a slug of rum next to the tomb. It soaked into the gravel, leaving the scent of molasses and cloves lingering in the air like a final tribute. Tobias wondered with a shudder if these men were pirates themselves.

He'd had little time to dwell on it, as a Mason engaged him in conversation shortly after Tobias overheard this exchange. The man wore a fine wool suit, well cut and fashionable, with a frock coat that gracefully skimmed the back of the knees of his trousers. Tobias usually dressed in working man's attire for his days in the cemetery, loose-fitting tweed trousers and a jacket, although on this day, he wore a suit. It was one he used to wear as a shop owner before he became a cemetery sexton, though now he saved it for Sunday Mass. His wife, Mary Catherine, would have his hide if he showed up to work on the day of an interment of such prominence in anything less. Tobias felt rather nattily clad until he beheld the sartorial superiority of the man. The Freemason was eager to engage Tobias in conversation, and Tobias found this agreeable.

Funny how he spoke to almost no one these days, save his family and his close friend, the proprietor of his beloved bookshop, Chapter and Verse. Yet within the walls of the cemetery, he came back to life, if only for a short time. He felt at home here as much as he did in his cottage on Bienville Street. Though he knew precisely why this was, he found it disconcerting that he was more comfortable with mourners than with those unaffected by death.

"Not a business in New Orleans stayed open today. Everyone's here to pay their respects," the man told Tobias. "I suppose you heard the cannons fired for him?"

Tobias assured him that he had, and added that he'd also noticed the flags flown at half-mast.

The Mason nodded.

"He was a proud man, Dominique You." The man seemed uneasy in the cemetery, as Tobias found most people to be. He suspected the Mason's attempts to converse stemmed from a compelling need to fill the silence. Tobias noticed the man's unconscious fidgeting with the intricately designed collar that nestled just below the tie on his starched white linen shirt, an adornment indicating his status among the Brotherhood. He spoke with a French accent, and his eyes told the story of a man who accepted the inevitable tribulations of life while still finding joy in living. Tobias was envious of him.

"Had not a penny to his name at the end but did not tell a soul of his troubles." The man gazed wistfully at Dominique's tomb.

Tobias would have left him to his thoughts, but he continued. "We would have come to his aid, I can assure you of that. But Dominique was never one for charity. Tough old sailors rarely are. At least we could honor him in this way." With a tip of his top hat by his white-gloved hand, the man moved on, presumably finding Tobias too taciturn.

Yet for all the military fanfare and grandeur surrounding the funeral, a mere nine months later, the tomb lay quiet. Tobias had seen no visitors at the tomb since that day. Dominique You had never married, and although he had been an upstanding citizen in the twilight of his life, he did not appear to have close friends, at least not that Tobias had seen. Close friends visited a grave from time to time, but not even his brothers from the Masonic lodge had come. And those had been the folks most upset by his death, at least if public grieving was any indication. Then again, Tobias had seen a lot of grief in his tenure at the cemetery, and it had been his observation that even members of the sterner sex could make an enormous fuss over the coffin and then never come back.

The people who looked the most distraught, as if they did not care to go on living, usually got over it by morning. It was the ones who never took their eyes off the coffin, even as it made its way into the vault, that you could be sure would put flowers there for years. Real grief was mostly invisible. It consumed a person from within, leaving only an outer shell that appeared to the world as a whole being but was hollow inside. Tobias recognized it in others because he was just a shell himself.

Tobias wondered once again why the Freemasons had chosen this spot for

You's tomb. It seemed a poor location in the cemetery to build, but it was not Tobias's place to say so. It was kind of the Freemasons to construct it for their brother, even if they had decreed it was to be sold in fifty years. This stipulation did not surprise him, as he knew people sometimes purchased tombs this way. The odd part was that an entire tomb was dedicated to a single person, when so many held multiple family members.

Tobias would have thought a man with no surviving family and little money would not need a whole tomb to himself. But perhaps his contribution as a war hero had moved some hearts to loosen their purse strings and fund this stand-alone vault. This was a monument to Captain Dominique You, and Tobias would do his part to honor his memory by mucking out the mess around the man's final resting place.

He finished raking the gravel around the front, repositioning it as best he could amid the puddles that stubbornly lingered even with the scorching August sun. He could not do much else until the water drained, which might take a while in New Orleans. In the meantime, he could wipe away some of the mud that had splashed onto the tomb from the rainstorm. He pulled a clean rag out of his pocket and decided to concentrate on the nameplate on the front of the tomb.

It was then that Tobias noticed the oddest thing—the marble plate was not flush against the bricks. Tobias chided himself for not observing this before, but as he studied it closely, he realized that it appeared to be placed properly from the front. It was not until he looked from the side that he could see the marble stone was bowing. This was indeed curious, as he himself had placed the outer tablet. As sexton, it was part of his duties to affix the plate upon the bricks after the body was interred and the tomb bricked up.

He had seen marble bow when exposed to extreme heat, but thick nameplates typically did not deform so quickly. It was a blessing in disguise that the rain, which would inevitably flood the cemetery in the summer months, had forced him to spend time around this tomb, allowing him to observe it more closely. Had the Freemasons chosen a more optimal spot to place the tomb, it might have been many years before he had noticed this subpar workmanship. And since the inhabitant had no living family members, it might not have been until the fifty years were up and the sexton opened the tomb for a new burial that the faulty nameplate was discovered.

But surely he would have noticed if something was amiss when he placed the nameplate. He leaned in for a closer inspection and blinked rapidly. He thought perhaps it was a trick of the bright sunshine, but as he stared at the marble slab, he discerned a hairline fracture running the length of the stone. Dominique had been interred less than a year ago. This nameplate should not display such signs of degradation. Had he somehow damaged the stone when bolting the nameplate onto the brick vault? Utterly perplexed, Tobias pondered what he should do. He was exceedingly curious whether his workmanship was to blame for the bowing and cracking or if it was a defect in the stone itself.

He knew he should probably wait until he had help, but his inquisitive nature got the best of him, and he rushed off to retrieve his wrench. Removing the large bolts holding the nameplate in place would not be easy. He half-expected he would not be able to get them to budge at all, but he was relieved to find them coming loose without applying heat. He knew the stone would be too heavy to maneuver on his own, but he planned to slide it down to the ground once it was free from the brick on the front of the vault. With less effort than should have been required for such an undertaking, Tobias freed the marble slab and eased it down about a foot until it rested upright against the tomb. To conduct a proper inspection, he would need to see the back of the slab. The stone was indeed heavy and should have been cumbersome for two men to handle, yet Tobias was able, with some difficulty, to lay the slab on the ground so that the back was visible.

He instantly understood why he was able to maneuver it unassisted. The back of the marble had been carved out, and the stone, too thin in the center to withstand the intense heat, had bowed as a result. The thinned-out stone also accounted for the hairline fracture Tobias had noticed. This nameplate was not the solid, thick slab he had affixed to Dominique's vault nine months ago. The slab had been altered and reattached, unbeknownst to him. Tobias did not need to ponder why someone had done this because nestled within the carved-out space was a book.

Chapter Two

New Orleans

August 1831

*I*t *must be a map to the pirate Lafitte's treasure.* This was Tobias's first thought when he saw the leather-bound book. What else would an old pirate go to such lengths to hide? It had to be something of extreme value to warrant this level of precaution. Tobias tried to imagine the stealth and planning that would have preceded stashing the book. The culprit had to enter the cemetery at night and remain undetected long enough to remove the nameplate and hollow out the marble to hide the book. Then he would need to re-bolt the stone to the outside of the brick tomb. Tobias was confident that one man, even a hearty one, would be unable to perform such a task unaided. Who might have done this? Dominique You was dead, of that Tobias was certain, as he was most definitely in the tomb when the opening was bricked up and the nameplate attached.

He looked around to ensure he was still alone in the cemetery. He'd often felt as though someone was watching him when he was working in St. Louis No. 2, though he'd always chalked it up to his active imagination. But now he felt that unsettling, persistent sensation that another was near. *Keep your wits about you, Tobias,* he reprimanded himself.

Tobias was a man of insatiable curiosity, a personality trait that had gotten him into trouble more times than he cared to recall and that stoked his passion for adventure stories. He always needed to know what came next. Although a patient man, a more circumspect man, might have made a different choice, Tobias hardly hesitated a moment before reaching for the book. It was a slim volume, bound in worn brown leather. It did not appear damaged at all, and Tobias could only surmise that the book had been well insulated from the elements, tucked away in the niche carved into the marble, the overhang of the parapet roof above the tomb providing an extra layer of protection.

He stared at the book in his hands. This object should not exist. And yet here it was. Tobias gently stroked the soft leather of its cover, as if trying to discern the secrets contained within through touch.

And now a battle raged inside Tobias. For he was a devout Catholic, and he knew right from wrong. Not that he never made poor choices, but the guilt that inevitably went hand in glove with those choices usually propelled him straight to the confessional. Should he open the book?

As far as Tobias could figure, whoever hid this book intended the sexton to find it. After all, it was the sexton who would remove the nameplate to unseal the brick opening of the tomb when it was time to inter a new coffin. Tobias, of course, knew that since Dominique You had no known surviving relatives, it was unlikely that such a task would be required of him anytime soon. But what about the Freemasons' contract to sell the tomb after fifty years? At that time, the nameplate would have been disturbed when You's remains were removed from the vault before the new owners buried a body within it. They would replace the nameplate and engrave it with their family's inscriptions. No doubt, the sexton was the intended audience of this book. At least, that was what he told himself, and so convincing was his logic that he almost believed it.

With trembling fingers, he flipped open the cover and examined the first few pages. He hoped to find a series of maps. Was it naive of him to anticipate an "X" marking the spot of the treasure? He even had an idea of what the map would show, more or less. He knew that Jean Lafitte and his band of pirates, which of course included the infamous Dominique You, had operated for some time in Barataria, a swampy region of inlets south of New Orleans where Lafitte set up the base of operations for his "pirate kingdom." Lafitte abandoned it years ago, but rumors persisted that treasure had been left behind.

Tobias leafed through pages filled with writing and utterly devoid of treasure maps. The hand was fine and firm. Unfortunately for Tobias, it was written in French. Much of New Orleans was inhabited by French Creoles, so the language was more common than English. At least it had been until recently, thanks to the influx of Americans moving to the city after Napoleon sold the Louisiana Territory to the United States. English was now becoming more widespread. Many New Orleanians could read both languages, but not Tobias. He was from a modest Irish family that did not speak French, and he considered himself inordinately blessed to have received a rudimentary education that taught him his letters, thus opening up the world of books to him. But not this book.

He let out a frustrated sigh, glancing up at the sun, hours away from setting. He pocketed the journal and picked up the rake—time to get back to it.

At the end of the workday, Tobias walked past the brick and stucco buildings of the Vieux Carré as he made his way home, lost in thought. The book did not contain a map, but surely the writing described where to find treasure. If he followed the instructions he was certain must be contained in the pages and found it, could he keep it? What if he just kept some of it and donated a large sum to orphans? Or widows? Or the destitute? Would that be morally permissible?

He hardly slowed his pace as he doggedly wove through the throngs of pedestrians darting in and out of the pastel-painted structures and the street vendors selling their wares.

"Yellow Jack is comin' callin'!" A newsboy waved his broadsheet at Tobias, eager to garner his attention and coins. "Read the weekly death count!" His tenacity was not deterred by Tobias's tightened jaw and increased pace as he swept by the lad.

Deeper into the Vieux Carré he went. Had Tobias been the one to choose his residence, he might have decided upon the Faubourg Marigny, where many Irish were now living. His father built the cottage on Bienville Street in one of the city's oldest neighborhoods. Tobias's parents had immigrated with a wave of like-minded settlers who preferred leaving Ireland to facing British persecution. The elder Whitneys were proud of their Irish heritage but eager to assimilate into their new home, so in place of a traditionally Irish name, they chose a biblical one for their only child—Tobias, meaning "God is good."

Ordinarily, Tobias found the gumbo of races and cultures around him invigorating. Not one to engage others in conversation, Tobias preferred to listen and observe. He would often pause under the iron-lace galleries, gaining a respite from the brutal sun, and try to parcel out each language or dialect he heard in the cacophony of the busy streets. Although incapable of comprehending individual words, he could distinguish between Parisian French and Creole French. These sounded far different to his ear than the Spanish, Italian, and German he often heard spoken. The Caribbean and African dialects were still a mystery to him. But on this particular August evening, he paid as little mind to the sounds around him as he did to the sights, so focused was he on the book.

"Mr. Whitney, care for a baguette to bring Mrs. Whitney for supper?" Madame Dupont proffered the long loaf of bread as Tobias passed by her bakery, a narrow ochre building with the store on the ground floor and the Duponts' living quarters above.

A longer-than-polite pause ensued before Tobias realized the woman was addressing him. "No, thank you, Madame Dupont." This evening, Tobias was immune to the heavenly aroma of freshly baked bread and the warm, sugary scent of pralines that wafted through the narrow doorway and open shutters. In his haste to return home, his boots accumulated mud and other unsavory substances as he failed to walk along the planks while crossing the cobblestone street.

"Eh là! Pousse-toi, couyon!" The harsh words jolted Tobias out of his stupor. He had stepped in front of a barouche, and the startled driver was cursing at him in Creole French. Tobias caught the gist of the angry words and the driver's assumption that Tobias was a fool who needed to get out of the way quickly. He hopped back onto the banquette and vowed to pay closer attention to his surroundings. He would never learn the secrets of the book if he were run over before making it home.

Walking a bit more cautiously now, Tobias considered his options as he neared his cottage. As luck would have it, the most obvious choice was the least appealing. Was there any other course of action? Surely there must be alternatives, but try as he might, he could think of none. Downtrodden yet still determined to succeed, Tobias steeled himself for the distasteful task ahead. He needed to ask his wife for help.

* * *

"Ugly as homemade sin, it is!"

Tobias could hear his wife's words from the street before he even alighted the stairs to the front porch. *Mary Catherine's spitting nails*, he thought. This was not unusual, as fury was her go-to reaction for most of life's minor annoyances. Fortunately for her sons, Mary Catherine was not a hitter most of the time. She instead relied on tongue lashings, which proved far more effective. Most sensible people were terrified of her.

The ones with no sense, or those who took her at face value, saw her as anything but formidable. Mary Catherine barely reached five feet and had a delicate, nymph-like build. She had giant green eyes that, while mesmerizing, defied you to look away when she held your gaze. Surprisingly, her eyes were not her prominent feature. It was her hair that people remembered most. Her curls were as fiery red as her temperament, and her own father, who was somewhat terrified of her as well, used to say that the Good Lord had given the world a fair enough warning about Mary Catherine with the color of her hair. The rest was on them if they stoked the flames.

Tobias ascended the wooden stoop of his white plastered brick-between-post cottage, pausing before opening the green-painted French door. The façade of his home was symmetrical, with four such doors that could be opened to assist airflow, but even with all of them presently closed, Mary Catherine's voice carried easily beyond them. All was not well in the Whitney house. With a deep breath, Tobias screwed his courage to the sticking place and crossed the threshold.

"Whatever made you think you could bring such a thing into the house? Don't use the sense God gave you, do you?" She was directing her ire at their son, Shane.

"But Ma, it was free! I didn't pay a penny for it!"

Mary Catherine crossed herself. "Jesus, Mary, Joseph, and all the saints, tell me you didn't nick it!"

"Of course not!"

"Then where did you get such a hideous cap?"

"I found it on Chartres Street, lying in the gutter, for anyone to take. I look right dandy in it!" Shane preened a bit so that his mother could get the full effect.

"Makes you look daft is what it does. Take it off. You're sure to get the mange from it, if you haven't already!"

Shane opened his mouth to respond, but his mother cut him off. She was wound up now, and there would be no stopping her until she ran out of breath. Her mercurial outbursts, for all their frequency, rarely lasted longer than it took for her to refill her lungs. Her loved ones had learned long ago that by the second breath, she usually ran out of steam and ceased her tirade, unless she was particularly riled up, in which case, Lord help you. Tonight, she was boiling over.

"Of all the nonsense—a hat from the gutter! And to think I was just listening to Mrs. Nolan crowing about her boys, thinking to myself, this cow talks about her children like they are the angels incarnate, when my boys are good, wholesome lads, with nary a strike against them! And all the while my second-born was picking up refuse off the street—the *street*, mind you, and putting it on his head! Looking like something the cat dragged in! And I thought your father and I raised you boys right!"

Shane was only ten years old, so he was not certain that his raising was complete, but he chose not point this out to his mother, who was by now turning the most amusing shade of puce. Her boys dearly loved agitating their mother, and since she seemed to enjoy yelling at them, they figured it was their filial duty to find ways to anger her.

Tobias had witnessed this exchange without uttering a word. He found it best for their marital harmony to let Mary Catherine finish berating her current victim before inserting himself back into their domestic world after a day of work. Shane noticed him first.

"There ya are, Da!" He grinned at his father, thrilled for the distraction that made Mary Catherine peel her narrowed eyes from her son and turn them to her husband instead.

Mary Catherine looked fierce as always. Her brow was creased in consternation, and her lips were a tight line now that she had taken a moment's break from chastising Shane, who took advantage of her shift in focus to stash the cap in his shirt.

The boy more closely resembled Tobias than Mary Catherine. He had his father's tall, lanky build, dark hair, and brown eyes. His brother, Connor, had a similar build and coloring. They looked so much alike that people sometimes mistook them for twins, even though they were two years apart. His younger sister, Kathleen, and the twins, Riley and Imogen, had favored their mother, with their red hair and shorter stature.

"Tobias! I did not hear you come in!" declared Mary Catherine. All thoughts of mangy caps fell by the wayside as the corners of her mouth turned up into a grin, and she crossed over the sitting room to embrace him in a warm hug. Tobias had often reflected that from her hugs to her temper, there was nothing cold about Mary Catherine.

"Evenin', Kitten!" he addressed her by the nickname he'd given her during the early years of their marriage. "There ya are, Shane! Where's Connor? Still at Dufilho's?" Their eldest son worked after school at the apothecary shop.

"Aye, and don't get me started on that boy! Left his room looking like a hurricane blew through, he did! As if the good Lord had nothing better for me to do with my time than follow that lad around and care for his things! I will give him a talking to when he gets home, of that you can be sure! I have a mind to keep his supper from him. Just watch!"

Shane smirked. "Ah, go on now, Ma! You'd sooner stuff us fit to pop than let us go hungry!"

Mary Catherine gasped and turned to her husband. "Would you listen to your son? Never, in all my days, have I heard such cheek from a boy!"

Before Tobias could speak, she rounded on Shane, wagging her finger inches from his nose. "After all we've done for you, and our parents before us! Do you even know the hardships my family had to endure to get here in the first place?"

Shane had heard this story countless times, so he nodded and said, "When you were little, you traveled here with your family on a cotton ship returning to New Orleans."

"Just making our way from Ireland to Liverpool nearly killed us, and then we'd no money to speak of for our transport, so what were we to do?"

"You got a crossing as ballast," Shane offered.

"That's right we did! We were human cargo for the return trip, we were!"

"The ship needed to make up the weight after they unloaded all that cotton, so they let people make the journey back," Shane said.

"Aye, we barely survived the passage, but my parents were determined to give me a better life and my children after me! But who knew my children would act like riffraff? And after my father worked his life away as a stevedore at the port. And my mother cooked for the Ursuline nuns to earn enough to put food in her own children's mouths!"

Shane nodded earnestly.

"And I was too little to stay on my own, so you know what I did?"

"You went to work with her in the convent kitchen," he said.

"And those nuns eventually let me learn right alongside their paid charges, even though my parents would never have been able to afford tuition. The sisters saw I had an inquisitive nature, they did!"

Tobias added to the story. "They recognized you were a bright girl with a quick wit, and they were never ones to deprive a promising mind of an education, no matter her ability to pay." He knew his wife was very fond of the French order of nuns who had arrived in New Orleans over a century before. They'd established a hospital and a school where they educated girls from wealthy families.

"But Ma, Granny always said the nuns agreed to let you learn because you asked too many questions and got in the way while she was trying to cook."

"Shane Whitney, you take that impudent tongue of yours out of doors this instant!"

Shane grinned and headed out back to the courtyard before his mother changed her mind.

Tobias chuckled.

Mary Catherine gave him a stern look, then softened. "It's true enough, I suppose. But still, that boy needs to watch his saucy mouth!"

Tobias looked fondly at his wife. She wore a simple calico gown with an apron on top, her curls escaping the mob cap's futile attempt to contain them. Tobias thought she looked lovely in her plain attire. For all her spitfire, she was his soulmate.

However, he did not relish asking for her help, despite her fluency in both French and English, thanks to her education by the nuns. It was not that Tobias did not wish to confide in Mary Catherine, but he suspected his wife would disapprove of how he had acquired the book. Although he hoped she would come around to his way of thinking and translate it for him, he knew that there would be a tremendous amount of scolding to get through before she acquiesced. It was simply her way. And although he loved her, sometimes he just did not care for the noise.

"The most remarkable thing happened at the cemetery today." Tobias had decided he should wait until after supper, when things around the house were a bit more settled, before broaching the subject of the book with Mary Catherine, but his excitement got the better of him. Before he could stop himself, he was relating the day's adventure. He finished the story and eagerly awaited her reaction.

She stared at him.

Tobias swallowed and shifted on his feet. He watched the color rise in her cheeks and knew he had unleashed hell's fury. He weathered the storm, trying not to focus on every single word but making out the key theme that he was the devil incarnate for desecrating a man's grave and stealing from him while he was trying to enjoy his eternal slumber in peace.

"There now, Kitten, don't get yourself in a state about it," he soothed.

"Don't you 'Kitten' me, Tobias Whitney! Why, I ought to summon Father Hedrick right this second. You need to go straight to confession, or this pirate's ghost will haunt you, you can be sure!"

Tobias silently scolded himself for his careless approach. He needed to handle this request with delicacy if he wanted to persuade her to cooperate.

"I need your help, Mary Catherine."

Her green eyes grew wide at his use of her Christian name. Tobias invoked it only under the most serious circumstances.

"Whoever hid the book in the nameplate meant for me to have it. Or at least meant for the sexton to find it. It makes no sense otherwise. I simply want you to tell me what kind of book it is. You can take a quick look, can't you? I know your French is superb."

When Mary Catherine responded, not by bellowing but by holding out her hand to receive the book, Tobias silently thanked the Lord above. He had won.

Chapter Three

New Orleans

August 1831

Mary Catherine settled herself in a sturdy chair at the cypress dining table and opened the book. Tobias watched intently as her eyes skimmed the pages. He had assumed she would read it aloud. The suspense of not knowing what she was learning was too much for him to bear.

"Well, Kitten? What does it say?"

Mary Catherine's features remained placid despite his uncharacteristically brusque tone. "It is Dominique You's private journal."

"Then, surely, it must speak of treasure?" Tobias leaned his palms on the table, inches from his wife and the journal.

Mary Catherine turned her fiery eyes on him. "Will you let me read, man?!"

He pulled out a chair and sat down. He observed her forehead wrinkle, then her mouth fall open. When he thought he would expire from curiosity, she finally addressed him.

"Well, it's a pirate's tale, all right. No doubt about it. But it's not about Dominique You, God rest his soul in his desecrated tomb! It's about another pirate—Captain Lafitte, his brother."

"Do you mean to say that Jean Lafitte wrote the journal?"

Mary Catherine shook her head, "No! Dominique You wrote an account of Captain Lafitte's life."

"But, Kitten, why would he do such a thing? I imagine pirates are tight-lipped about their exploits, especially those that are illegal. Why would he commit them to paper and place the book where someone would no doubt unearth it?"

"Because Dominique You wished to tell the world Captain Lafitte's story."

"But if that's the case, then why go to the trouble of hiding it in the tomb?"

Mary Catherine paused before answering, "All is not what it seemed with the captain."

His thoughts crashed into one another as he waited for her to continue.

She leaned in close and whispered, "Captain Lafitte did not die in 1823. According to his brother, he died last year."

"But I thought—" The first of Tobias's myriad questions was interrupted when their oldest son entered the house.

"Connor!" Mary Catherine jumped up from her seat and began fussing over her boy, having completely forgotten that she'd meant to give him a stern talking to about the unkempt state of his belongings. Once Shane bounded into the room, the noise level increased as Tobias's wife and sons began talking all at once and ever louder to be heard above each other.

"What's for supper tonight, Ma? I'm starved!" Connor asked.

"I'll just bet you are, poor lamb, with your studies and then working. Don't you fret now, I've got redfish and colcannon, all ready!" She ushered the boys to their chairs and began serving the meal.

After dinner, it was the Whitney family's custom for Tobias to read to the children, offering Mary Catherine a respite from domestic duties.

An avid reader, Tobias was ever thankful that manufactured goods of all kinds flowed into the city like water down the Mississippi River, including books. He had neither the income nor the inclination for the rest of the offerings along Chartres Street, but he could pass an eternity perusing the latest publications at Chapter and Verse, one of Tobias's favorite places on Earth.

But this evening, Tobias rose from the dining table and announced, "I must go out. Connor, you can do the reading in my place, eh?"

"You want me to read it?"

"You've never asked him before," said Mary Catherine.

"I could do it! " Shane insisted. "You said my reading was coming along nicely, Da!"

"That's very true, but Connor is older, so I think it should be him. It's only this one night, mind you. I'll resume tomorrow. We are to read three chapters tonight. You remember where we left off?"

The boys were accustomed to their father's precise scheduling of pages they would enjoy each evening.

Connor nodded and said, "Aye, that I will, Da. I'll not let Shane talk me into reading ahead."

Shane frogged his brother's arm.

Tobias pulled the tattered book out of his pocket, where he kept it for reading during his breaks at the cemetery. The action-packed adventure story had been a family favorite since its publication five years earlier.

"*The Last of the Mohicans?*" asked Mary Catherine. "How many times have you read that one so far this year, do you suppose?"

"This is our third time this year, but our tenth time overall," answered Connor.

Tobias put on his cap and approached the front door. Mary Catherine looked at him with a single raised brow.

"I am popping down to Chapter and Verse. I shall fetch you some writing paper for your translation," he explained. "And a new inkpot as well. Ours is running dry, I'm afraid."

"So I'm to translate this whole book. Is that your intention?" Mary Catherine tried to inject her usual exasperation into this query.

Tobias grinned and gave her a roguish wink.

"Well, I'd better get to it, then," she replied, fighting to mask a smile.

Tobias strolled through the Vieux Carré, heading toward Chartres Street. The afternoon rains, so predictable this time of year that Mary Catherine had declared she could set a clock by them, had come and gone, soaking the ground and making a mess of the roads. Brown sludge ran in rivulets through the divots in the cobblestones, pooling on either side of the street.

Unfortunately, the storm had failed to ameliorate the intense August heat. Even at this hour, it was still "hotter than the hinges on the gates of Hades," as Mary Catherine was fond of saying.

Tobias's shirt and trousers clung like a second skin by the time he approached his destination, a light blue-painted building with a faded sign hanging from an iron hook over the entry. The slim wooden door of the shop emitted a comforting creak when Tobias opened it. Chapter and Verse was a charming shop that carried newspapers, broadsheets, all manner of writing paraphernalia, and, of course, books. So many wonderful books could be found inside its walls.

As he stepped across the threshold, he allowed himself a moment to breathe deeply. The familiar, intoxicating scents of leather and ink greeted him, along with the sweet, earthy aroma of beeswax from the polished, ornately carved shelves that ran the length of the walls, stretching from the floorboards to the ceiling. The shelves were stacked with volumes, their spines displaying myriad languages. Most were leather-bound, but some newer volumes were cloth-bound, sporting simple gold lettering. Tobias ran a finger over one of the cloth-bound books, marveling at the technology that could now produce a book from linen or cotton. While he was partial to leather-bound volumes, his reduced circumstances as of late made him grateful for the lower-priced option.

He said a silent prayer that the good Lord would protect this place from fires like the ones that destroyed much of the city several decades before. He could not bear to think of all these beautiful books disintegrating into ash. The first volume to catch his eye was *The Hunchback of Notre-Dame.* He had been eager to read it since its publication earlier in the year, but alas, it was in French. Tobias toyed with the notion of convincing Mary Catherine to translate it for him after she finished her current task, but decided it was better to abandon that idea for now.

He was moving deeper into the shop when the proprietor, a French Creole man named Denis Loutrel, noticed him. "Mr. Whitney! Good evening to you!"

Tobias smiled and returned the greeting. "And how is your health of late?"

The stooped man unconsciously rubbed his gnarled hands. "You know, some days are better than others—so it is with the gout, n'est-ce pas? But enough of an old man's complaints. Tell me, what brings you here so late in the evening?"

Tobias told him the items he required without mentioning their intended use. He was not ready to reveal what he had found, even to his friend. While Mssr. Loutrel gathered what he'd requested, Tobias perused the shop. He was gazing longingly at the new steel pens on offer when Mssr. Loutrel returned.

"Ingenious design, are they not? You simply insert the steel nib into a wooden pen holder." He demonstrated the process for Tobias. "And you just discard them when they break or become dull from use."

The concept seemed scandalously extravagant to Tobias, but the uniformity of writing such an appliance offered appealed to his fastidious nature. "I should very much like to try writing with one."

"Shall I add a few to your order?"

As tempting as it was, Tobias knew Mary Catherine would balk at the purchase. She had made her opinion on the matter clear on an earlier occasion, when she'd declared, "The good Lord gave us birds for mattress stuffing and writing. Otherwise, what's a body to do with all those feathers?"

"Perhaps another time," Tobias said.

"Ah, well, here you are, one inkpot and one book of writing paper."

Tobias looked at the lovely, dove-gray leather-bound book of blank pages. "Thank you, this will do nicely." He had considered requesting the more frugal cloth-bound option, but he feared Mary Catherine, never one to take to newfangled contraptions, would scoff, and keeping her enthusiastic about the project was of paramount importance. The journal Mr. Loutrel had chosen would be perfect for Mary Catherine's translation.

"Tenez, Mr. Whitney. I hope you put these to good use." Mssr. Loutrel smiled at Tobias, but then his demeanor became grave. "Hand to heart, I thought you had come to accept my proposal. I suppose I'll console myself with a sale instead."

When Tobias did not reply, Mssr. Loutrel continued, "I trust you need more time, but that is the one thing a man of my age does not have. You would be good here. Running this shop is in your blood, after all. And you are the best at pen cutting I have ever seen."

Quill pens were favored by many because their tips allowed for fine strokes, but only if the point was cut well and maintained. If used regularly, a quill pen required constant mending, and Tobias could both make and repair them. It was a skill he had learned from his late father when he had owned this store.

Mssr. Loutrel soldiered on. "I know you are concerned about the expense, but as I've assured you, we can work out a situation agreeable to us both."

Tobias had heard this argument many times before and dreaded what he knew was coming next.

"Besides, it would do you more than a bit of good to be around people again, instead of spending your days with the dead at that cemetery. Sooner or later, you will have to get on with living."

Tobias felt the familiar heat creep up to the tips of his ears that always accompanied an allusion to his children. "I've not got the funds together quite yet, but soon, Mssr. Loutrel, soon." Tobias bid his friend a good evening and headed out into the sultry twilight.

The streets were less crowded now, as shops were closing for the night. The glow from the oil lamps cast otherworldly shadows on the facades of Spanish-style architecture with wrought-iron balconies and terrace roofs that had replaced the original French structures after the fires. The dim, hazy lighting, combined with the clicking of his heels upon the cobblestones, produced an atmosphere that some might find foreboding but that Tobias barely noticed as he made his way back to his cottage.

His mind was busy conjuring memories from three years ago. This often occurred when he was sleeping, and the memories—more like dreams— were so vivid that they woke him. Then, in the middle of the night, when he felt the most vulnerable and the most alone, when he had an uninterrupted block of time to question his decisions and pass judgment on them, Tobias would lie in the dark and wonder how his life had changed so profoundly, so quickly. He would berate himself for not being able to move forward, to rejoin the living, as Mssr. Loutrel had urged him to do. A few uneventful nights would pass, and then his dreams would torment him anew.

Tobias knew he could not control the content of his dreams, but he could master his thoughts in his waking moments. And he had grown accustomed to using them to punish himself. When someone referenced his children, rather than pushing away the painful memory, he fixated on it, reliving each detail as if it were happening to him in the present. He felt the sting of his bad decisions. He suffered every pang of regret as if for the first time. He regularly dredged up those gut-wrenching, soul-twisting moments and experienced them over and over. He acted as the Furies to his own Orestes, forever condemning himself to suffer from guilt. And he was about to subject himself to the pain once again. He took a deep breath and went back to that darkest place in his mind, another self-inflicted installment of his endless penance.

It was a lovely autumn day in 1828. The cloudless sky was the most alluring shade of periwinkle, and the temperature was finally bearable. The weather was as perfect as Tobias's life. He recalled thinking that this was God's way of rewarding the inhabitants of New Orleans for persevering through the oppressive heat, humidity, and swarms of mosquitoes during the summer months. Those who had the means to flee the city for more comfortable environs did so. Everyone else had to endure the summer and dream of perfect autumn days like the one he was now enjoying. But a heavenly reward was not in Tobias's future. The exact opposite was in store for him.

Tobias recalled reading the headline of the *Louisiana Advertiser* when he arrived at Chapter and Verse. "City Out of Peril—Yellow Fever Subsides as Cool Weather Advances." The disease typically appeared every summer in New Orleans, although some years were more severe than others. Tobias recalled a terrible year in 1817. Yellow Jack, as some called it, had not been good to the city in 1828, but things had settled down by October. Folks were breathing a sigh of relief that the overlapping seasons of hurricanes and yellow fever were nearing an end, and everyone was looking forward to the cooler months.

The Whitneys' neighbor, Mrs. Ross, had come rushing into the shop only a few hours later.

"Mr. Whitney! You must return to your cottage immediately! Mrs. Whitney needs you there at once!"

"What's wrong, Mrs. Ross?" he'd asked.

"It's Connor—he's taken ill. I told Mrs. Whitney I'd fetch you as soon as I was able."

She had barely spoken the words before he grabbed his cap and rushed out of the door, all but sprinting back to Bienville Street.

Connor was nine years old and a generally hearty youth, but Tobias and Mary Catherine were beside themselves with worry. Mary Catherine barely left the child's side as she tried to bring down his fever with cool rags. The Whitneys summoned doctors to Connor's bedside. They attempted to expel the noxious humors from the child's body and restore balance through bleeding and by inducing vomiting, but their efforts were to no avail.

"His eyes—" Mary Catherine had clutched Tobias's sleeve and pulled him over to where their son lay. His worst fears were confirmed when he saw the yellow tint to the whites of his eyes.

Kathleen was next. The disease ravaged her tiny body with fever and chills, convulsions, and vomiting. Slight of build like her mother, the three-year-old succumbed quickly to the disease, dying within days of taking ill. Her final hours were horrific. As much as they hoped and prayed for a cure for Kathleen, they knew when the bleeding started that it was hopeless. Tobias would never forget the blood. He found it hard to fathom that a tiny body could have contained so much. At the end, it seeped out of her eyes, nose, and mouth. She vomited blood black as coffee, and then she was gone.

Connor, meanwhile, lay in a fever-induced delirium, lingering for days at the edge of death. Tobias and Mary Catherine were desperate to save him from the ghastly ending that Kathleen endured.

They were at their wits' end when another of their neighbors, Mrs. Nolan, gave Tobias a glimmer of hope. "Dr. Thompson's the man you need to cure your boy."

"Dr. Thompson? I've not heard of him," Tobias said.

"He is a miracle worker, I tell you! My Christian was at death's door, he was. Dr. Thompson brought him back to us," Mrs. Nolan said.

"But we've employed several physicians already. They've done all they can," Tobias said.

"Ah, but you haven't tried Dr. Thompson. He's new to the city. Sets up shop right outside the Cathedral of St. Louis. What harm could it do to go see him?"

Although Tobias was skeptical, particularly since Mrs. Nolan could not tell him what kind of doctor he was, he and Mary Catherine went to the cathedral. Dr. Thompson was standing outside, atop an overturned crate, hawking his life-saving remedies to a crowd of worried New Orleanians, equally desperate to protect themselves from Yellow Jack or cure an already stricken loved one.

"My good ladies and gentlemen of New Orleans, I know you suffer, but do not despair! Relief from Yellow Jack is near! I hold in my hand the answer to your prayers!" He proffered a small bottle, which he showed to the crowd. The spectators jostled one another for a closer look.

"I myself prepared this elixir with ingredients known only to the most learned medical men, ingredients harvested in the primeval wilderness of Guiana, from the bark of the Cinchona tree. It will purify better than any blood-letting your local physician might do and restore humoral balance better than any vomit he could prescribe. Take it at dusk and dawn, and you will be protected from the dreaded disease! Only five dollars per bottle!"

"Five dollars!" A man in the crowd scoffed. "Is it made from liquid gold?"

"Can you put a price on your health? On your very life? Indeed, the fee is a pittance compared to the privilege of breathing another day!"

"But who's got that kind of money?" the man asked.

"It'll cost you a pretty penny more to buy a spot in St. Louis Cemetery, will it not?"

There were shrugs and grunts of acquiescence from the crowd.

"You might feel the sting of my price, but it will be mild compared to the sting you'll feel watching your wife or your child, sweating and delirious, succumb to the fever, the whites of their eyes yellowing, knowing they will pass, and that you did not care enough to save them," Dr. Thompson insisted.

Mary Catherine tugged the sleeve of Tobias's coat. He looked down into her eyes, wide with terror, and knew he would pay whatever price Dr. Thompson asked.

The Whitneys made their way to the front of the crowd.

"We'll take the elixir," Tobias told him.

Dr. Thompson handed him a bottle. "May it keep you in good health!"

"Will it work on a child who's already suffering from the fever?" Mary Catherine asked.

Dr. Thompson smiled in a way Tobias supposed was meant to be sympathetic, but that seemed predatory. "Ah, no, I am sorry to say it will not. My elixir only works on the healthy, to keep their humors balanced and protect them from the bad miasma."

"Is there nothing you can do? It's our son, you see. He's gravely ill," Mary Catherine persisted.

"Oh, your son has the fever. Well, that is a problem." Dr. Thompson wrung his hands, as if distressed by their plight. "But do not despair! I would never leave you without hope. He dug into his bag and pulled out a glass jar sealed with a cork. "Here is my Yellow Ointment. Now, you must listen to me very carefully. Your son's life depends upon it. You are to rub it on his gums every hour on the hour. It may take a day or perhaps even two, but he will recover. When he takes the turn for the better, give him my elixir at dawn and dusk to protect him from further infection."

The ointment was far more expensive than the elixir they had already purchased, but they decided they must have it. Connor eventually recovered. Tobias and Mary Catherine were unsure whether the ointment had helped or God had intervened on their behalf, but they were grateful that at least one of their children had survived.

Then the twins fell ill. They were infants—less than a year old—and upon consulting with Dr. Thompson, Tobias and Mary Catherine were told they must purchase one of his special fever powders that children of such a young age required. The powder was even more costly than Dr. Thompson's other remedies.

"We can't afford it, can we?" Mary Catherine looked at Tobias, her eyes pleading.

"We will manage the cost," he said.

Riley and Imogen did not make it. The Whitneys were already in dire financial straits after paying for doctors to attend their sick children, buying cures from Dr. Thompson, and spending a small fortune on an above-ground tomb for Kathleen. The law decreed the tomb could not be reopened to admit the twins until at least a year and a day after a body had been placed within, to ensure the body had enough time to decompose. This necessitated their renting two additional tombs in the wall vaults surrounding the cemetery to house the twins temporarily. Tobias, wracked with guilt over not keeping his children healthy and now making what remained of his family nearly destitute, placed the blame for all that had befallen them squarely on his shoulders. He could have kept them healthy, but he had been remiss.

Local physicians from La Société Médicale de la Nouvelle-Orléans and their English-speaking counterpart, the Physico-Medical Society, agreed that yellow fever was caused by vapors rising from garbage exposed to heat and water. Located in the middle of the heavily populated Vieux Carré, the Whitneys' cottage was surrounded by just such an unhealthy miasma. Tobias was fortunate to own Chapter and Verse, having already taken it over from his father. He had the means to move his family out of the city for the summer months. It would not have been easy to afford such an extravagance, but they could have managed. Ironically, it would have cost far less than what they had spent on elixirs, ointments, and powders. Instead, his selfish choice to keep them near cost him three of his five children. Losing them only days apart was more than he could bear. And try as Mary Catherine might, no one could convince him that the fault was not entirely his.

After the death of his children, Tobias had a critical decision to make. He needed money. He could sell his home or his shop. Although he loved Chapter and Verse dearly, the choice was easy. He had a potential buyer at the ready. Mssr. Loutrel had assisted in founding the French-language newspaper *L'Abeille de la Nouvelle-Orléans* the previous year and was seeking a new venture. He had approached Tobias earlier that year with an offer to buy the shop. Tobias had declined, but after the events of that fateful October, he sold his shop to Mssr. Loutrel and took a job performing maintenance for St. Louis Cemetery No. 2.

Chapter Four

New Orleans

August 1831

By the time he neared his cottage, Tobias had caught up with the lamplighters as they concluded their work. He slowed his pace so as not to walk before them, instead letting the flickering lights chase away the gloaming. Dusk was a harbinger of night and the dreams that accompanied it. He shuddered, then breathed deeply and expelled the breath, and with it, he hoped, the memories, at least for a time. He feared they would find him again in his slumber.

But perhaps they would not. Perhaps they would be pushed out by other thoughts. His mind drifted to the mysterious book he had found. It stirred something within him. He and Mary Catherine were embarking on a new adventure. It was a thrilling experience he only felt when he turned the page of a particularly gripping scene of one of his adventure novels, and he couldn't wait to find out what came next.

For the past three years, he had been in a daze, and although he recognized this, he had been at a loss as to how he might shake loose from it. Now, as he walked past the neighboring cottages, he found himself noticing details that he had not consciously taken in recently. The cooking smells of fried onions and peppers, the scent of wet cobblestones after the afternoon storms, the musky citrus fragrance of the Angel's Trumpet flowers growing in the cottage gardens, even the fetid privy smells emanating from the courtyards in the back of the houses and the dung from the horses in the street mixed into a distinctive scent that was unique to Tobias's neighborhood. In the cemetery, he only took notice of the smell of death. But at this moment, he smelled life in all its incarnations. And for that, he was grateful.

Tobias walked up to his cottage and allowed his gaze to linger on the cantilevered canopy that extended from the steep wood-shingled roof. The canopy provided cover from the rain and a bit of protection from the sun, both of which were needed more often than not, particularly during hot summers when a scorching day could give way to a deluge in an alarmingly short span of time. He recalled one summer afternoon when he and his family were returning home from mass. They were not far from the cottage when the thunderclouds opened, and the rain came down in fat droplets.

"Hurry up, children, before we are all drenched to the bone!" Mary Catherine commanded as she scooped up Kathleen and prodded Shane and Connor to quicken their pace. Tobias, who had been carrying Riley in one arm and Imogen in the other, followed closely on her heels. They hastened past the last few cottages before reaching their own, Mary Catherine yelling all the way. "Connor Whitney, watch that puddle! You will ruin your Sunday clothes! Shane, enough with your tarrying! I've seen a snail move faster than that!" They'd raced up the steps and huddled together under the small canopy. As Tobias was fumbling to open the door, Mary Catherine had laughed and said, "You look like you just took a dip in Lake Pontchartrain!"

He'd looked at her soggy bonnet, the curls plastered to her face, and replied, "And you, love, are wetter than a duck's backside!" Connor had roared with laughter, and the rest of the children followed suit. By the time they were all in the front room, even Mary Catherine was clutching her sides, gasping that they ached from laughing so hard.

The memory jolted him. It was a fond one, yet he'd allowed himself to dwell on it. He found it most uncomfortable, but he'd done it regardless. He lingered under the canopy, letting the drops of leftover rainwater splatter onto his cap. The sound of Mary Catherine's voice inside the cottage eventually roused him.

"Never have I seen such lollygagging! You boys are as slow as molasses in January!"

"Alright, Ma! We've our nightclothes on! Can you quit your cawin'?"

"Connor Whitney! Don't you 'alright, Ma' me, young man! And watch that smart tongue while you're at it!"

Tobias entered the front room of his home, and Mary Catherine turned to him.

"Tobias! You're finally home. You would not believe the acts of hooliganism your sons have performed this evening."

"My sons, eh? Well, now, don't worry about such things, Kitten," he soothed. "I've got all you need for your translation. Have you read any further since I've been gone?"

"Read? As if I have time for such frivolity when the dishes need washing and clothes need mending. Is that what you think I'm up to when you're gone? Whiling away my time in the lap of luxury like the Queen of Sheba?!" Her challenging glare demanded a response.

"No, no, Kitten," Tobias assured her. "I just wondered if you had managed a peek or two."

"Well, I might have cast a glance."

"And what did you learn?"

"It is quite a tale, I'll tell you that much. Make quick with the ink and writing paper, and I shall begin putting it down for you."

He handed Mary Catherine his purchases from Chapter and Verse.

She turned over the dove-gray book in her hand. "This is a right fine book." She gave it a sniff. "Good leather—the way books were meant to be made—none of that cloth-bound foolishness people buy now to spare a few coins!"

Tobias was glad he had not tried to economize with a cloth-bound book. He fetched her a quill pen with a nice, sharp tip.

"Hmm…wouldn't mind trying a steel nib for a project such as this," she commented.

The woman delights in vexing me! he thought.

"Might as well save some oil by working in the kitchen while you read to the boys," she said. "They didn't get to it when you were gone—spent their time tearing this house apart instead!"

"You wouldn't mind if we read out here, just for tonight?"

Mary Catherine didn't look up as she gathered her writing things on the table. "Oil is costly! But I know how much you cherish your reading sessions with the boys, and you can't very well read in the dark, nor can we justify lighting two lamps when one will do. So just for tonight, we'll share the space."

Tobias clasped her hand in his and squeezed it. She returned the gesture. He called the boys into the dining room, and despite their mother's recent accusations to the contrary, they arrived promptly.

"Here ya go, Da," said Connor, handing him *The Last of the Mohicans*.

"Connor probably would have messed it up anyhow," said Shane.

"What would you know—"

Before an argument could commence, Tobias began reading to them about the harrowing journey to the caves. The boys were soon enthralled with the story, even though they knew exactly what would happen next. Escaping into a book, especially this one, was a comfort to them all. They welcomed the words as they would an old friend come to visit.

Tobias was distracted this evening, glancing over at Mary Catherine every few minutes. She was hunched over the journal he'd found, her shoulders tense with concentration. After a few moments, she scribbled away in the new book he'd given her. Then she would return her attention to the journal, and the cycle would continue.

It occurred to him that despite the best efforts of the Ursuline nuns, Mary Catherine's penmanship left much to be desired. Tobias wondered how easily he would be able to decipher what she wrote. Dominique You had penned the original journal in a deliberate and neat hand, but Mary Catherine's writing would more likely resemble chicken scratch. Ah, well, he would figure it out, but there was another thought bothering him. How accurately would she translate the journal? He knew her to be exceedingly bright, but Mary Catherine had a flair for the dramatic, as evidenced by her colorful language that reached its creative pinnacle when she reprimanded her family. He also knew that she was a stickler for grammar and wondered if the version she would present to him would be just as Dominique You wrote it or if Mary Catherine would make extensive changes. There was no way of knowing, so Tobias decided to push such thoughts from his mind.

"That's our stopping point for tonight, lads," Tobias said, closing his well-worn copy of *The Last of the Mohicans*, amidst groans and protests from his sons.

"None of that now! Mind your father," said Mary Catherine, guiding the boys to their beds and tucking their coverlets snug around them. The cottage had no interior hallways, so the boys' room was directly off the dining room. The close quarters meant Tobias and Mary Catherine had to whisper if they wished to converse privately.

When the boys were settled, Tobias could wait no longer. "Kitten, may I read your translations?" he asked.

"I suppose now's as good a time as any," she answered.

Tobias could tell the story engrossed her, and despite her bluster, she was now an eager participant in this adventure. Mary Catherine continued to read the original journal while Tobias picked up the dove-gray volume and got his first glance at his wife's translation. Her sloppy handwriting would finally unlock the mystery and reveal the treasures within.

Mary Catherine Whitney's Translation of the Journal of Dominique You

To The Reader of This Journal

My name is Dominique You, and I have a tale to tell. A tale I gave my word would follow me to the grave. I have kept that word, in a manner of speaking, as this book lies within my tomb. Secrets cannot stay buried forever, and one should never trust a pirate. What's the word of a pirate worth, after all? Not a half cent, I would say. When this book sees the light of day once more, the real story of Jean Lafitte will finally be told, as well it should, or so

I think.

I have lived a life that few could imagine and even fewer would believe. I have sinned against my fellow man, and for those actions, I have repented. Jean never liked us to call ourselves pirates. He would bristle even at the mention of him being called a "Gentleman Pirate." We were corsairs, to his mind, educated and civilized ones at that. But pirates we were, or so was I for much of my life. Until I saw what was coming and changed my ways. I have tried to serve my fellow man and live a good life in the end. I tossed aside the sea and turned my head toward the land. New Orleans became my home. And though I have less than nothing to show for it now, I can die a proud man. And die I shall, before this year is through. Of that I am certain.

Before my maker calls me away from this world, I shall record what I know of the life of the man so many call the Terror of the Gulf. He was the greatest corsair since Blackbeard himself. People talk of his misdeeds, not of his kind acts. They remember his defeats and forget his victories. He is a hero who saved this city from the British, yet people know him as an outlaw. Upon his death, no one mourned him, save his closest friends. Our brother, Pierre, who stood by his side throughout so much of his life, died alone in Santa Cruz. But even still, he has a headstone to mark his life, simple and crude as it is. I, who have not a fraction of Jean's courage and cunning nor Pierre's wisdom and wit, have this tomb. I do not deserve such grandeur, but my brothers from the Concord Lodge have seen fit to honor me with it nonetheless. I shall be forever grateful for the gift of this tomb, but I cannot rest in it knowing I enjoy such a memorial while my brother's true story is lost to history. Therefore, I shall prevail upon my fellow lodgers one last time and entrust them with a task of utmost importance to me. I have instructed them that upon my death, they are to secret this volume, unread by any man, in my tomb following my burial.

For fifty years, it will slumber alongside me until awakened when my tomb is sold. Then the story will be told. Surely, Jean would not object to a secret emerging from hiding after so long a period, when all involved will be enjoying their eternal reward. I feel I will have done my duty to him and kept my word. For all the good a pirate's word is. Never trust a pirate!

If I am addressing the emancipator of this document, I thank you. Tell this tale. Let all who will listen learn the secrets I am about to reveal! It is not for my sake that I ask you to do so, but for the sake of my brother.

Forgive the haste with which this journal was written and the errors that undoubtedly accompany it. I am not a well man, and I know my time is limited. I have not the luxury of transcribing my pages anew should I mark out words. I hope the reader will forgive this and that it does not compromise the legitimacy of the document in his eyes. The good Lord will take me soon, though I pray not until my work is complete.

I swear upon my honor that the words within this book are true. The facts were spoken to me by the man himself, or else written to me in letters by his own hand. Those letters were written in a code only we could decipher. Jean was not a man to hold back, and I would reckon he thought of me as his confessor, especially in my twilight years after I had made my peace with Our Maker. I was a good bit older than he and understood the world in which he operated. I knew more than most men what he had been through and why he did the things he did. He told me all. No matter if it made him look like a hero or a villain, whether he was proud of his actions or ashamed. I listened.

I was able to consult other accounts of his life, such as newspapers and the like, to aid me in writing this document. My facts are accurate. Anyone with doubts now will cast them aside upon reading these pages. The truth will emerge. The world thinks Jean died in 1823, when yet he lived another seven years, leading a life no one could imagine, performing deeds no one would believe. For this is his story, and I pray God gives me the time on this Earth to tell it all.

Dominique You

23 September 1830

* * *

The translation ended. Tobias took a moment to consider what he had just learned before speaking. "Mary Catherine, this is incredible!"

"That it is!"

"If I had not noticed that bowed marble, Lafitte's secrets would have remained hidden for years."

"But you did find it, just a mite sooner than intended."

"Incredible," repeated Tobias, shaking his head.

"Fifty years have not yet passed." Mary Catherine voiced the worry that had been nagging Tobias.

"Dominique You died only last year."

"Still, you noticed the marble for a reason. Near as I can figure, it must have been God's will." Mary Catherine crossed herself.

"Captain You kept his word, did he not? He and Jean Lafitte have both passed. Could there be any harm in learning his secrets now?" Tobias raised an eyebrow in question.

Her silence hastened his decision.

"I must know what happens next."

Mary Catherine told him about what she had read during his time with the boys, and when she had concluded, he excitedly declared, "Kitten! What are you waiting for? Pick up that quill and continue!"

"Tobias Whitney, I will not be ordered to burn midnight oil by the likes of you! I have a house to run and cannot do so without the sleep the good Lord intended for me!"

Tobias spied her struggling to keep back a smile that threatened to turn up the ends of her lips. He knew she was pleased that he had found something to interest him once again, and he suspected she found his excitement contagious. He felt emboldened to press on. "It will be worth it in the end! You'll have the journal translated before the week's end!"

"And the cleaning—just who do you suppose will do that while I spend my days buried in a book?"

"Blast it all, let it stay dirty!"

Mary Catherine's eyes widened, as Tobias was not one for swearing, but she soon found her voice. "And the cooking? A body needs to eat!"

"Put the beans on tomorrow morn. You won't need to mind them for the rest of the day, except to give them a quick stir."

"But tomorrow isn't Monday! You know good and well I always cook my red beans and rice on washday!"

"Beans can be for tomorrow, and the next day, and the next if need be!" He slammed a fist on the table for emphasis. *Lord, that woman could try the patience of a saint.*

Mary Catherine sputtered on about the barbarism of cooking red beans too many days in a row, insisting that she would, under no circumstances, neglect her duties to her home and family to translate some pirate book. Yet they both knew this was precisely what she would do.

Chapter Five

Mary Catherine Whitney's Translation of the Journal of Dominique You

The Death of Captain Lafitte

I shall begin at the end. For the end is where the tale starts, at least this tale. Forgive my writing in riddles, but the world believes Captain Jean Lafitte died in 1823, yet I know he did not. To understand the man's life, one must understand his death or, I should say, the account of his death as reported by his crew.

It was 4 February 1823 in the Gulf of Honduras. Jean Lafitte was captain of a forty-three-ton schooner named the *General Santander*. It was a cloudy morn, but at first light, an officer sweeping the horizon with his glass spotted a schooner and a brigantine. They were off the coast of Omoa in Honduras. This is near where the Spanish have a fort to protect the riches of silver brought there from the mines of Tegucigalpa. When the vessels turned to run, the *General Santander* gave chase, thinking they were Spanish merchant vessels and as such were ripe for the picking. Jean had a letter of marque from Great Columbia that permitted him to raid Spanish ships. Jean furled his awnings, set his big square sail, and cruised through the water.

"After 'em, boys!" he shouted to his crew, his right arm raised high above his head, clasping his beloved blade. "Make those

Spaniards know the General's fury!"

The *General Santander* pursued both vessels for nearly a day. Jean caught up to the brigantine late that night, and shots were exchanged. The *Santander* lost her fore-topmast in the fray. Just when Jean felt certain the brig would strike her colors in surrender, her captain signaled, with lanterns raised in her rigging, to the schooner to double back and assist them in fighting the *General Santander*.

Now Jean realized he had been tricked. These were not Spanish merchant vessels, but Spanish warships! His only option was to fight hard, though he knew he was outgunned. Jean and his crew counted muzzle flashes and figured the brig had twelve cannon and the schooner had six. They mounted a frontal counterattack. Jean's schooner came under heavy fire. A furious battle raged! The enemy schooner was equipped with a swivel gun, the better to rain its deadly fire directly upon its targets, and rain down upon the *Santander* it did, like hell's fury. Jean knew he would fight to the death if he must, for honor was everything to him.

The vessels clashed until after midnight, with cannon flashes lighting up the night sky amidst the thunderous boom of grapeshot striking the wooden ship. Jean managed to survive the skirmish with only some splinters from the shot hitting his schooner, but his chief lieutenant suffered a lethal wound. Jean was a man who was no stranger to death, and he knew from the man's shallow breathing and unfixed eyes that he would not live to see dawn.

It was then that Jean realized what he must do. He had for some time felt the noose tightening around his neck and knew his luck would not hold out much longer. Luck never gives, it only lends, as they say. It was only a matter of time before Jean's ran out completely. At this moment, fate had handed him an opportunity he could not decline. He devised a plot to make the world believe he had been killed.

My brother could only envision dying one way, and that was

at sea. "The sea is my life. So shall it be my death," he told me on more than one occasion. Therefore, with the help of his crew, who were loyal to him 'til the end, and encouraged by his dying chief lieutenant, Jean devised a clever ruse to make all believe that he had been mortally wounded in the battle. Petty Officer Francisco Similien assumed control of Lafitte's schooner. At one o'clock in the morning, he ordered the *Santander* to give up the fight and chart a course for Cartagena, away from the dangerous vessels wishing to do them harm.

As Jean predicted, the chief lieutenant died from his wounds, and it was decided that they would declare Jean deceased as well. It took several weeks for the *Santander* to limp into port, damaged as it was from the sea battle. Since a body could not have been kept aboard for so long a time, the crew reported that the bodies of those lost in the skirmish had been buried at sea, among them Captain Jean Lafitte. Meanwhile, Jean acted the part of the boatswain, as that man had been one of those buried at sea, having succumbed to injuries received during the battle. It took little effort for Jean to assume another man's role. He knew how to perform any job aboard a ship, and he had, of necessity, become masterful at disguising himself. No one had reason to suspect the story was untrue. Jean had successfully "died" and could now go on living.

Even if certain people did not trust his crew's account, it was of no real consequence. Jean needed only to plant the seed of doubt to loosen the noose. He required the smallest window to slip through to escape the dangers of his old life. He would be safe in his new life. Or so he wanted to believe. So we all wanted to believe.

Not long after Jean's "death," I received a post containing an account of Jean's final acts of bravery aboard the *Santander* as described by his crew members when they reached port. The death of my brother may not have been true, but the manner in which he was described by those who knew him so well could not have held more verisimilitude.

Their report asserted that in those dark hours of night, when the battle raged furiously, Captain Lafitte suffered a grievous wound. A cannonball ripped through his right arm, rendering it a ruined, gory mess and shattering the sword he gripped in that hand. A lesser man would have been out of the fight after suffering an injury such as this, but not Captain Lafitte! Amidst thunderous cannon shots and agonized screams, in the darkest of night, could be heard his stentorian voice, urging his men to keep up the fight!

But he was not one to ask of others what he himself was ill-prepared to do. Despite the blood streaming down his right side, seeping into the deck upon which he lay, he was just able to clamber to his feet, grip the blade in his other hand, and raise it in defiance. Both sides continued to clash until the sea ran red with blood from the crimson rivulets that flowed from their scuppers.

Night waned, but the battle only intensified. The Spanish warship blasted cannon at the *Santander*, and one found its mark too close to the captain. It splintered the wooden deck next to where he was standing. He was impaled through his abdomen by a piece of wood from his own ship. It pinned him to the deck, as if to lay claim to the beloved captain forevermore. This wound was lethal, but Lafitte was not one to succumb without a fight. And though he suffered wracking waves of torturous pain, he spent his last moments on this earth concerned about his men. He would not have them suffer his same fate. Rather than urging them to fight to the death, he implored them to end the battle and save themselves. Too much blood had been shed. He would be responsible for no more deaths.

With his dying breath, he wiped away the blood that seeped into his eyes, the better to see his beloved crew one last time. He looked up into their worried faces, smiled that roguish smile of his, and, through teeth clenched in pain, said, "We had a good run, boys! 'Til we meet again!" Then he expired.

The papers hailed my brother as a hero. He had found himself outgunned by far superior forces, yet he fought courageously to the death. He could not have asked for a finer ending.

His crew took liberties with the story, of course, but they perfectly captured the valor of the man. Had he truly been mortally injured, I have no doubt he would have fought to the death, sacrificing himself for the sake of his honor and the protection of his crew. That was the kind of man he was, and his crew respected him for it. Jean was brave and bold, and never ran from a fight, save for this one instance, when fortune necessitated his retreat so that he could survive to fight again.

Should the reader feel compelled to question Jean's motives for allowing the world to believe he had perished in that sea battle, I shall explain what egregious miscarriages of justice he had suffered to that point, and all will be made clear. As I have already stated in this document, Jean never thought of himself as a pirate. He was a privateer. He always had the sea in his blood, and he always knew he would make his way in the world as a man of the sea. Yet not as a pirate. Never as a pirate. If the reader is not well-versed in seafaring, allow me to explain the difference. If the reader is already familiar, please indulge me with this elucidation.

A pirate is a rogue who sails the seas looking to plunder ships. He cares not what flag the ship sails, nor the purpose of the voyage. If there are spoils to be had, the pirate will take them. A pirate ship will raise the bloody flag and demand that the ship surrender. No surrender means no quarter. Cargo will be taken, and no crew will be spared. Pirates are subject to being hanged if caught in the act of piracy. They are outlaws. Pirates are not to be trusted.

Corsairs and privateers are not outlaws. They have been issued a letter of marque from a nation, permitting them to target ships from unfriendly nations. There is a code under which corsairs operate. They do not shed blood indiscriminately. They will take a ship and its cargo as a prize, yet the crew should come to no harm at their hands.

All of us brothers, Jean, Pierre, and I, thought of ourselves as privateers, though I have gotten right with God and now know I sometimes acted the pirate. Yet not Jean. Never Jean. Even when we could not receive letters of marque for our country, even when we were privateers for other countries, we never knowingly targeted American vessels. Some will say otherwise, but they are wrong. For we are loyal citizens and also Freemasons, even Jean, but that is a tale I shall tell later.

There is a story that goes 'round that Jean attacked an American ship. They say he brutalized the captain. Yet this is false. Jean was not such a man. He lived by a code. It was one he would not break. However, there were also pirates plying the waters of the Gulf of Mexico. Not as many as there were a hundred years before, but they were still there. On more than one occasion, they would commit dastardly crimes in the name of Captain Jean Lafitte. The survivors of their mistreatment would report to the world how Jean Lafitte abused them. They would recount his heinous acts, and all would believe them. Why should they not? The survivors no doubt believed the lies they were telling. Why should they question the person who revealed his identity to them? Never trust a pirate!

And what could Jean do about such things? He could not stop the slander. He could not say, "This was not my doing!" By this time, he could no longer show himself in public, for he was a wanted man. A wanted man who had saved New Orleans from the British! His good deeds were too soon forgotten. People would rather believe the worst about a man. Such is the nature of men. But not all men. Some remembered. Some remained loyal. That is a tale I shall tell later.

Jean did not commit the detestable acts of which he was accused. It was not his custom to shed blood for the enjoyment of it. When he took a ship, he treated those aboard humanely. He never ransomed the crew. He released them. People are not cargo. The latter is fair game and the just spoils of privateering. Not the former.

There are many stories I can tell that prove his character. But why believe me when the newspapers say the same? I have searched for news of Jean since my return to New Orleans, ever curious to know what lies people write about him. But sometimes they speak the truth. The *Louisiana Chronicle* is one such paper that printed a story about my brother mere days before he "died." It relates the account of the captain of the American schooner *Columbus Ross* when he encountered Jean's *General Santander*. Did Jean capture the *Columbus Ross*? He easily could have. He had already seized two Spanish vessels on that particular voyage. But Jean would not act against an American ship. Instead, the captain of the *Columbus Ross* insists that Captain Lafitte treated him and his crew with the utmost politeness, never once demanding to see their papers of cargo, though the ship held a fortune. Instead, Jean convoyed the ship for two days, helping it safely navigate through dangerous waters known to conceal Spanish pirates. He replenished their stores of ammunition and offered them any other supplies they might require. This was the real Captain Jean Lafitte. He was a man who would save the innocent from wicked pirates, not for gain, only in the interest of doing what was right.

But the world did not know this about Jean, and he was forced to make his way over and over again, never afforded the luxury of a home, despite the riches he acquired. He was always moving, always starting over. It was becoming harder for him to find a safe place to land. Fewer countries were issuing letters of marque, and Jean was not willing to resort to acts of piracy. He lived by a code.

That is not to say he always followed the letter of the law. He did not. Smuggling was in his blood, as it was in Pierre's and mine as well. However, smuggling does not harm those except the wealthy and benefits many people, I say. People around New

Orleans, and especially those around Barataria Bay, still have a fondness for Jean Lafitte because he brought in goods for them to buy cheaply, items they required but could not afford due to the unjust embargoes imposed by our country in those days. Jean helped people get what they needed.

"Pirates are parasites, privateers are philanthropists," he told me on one occasion. Many thought of him as Robin Hood of the Bayou and called him by that name. That is a tale I shall tell later.

The years leading up to Jean's "death" had not been good to him. The world was changing, and the prospects for a privateer were shrinking quickly. Jean was struggling to make a living. He was in dire straits. He had no choice but to accept a letter of marque from Great Columbia. He was granted a commission in their navy and furnished with a schooner, the *General Santander*, named in honor of the vice-president of Great Columbia. He would prey only on Spanish merchant ships. Spain was his enemy for many reasons. But, Reader, hear me when I say to you that Jean never attacked American ships. It was a line he would not cross, so help me God. Yet the Americans came for him. They wished to believe he was a pirate. They wanted to make an example of him, to dissuade those who would terrorize the seas. They chose to forget all he had done for them. They chose to forget he was a patriot.

The Gulf, the office in which he plied his trade, was awash with American vessels like the *Alligator* and the *Grampus*, part of the pirate-hunting squadron under Commodore David Porter. The British were also active in the area, patrolling the waters to combat pirates and privateers alike. It made no difference to them that Jean was a legitimate privateer with a commission in a navy and a letter of marque to prove it. He was the Terror of the Gulf! They aimed to put an end to him. It was not safe for him to be about in the Gulf or the Caribbean, even as a legitimate privateer. He had enemies lying in wait all around. They drove him off his land in Barataria and again in Galveston. They hunted him at sea.

In 1823, he was a man whose country had abandoned him. He was a man with a price on his head. He was a wanted man with no home and no legitimate prospects. A lesser man would have turned to pirating, but Jean was not such a man. He did what he needed to do to survive, to remake himself so that he could live out his remaining days in peace. Peace was the one luxury he could never afford.

* * *

The next day, Tobias entered St. Louis No. 2 and made his way to Dominique You's tomb. The gravel around it was now evenly dispersed, thanks to Tobias's efforts from the previous afternoon. The nameplate lay on the ground where Tobias had left it. The tomb itself looked generic—just a plain brick facade, with nothing to distinguish its occupant. There could be anyone buried within it. Tobias felt heat creep up his face. "You deserve better, Dominique You," he said.

The morning was overcast, with rain clouds threatening. There would be afternoon storms. He wanted to have the nameplate back on You's tomb before the weather turned. The nameplate was far too heavy for him to reaffix to the tomb by himself, even with a good portion of it carved out. He could have requested assistance from one of the day laborers who usually helped him with such tasks, but he did not wish to have anyone else in the cemetery know what he had uncovered in the tomb. Instead, he went back out through the iron gates and approached some neighborhood boys who had taken to loitering near the cemetery most days. They were a rough-looking group, all patched-up trousers, unkempt hair, and faces that needed washing. Yet they allowed Tobias to pass unmolested twice daily, so he figured they were not as tough as they wished to appear. This morning, he decided to test his theory.

"Fancy making a few quick coins today, do ya, lads?"

The three boys, slouching against the brick perimeter walls, straightened at this unexpected offer.

"And what's your grand idea, then?" the tallest of the boys asked, suspicion rolling off his scrunched-up face in waves.

"Ah, now, it's nothing against the law, I promise. I just need a few extra hands to help with a quick bit of marble lifting."

"Tis nothin' to do with movin' bodies, is it?" asked one of the smaller boys.

"Not at all, you'll see. It will be the quickest coins you'll ever make." After an exchange of looks among the trio, the boys followed Tobias into the cemetery. He led them to Dominique You's tomb. The boys shuffled nervously from foot to foot, clearly unnerved by the proximity to the body within. Tobias explained what he wanted them to do, and just as he suspected, the boys were wholly uninterested in the hollow portion of the marble. If anything, they seemed relieved the nameplate was not as heavy as it looked and were able to perform the task quickly.

"Damn! This place stinks to high heaven! How do ya stand it here all day?" asked the tallest boy as they finished up. The other two nodded in agreement, not removing their fingers as they pinched their noses closed.

"Mind your tongue!" Tobias snapped, causing all three to jump. "I'll not have you offending the souls resting here with your profanity." He fished out the coins and handed them to the boys' outstretched hands. They shoved them deep into their ratty pockets and hurried towards the cemetery gates. Tobias could hear them exclaiming as they left.

"Told ya, he's a right old coot!"

"Talks about 'em like they can still hear ya!"

Tobias paid them little mind. He had heard such comments before. He looked around. The cemetery was once again still and quiet, yet he had the oddest sensation that he was being watched. It was one he'd felt quite often when he first began working in the cemetery. He'd assumed it was simply part of growing accustomed to spending days amongst so many souls at rest. So why did the sensation linger? He shook his head. *Just my imagination,* he thought. What was he expecting—a pirate to pop out from behind a tomb? Surely no one knew about his discovery, with the exception of Mary Catherine.

Yet, he had left the nameplate off the tomb overnight. If someone had been watching the tomb, they might have realized he had found the book. But why should anyone do that? Dominique You had received no mourners since he'd been interred. *No,* Tobias thought, *I've simply been reading too many adventure tales and fancy myself in one.* He resumed his duties, failing to notice the man lurking in the shadows nearby.

By late morning, he was ready for a respite from his toil, although it was far too early to leave for the day. He decided he should not stray from his usual daily routine and settled himself in his favorite spot in the cemetery, sitting upon a bench he had placed there for the express purpose of reading. It was a lovely area, shaded by magnolia trees and surrounded by fragrant bushes, which today were making a valiant effort to camouflage less aromatic scents. It might be considered an idyllic spot if one could disregard the underlying fusty odor of decay and shift focus away from the tombs. And while most might not think of a cemetery as idyllic under any circumstances, it was the place Tobias had felt most comfortable for the past few years. As he settled on the bench, he realized that if he looked past the tomb directly in front of him, he could spy Dominique You's tomb. It was curious that he had not noticed this before, but as it was not within his direct line of sight, Tobias supposed he'd simply never taken note of what lay beyond.

He reached into his pocket, momentarily wishing he could retrieve the dove-gray journal instead of the volume currently occupying the space. Still, this particular book never failed to bring him contentment. The somnolent summer morning was quiet, save for the cooing doves, the screeching cicadas, and Tobias's voice as he read aloud the same three chapters of *The Last of the Mohicans* that he'd read to the boys the previous night.

Chapter Six

Mary Catherine Whitney's Translation of the Journal of Dominique You

The Early Days of a Privateer

It was a sad state for a man of Jean's ilk to find himself at forty-one years of age and hiding from the world. I'd never thought it would come to this. Few knew all he had accomplished and the challenges he had overcome. I knew.

Those who knew Jean in his earliest years did not doubt he would succeed, for he was destined for greatness. "There's fire in his belly and steel in his spine," our father used to say of him. I saw the promise from his youngest years. I believed he had the bravery to survive on the high seas.

We were not ones to talk about where we were from to others. We told disparate tales to suit our needs. Some thought we were born in Saint-Domingue, others believed we were from France. Some even thought we hailed from Spain, but those were the ones who did not know us well. Some thought we were brothers, but most did not. They knew of Pierre, but not of me. I was just part of his crew to most. I was happy for them to think it was so. When you live the life we did, it does not pay to have your business all about. We told people what we wanted them to believe. All the better to protect ourselves.

It gave us no pleasure to deceive. We did what we had to do to shield ourselves from enemies who wished to do us harm. This is why I say never trust a pirate! If their mouths are moving, they are lying! If Jean were reading this, he would reprimand me for calling us pirates. I mean him no offense. Though we may not have been pirates ourselves, we learned their ways. We put their lessons to good use. Those lessons kept us alive.

Secrets won't stay buried forever. Nor should they. It's time that ours are told. The world will know the truth. We were born in France, in the village of Bages. A more charming place cannot be imagined. It is home to fishermen and winegrowers. There are oyster beds and the most beautiful flora and fauna a man could wish to see. Lavender and roses were nearly always about, as were the prettiest songbirds, though I do not recall their names. We ate well from the bounty that surrounded us. I can still smell the heavenly aroma of the day's pot-au-feu simmering on the fire.

Jean and I share a father. His name was Pierre Lafitte. I am some years older than Jean. Dominique is not my given name, nor is You my surname. I was christened Alexandre Lafitte. I became Dominique You, but that is a tale I shall tell later. My mother died in childbirth. My father then married Marguerite Destreil, who bore him six children. Not all survived. Jean was the youngest boy, born in 1782. Pierre was two years older than Jean.

Many men in the region were involved in trade. Our father was among them. We lived a quiet life in Bages until revolution came in 1789. It swept all of us up in its wake. My family would have been content to mind our own affairs. We cared not for the machinations of those in Paris. Unfortunately, peace was not meant for us. There was much turmoil. The repercussions of unsettled politics bled into all regions of France. We could not hide from it, even in our little village. The years of unrest cost many men their livelihoods. The Lafittes were among those who suffered.

My father was a ruined man. Many left France for the United States, and some went to the Antilles. They were eager to find new opportunities. My family was one of them. I went along, though I did not remain there long. It was time for me to make my way, yet I will not dwell on my life, save when the narrative is necessary to explain Jean's actions. This is Jean's story, not mine. I will only say that I would go on to fight for Napoleon before beginning my career as a privateer. It was in his army that I learned my skills as an artilleryman and became an expert cannoneer.

Jean and the family settled in Saint-Domingue, which they now call Haiti. Our father was often away or engaged with his business concerns. Jean's mother died, so he was raised on the island by his maternal grandmother. Jean was very fond of her. She was of Spanish and Jewish origin. She and her people were treated wretchedly by the Spanish. Her husband, Jean's grandfather, died at the hands of the Inquisition. Their property was confiscated, and they were no longer welcome in their homeland. Jean hated the Spanish for this, and for many other atrocities he was to witness in his life. His fondest wish was to chase the Spanish back to Europe and grant freedom to all of Spanish America. "Spanish dogs," he would call them, then spit on the ground to rid his mouth of the repellent word. He blamed their lying and cheating ways and their poor treatment of the slaves for the uprising led by Henri Christophe and Toussaint L'Ouverture in Haiti. It was a bloody affair in which many people were executed or forced to seek refuge in other lands.

His grandmother was a woman of strong convictions. She took great care in raising the children. She saw to their education herself when they were young, teaching them to read, write, and speak Spanish. She arranged for tutors as they grew. Jean could speak and write in Spanish, French, and English. He became a well-educated man who comported himself as a gentleman and could move about effortlessly in the highest social circles. Yet he also had to deal with men who were rough and often uncivilized. He could handle both with ease. He attributed this to his grandmother.

"That woman was a respectable lady on Sunday who could bring a grown man to tears on Monday," he said of her. He was indebted to her for showing him how to make his way through the world with dignity and strength.

His grandmother was a small, portly woman. She had poor vision, which necessitated her face to screw up in a squint most of her waking hours. A wrinkled visage was one of the most prominent features I can recall about her, besides her hair. It was white as snow and had been for many years.

When a neighbor asked her how she managed two strapping boys at her age, she would respond by peeling back her bonnet the slightest bit to reveal a shock of ivory locks and say, "It's those boys who made it so." There is likely some truth to this!

She took charge of these children who were not her own. She never raised her voice. Her calm demeanor in the face of savage children, such as Jean and Pierre, taught Jean valuable lessons. He learned them well. When, later, his crew at sea or in his camp would get rough with one another, Jean could quell it with only a stern look. If the threat of mutiny lay heavy on the air, his demeanor, austere yet unflappable, would quench those fires as well.

I was the brother with the choleric personality. I was known to have a jolly twinkle in my eye one minute, then a devil of a temper the next. Jean used to say I had a sack of rattlesnakes in my belly. All was fine 'til someone shook me up. Jean was not quick to anger like me. He was not a man to be trifled with, yet he knew how to contain his temper. His command of himself was like no man I have ever known. When forced to act in violence, he did so quickly and efficiently. Then his placid demeanor would return. I shall tell those tales later.

After fighting for Napoleon, I decided to become a seafaring man. I was often far from my family, but I would return to Saint-Domingue when I was able to do so. On one of my visits, Captain Puilijon, for whom I sailed, came to our home upon my invitation and regaled Jean and Pierre with his stories about life aboard a ship. There were many such guests in our house in those days. He educated them about the life of a privateer. Jean's grandmother disapproved of such talk, but Jean was not deterred. He saw privateering as a way to seek adventure. He wanted no other life. It was from Captain Puilijon that I and my brothers after me learned the lesson never to reveal our real names or place of birth. A privateer must protect his identity as he would his treasure. It is one and the same.

All save my family knew me by now not as Alexandre Lafitte, but as Dominique You. This was not an alias I assigned myself. It settled upon me like a fog that would not lift. I came to be known as Dominique You in my early days of privateering. I knew I should not share my true name when engaging in privateering, not with the country for which I acted, nor with those I fought against. Yet, at that time, I had no notion of what I wanted to call myself. I was new on the ships then, still learning the ropes. I was compelled to do whatever jobs were requested of me, not having earned my way to a better place. Such is how it goes. I did not complain but performed my given duties and whatever else was asked of me to the best of my ability.

The only information I was willing to reveal about myself was that I was from Saint-Domingue, which was my home at that time. When one of the other sailors needed me to perform a task, he would call to me by shouting, "Domingue, vous!" or in English, "Dominique, you!" Over time, they simply called me Dominique You. I felt the name suited me and was as good as any other, so I kept it for the remainder of my days. Even now, though I live the life of a solid citizen of New Orleans, am a business owner, and serve on the city council, all but a very few souls know me as

Dominique You. My name is my treasure. I do not care to share it.

Jean's grandmother wished for Jean and Pierre to become educated and make their way in the world in respectable professions. "Books will take you farther than a ship ever could," she would tell them when she caught me regaling them with tales of my adventures and all I had seen at sea.

They yearned to hear my stories. They ate them up like ambrosia. They would come into my room when their grandmother was away and beg me to tell them a story. I would spin a yarn from time to time, as all men of the sea are wont to do. Jean, especially, could not get his fill. Sometimes I would relate tales told to me about pirates and their deeds. He was not deterred by the violent acts of tossing a crew into the sea or the bloody battles that raged between ships at war with each other. I told them of my own adventures, as I had been privateering and had made trips to Cuba, Mexico, and South America by then. I believe it was my stories that made them want to become privateers.

As Jean and Pierre grew older, they wished for more than stories about the life of a privateer or the harrowing tales of pirates on the seas. I would oblige them upon my return trips to Saint-Domingue. It was from me that they learned the true ways and duties of a privateer. At times, I wonder, had I not filled Jean's head with the glory and escapades of privateering, what he might have made of his life. He was a bright boy, quick-witted and inquisitive. He could have excelled in his studies and achieved great things in numerous fields.

This was undoubtedly his grandmother's view. She wanted Jean to go into trade or become a merchant on Saint-Domingue. She never wanted a life at sea for him, and though she knew in her heart he would not be content on land, she longed to keep him near her. She knew he possessed a strong sense of egalitarianism and would stomach no injustice. Her intuition told her that Jean was destined to emancipate the suffering souls exploited by those who brutally reigned over them. However, she thought he might accomplish this remarkable feat through the power of his quill. She knew his intellect best.

Yet Jean loved adventure above all else. Though he had a strong sense of duty, his desire to chase danger through the deep blue waters was too strong within him. Sailing the seas, privateering against his enemies, afforded him the perfect combination of all that he valued most.

His decision to embark on a life of privateering was the culmination of many moments, but the one he recalled the most vividly was when I cast off on my first adventure as captain of my own ship. I have heard my story through his voice over more than one bottle of grog.

I can easily recall him telling the tale, a twinkle in his eye, glancing my way as he began. "Alexandre got in his head one day that he was ready to captain his own vessel. So what does he do? He fits out a brig as his very own privateer's ship. He was off to capture Spanish ships and make his fortune. Nothing but piss and vinegar, my brother was in those days!"

I boasted to our father that my brig could take on any ship at sea, though in truth I had but nine men in my crew, six small cannons, some muskets, and swords.

Our father was convinced I was mad. "Might as well throw his body to the depths now and save us all the trouble of waiting for word of him," he told Jean and Pierre.

But my brothers did not believe him. Jean used to tell the story of how he and Pierre snuck out of the house when I left on that first voyage. "In the darkness of night, we arose from our beds. We were quiet as church mice as we eased the door open with extreme care, so as not to elicit the tiniest squeak from its hinges. Then we made all haste to the pier where our brother was departing. We arrived in time to see him raise the jib and the main sails and glide through the inky waters to his destiny beyond. We returned home without rousing a soul, and no one was any the wiser."

Jean was always one to tell a colorful tale, but he was wrong about one detail. I spied Jean and Pierre at the pier that night. I knew I must return, if only to prove to them it could be done.

Had I not returned from that voyage, as indeed my father believed, perhaps Jean would have taken a different path. My demise might have convinced him that the life of a privateer was not a glamorous one. He would have seen the inherent danger of such a life. Yet I did return after two months at sea. Jean would tell the tale of the town buzzing with news that a pirate ship was docking and bringing with it the spoils of two captured ships!

"Pierre and I, never keen to miss an adventure, ran to the pier to witness the spectacle. Sure enough, we saw the captured crew being led off as prisoners. We knew not who the captain was, but he was clearly a man of importance, issuing orders that his crew carried out immediately. As the captain neared us, a gust of wind blew his hat from his head, and we saw that this man was our long-lost brother! We whooped and hollered with joy. After this, our course was set. We would be privateers just like Alexandre."

In the early years of the new century, I went back for a time to fight for Napoleon's righteous cause. It was in performing my duties as an artilleryman there that I suffered powder burns to my left eye. The scar of that injury would remain with me forever. I was proud of my service and wore this disfiguration as a badge of honor, as others told me it most certainly was. The scarring made me easily recognizable and meant I would never be able to disguise myself as Jean was so adept at doing. It did not matter much to me, as I was not the sort of man who could blend easily into a crowd. I am short of stature, yet with shoulders as broad as a man of six feet. My nose is a prominent feature on my face. It is hooked and crooked, giving me an odd mien. I was known to brawl in my day, having that fiery temper I alluded to before, and my nose bears testimony to that fact. Yet I was proud of all my features, even though none would say I had a pleasing countenance.

Despite my stature, I carried myself in a way that made other men know I could handle myself when need be. This helped me deal with the rough sorts one finds at sea. Those who were too ignorant to sense the danger that lay beneath the surface, who stirred it up thinking they could make quick work of a man shorter than they, those were the ones who suffered at my hands. A man learns lessons from combat. I do not only mean that he learns the skills of his post. He also learns how to survive. His instincts are honed, and his will to live is sharpened like a blade. The same is true for life at sea. A privateer cannot eschew violence, even if he is a good man who does not seek it out. Violence seeks the privateer. He must know how to inflict it to save himself.

I say these things not to paint a pretty picture of myself. I do so only to explain the world Jean grew up in and how it shaped him into the man he was to become. Jean followed me, as he was wont to do in his early years, and fought for Napoleon as well.

Upon hearing stories about France's valiant efforts to quell the British and Spanish, Jean and Pierre yearned to fight for the French. They felt it was their sacred duty. No matter how much his grandmother attempted to dissuade him from joining France's military, Jean refused to be swayed. It was in doing his duty to Napoleon that Jean learned fencing skills that would save his life on more than one occasion and garner not a little bit of fame on the streets of New Orleans for how artfully he could wield his dress sword. He served France bravely. These skills he carried through his life.

Ever restless for new adventure, Jean and Pierre came to realize that a marvelous opportunity was afforded them to begin their lives as privateers. They could be issued letters of marque by France to target Spanish and British vessels. Thus, they could achieve their dream of a life at sea while serving their country. To that end, they found themselves back in the Antilles, working as privateers, seeking to capture enemy ships and their treasures.

I understand I have been remiss in not painting a fuller picture of Pierre up to this point. I can only ask the reader to forgive my omission. I have not the time to correct my error by starting this document anew. I will attempt to make amends now. At first glance, their appearance was similar enough to declare to the world that they were brothers. Upon closer inspection, however, their features differed considerably. Jean had the swarthier complexion of the two. Pierre had paler skin but the same dark hair and eyes as his brother. They were both lanky boys who grew into tall men. Although I was some years older, they towered over me from an early age. They were athletic boys, although Jean was more keen on sports than Pierre. Jean's grandmother would often fret about feeding them enough to fill their long frames. "Might as well pour this stew into a hollow log for all the good it will do these boys," I heard her comment on more than one of my visits.

The two were nearly inseparable. I cannot recall a time when their opinion on a matter differed. They found trouble like a diviner finds water. Such incorrigibility must be managed and redirected, or chaos will ensue. To that end, the boys began their education with a tutor. I was not with them for their studies, yet I can only imagine the tribulations this unfortunate man must have endured at the hands of the Lafitte boys. I shudder to think of the herculean task of taming them. Jean told me tales of endless frogs placed in the man's pockets and spiders secreted into his bag when his attention was directed elsewhere.

Pierre, truth be told, had the greatest intellect of all us Lafitte boys. He excelled at his lessons. He could solve the most intricate puzzles with ease. He would nearly always win at a game of chess. He could plan six moves ahead of his opponent. He had a knack for anticipating what might come next. His foxy, keen mind could foresee what others might do and shift accordingly. Jean was the one who could dream the dream and imagine the grand plan.

Pierre was the one who made the plan come to fruition. I just did what my brothers told me to do. This was the pattern for all our schemes and business dealings as adult men.

Pierre was not as fearsome as Jean. For although Jean was calm of demeanor most of the time, his look was stern and could be frightful to those who did not know him well or those foolish enough to cross him. But Pierre nearly always kept his calm visage. He was rarely at loggerheads with anyone, though I do not mean to paint him as a pacifist. He would defend himself when necessary. All the Lafittes could do so. Pierre was quite fastidious about his appearance in a way that Jean and I were not. Jean cared not a whit how he looked, though women certainly found his manner pleasing. Pierre was careful and calculated in his grooming. He wore long sideburns in a classical manner. Though he fancied himself looking like a Grecian warrior, Jean and I teased that he more closely resembled a barrister.

I recall him responding once, "At least I don't walk around like a ragamuffin." That was for the best, as Pierre, more than either Jean or I, needed to be able to move about in the business world of New Orleans, particularly after he opened the blacksmith shop.

Now that I have corrected my error of omission as best I can, given the pressure of time, I shall return to my tale and explain how the Lafitte brothers began their careers as privateers. They went about it in a more clever way than most. This was mainly due to the combined talents of the two. They were calculated when plotting their new venture. Though they were new to privateering, they stood on the shoulders of giants in that they had been taught all the intricacies by the captains who visited our home in Saint-Domingue and by me. Please excuse my immodesty. I do not intend to come across as a braggart, and anyone who sees me knows I am not a giant! Yet I'd learned more than a little about the business of being a privateer, and I told them all I knew, advising them about mistakes to avoid.

By the time they embarked on their path, they had gained the experience of several lifetimes, which allowed them to burst onto the scene seemingly out of nowhere and take the Caribbean and Gulf by storm. Jean had all the makings of a solid privateer. He had bravery. He had experience in battle. He possessed the necessary combat skills, from swordsmanship to artillery. In addition, Jean had skills most privateers lacked. He was educated. He knew multiple languages. He could communicate with and command respect from men of all different ilk. He also had Pierre, whose intellect and business acumen were unmatched. 'Twas a combination of all the aforementioned qualities that made Jean Lafitte the greatest privateer the world has known. And New Orleans would be the place where his empire was born.

Chapter Seven

New Orleans

August 1831

"Red beans and rice again, Ma?" Shane asked when Mary Catherine placed the dish in front of him.

Connor's swift kick under the cypress dining table compelled him to add, "Good thing it's my favorite. I hope we have beans again tomorrow night."

"You two are good lads, I can tell you that. I know you must be wanting a different meal, but it's all I can manage these days, what with your father working me half to death on the translation!"

"Have you found it yet, Ma? Have you figured out where the pirate treasure is?" Connor asked.

"How do they know about the pirate treasure?" asked Tobias.

"Well, I suppose it's because your sons are quite good at pressing their ears to the door to listen to us talking. Maybe those ears need a good boxing?" Mary Catherine shifted her narrowed gaze from her husband to her sons.

"We're not trying to listen, honest, Ma, but you and Da talk about it almost every night, and since we sleep right next to the dining room..."

Shane finished his brother's thought, "Yeah, we can't help but hear you tell Da you're working your fingers to the bone day and night on this journal and that it will likely be the death of you."

"It's true, alright. And just what will my poor boys do without me? It's a good thing they've become accustomed to subsisting on nothing but beans and rice, I suppose, as the oil I'm burning through, working all night as I've been doing, will no doubt bankrupt us before long." She heaved a tremendous sigh and cast a sideways glance at Tobias, to be sure he was paying attention.

"Kitten, perhaps you might take a break this evening," he suggested.

Her tight-lipped, wordless glare was all the response he needed. He looked at the boys, who were trying not to laugh. They, too, saw through her angry demeanor. She was thoroughly enjoying the toil. Tobias sensed that she needed the distraction from their daily lives as much as he did. He also knew she enjoyed complaining immensely, so he played his part, offering sympathy for her sore hands, tired eyes, and general exhaustion. He lamented the stains on her tablecloth when she complained that the delicate embroidery was marred with black ink splotches. He apologized profusely for his treatment of her. All the while, he patiently listened to her carp about Dominique You's writing habits, which she found to be frustratingly subpar.

"The amount of scratch-outs! Did this man not rewrite a single page? And the ink splats! You would think he was writing in a burning house, trying to finish before the flames got him!"

At such assertions, Tobias found himself glancing down at the beautiful dove-gray journal, whose cover was becoming more ink splattered by the day, and pictured his wife's scratchy, barely legible writing and the smeared ink throughout the journal, the sign of a person who could not be bothered to sand her pages, let alone wait for them to dry. He decided it was best not to point out the similarities. Instead, he eagerly awaited the next installment of the translation, which would allow him to learn more about the gripping adventures of the privateer.

Mary Catherine Whitney's Translation of the Journal of Dominique You

New Orleans and Barataria

By 1804, all three of us Lafitte men found ourselves drawn to New Orleans. Refugees had been pouring in from the revolution in Haiti. The busy port meant people from all over the world called it home. New Orleans offered myriad markets for privateers. It was an ideal location to sell all that we captured.

Louisiana, especially New Orleans, felt like home from the moment we arrived. There were many Frenchmen, and they were eager to buy our wares, as they had been accustomed to purchasing smuggled goods and the merchandise of privateers, a tradition that dated back to colonial days. The unjust tariff policies of the Spanish and their poor treatment of the French in New Orleans made it a necessity, so many welcomed our efforts from the start.

Jean would reprimand me if I failed to explain that we did not intend to be smugglers. A privateer is eligible to receive compensation for the value of the contents of captured vessels. We chose to make those goods available to the people of Louisiana without the unjustly inflated customs duties imposed upon them. When the United States passed the Embargo Act, life became difficult for the law-abiding citizens of New Orleans. They could not get the things they needed without paying exorbitant prices, and often could not afford necessities. We could not have brought our goods to them at a reasonable price had we paid the unjust taxes imposed by the government. We initially attempted to do this. I would have gone another way, but Jean insisted we follow the law.

Eventually, he became disgusted with the corruption of the officials and their pretensions of moral superiority. He was pushed into smuggling by corrupt American customs officers who demanded extortion payments from him. He decided to bring goods directly to the people.

"Come get what you need—Robin Hood of the bayou provides!" This is what folks used to say about my brother and the goods he brought to them.

Any laws we broke, we felt were justified, because our actions always benefited others. Mind you, I do not mean to claim that our actions did not help us, as well. They did, indeed! We were riding high in our New Orleans days because, while we were not pirates, we were smugglers.

We required a place to sell our goods in New Orleans, and to that end, Pierre purchased a blacksmith shop on Rue St. Philip, along with living quarters for him and Jean on the corner of Rue St. Philip and Rue Bourbon. I did not spend much of my time in New Orleans. The real base of our operations was forty miles south of New Orleans, in Barataria. This is where I lived and worked. Barataria Bay and the surrounding area had always been a haven for pirates, smugglers, and legitimate privateers alike. There were outlaws there, along with decent folks who made their living from the abundance of seafood and wildlife, and many a Frenchman as well, mostly exiles from Napoleon's wars. It was an ideal place to go if you were up to no good and did not want the law looking over your shoulder. Barataria's name hints at its reputation. I'm told it comes from Spanish words meaning to deceive and cheap things. I cannot say if this is true, but both fit the place.

Barataria was already up and running when we arrived. This is precisely what makes Jean's actions even more brilliant. How do you come into a place filled with rough sorts who would kill you just as soon as look at you? How do you end up taking over such men and becoming their master? And especially when some have been there for generations? Only Jean could have accomplished such a feat and done it so quickly. He made it look like child's play. I wrote earlier that he was the sort of man who could talk to all types and command their respect, even the most dangerous and roguish of men. No one else in Barataria had such skills. Only Jean. So it was he who came to rule them all.

He began by accumulating vast knowledge of the region and all its secrets. The land is a maze of swamps and bayous, impossible to navigate without knowing your way. But we could navigate them with ease. Pierre and Jean, who never did anything by half measures, enlisted the help of our trusted officers and charted the coastline, drawing maps. Then they learned the interior of the region. They knew every nook and cranny, every oak and cypress grove.

"Barataria holds no secrets from me," Jean would say.

He knew those bayous better than some who had lived there all their lives. He utilized that knowledge to establish a network of secret transportation routes, spanning from the mouth of the Mississippi River to New Orleans and beyond. Some of the inlets and bayous were so shallow and winding as to be impassable except for shallow-bottomed pirogues, which we used to best advantage.

While learning everything about the area, he made himself indispensable to the Baratarians. Initially, he achieved this through his roles as an agent and banker. Jean would help privateers bring their goods to New Orleans through Barataria Bay. He was the man who got their goods liquified into profit. Jean was not content to move the goods that other privateers brought to Barataria. Jean had ambition. He was driven. He always wanted to build things bigger and better than they were before. Jean bought ships and hired captains to sail them, earning more from their plunder than he possibly could have had he sailed only one ship. He made sure all had letters of marque. We were privateers, as he always reminded us. Not pirates! Pirates are parasites, privateers are philanthropists.

These men, who came to rely on Jean, knew their trade, whether it was pirating or smuggling, but they were not skilled in the other aspects of business. I will not try to explain the complexities because I do not understand them myself. Jean and Pierre understood, and they could assist these men to the degree that they found they could not survive without the help of the two brothers who had only recently come into their lives. Everyone involved was earning more than they ever had before. Jean made this possible, so they followed him.

Jean used his charisma and natural leadership to convince the Baratarians to make him their leader for the benefit of all in the area. Mind you, this was no easy task. Barataria was a hornet's nest. It was not wise to stir them up. Men who had been at loggerheads with one another, who had warred with one another, all united under Jean. He created a company of privateers. They were never wholly tamed or civilized, but they were under his control. They were working for their mutual benefit.

Jean used to quote one of his books of war, saying, "The supreme art of war is to subdue the enemy without fighting."

I am not as well-read as my brother, and I cannot recall who said this, but Jean took it to heart and attempted to avoid violence in his dealings with these men whenever possible. But violent men, at times, will only respond to violent measures. In those moments, Jean did not shy away from what needed to be done.

I shall offer one example to elucidate my point. In Barataria, there was a man who called himself Grambo. He was a particularly roguish sort, cruel and quarrelsome. He refused to fall under Jean's yoke. He dared call himself a pirate when Jean insisted they were privateers. He had a group of men under his command, and he did not take kindly to Jean assuming control of the island. What was Jean to do? No amount of convincing would have led this man to accept Jean's authority, and he could not have a rival vying for power. He knew he must take bold and decisive action against this group or face insurrection. Even a whisper of mutiny on a ship cannot be tolerated, or chaos will ensue. So it was in Barataria. To that end, one of the men under Grambo's command opposed Jean's authority. Jean simply drew his pistol and shot the man through the heart, killing him on the spot, in front of all the men. No one questioned his authority after that, though Grambo would forevermore resent Jean and work against his interests. That is a tale I shall tell in time.

We used the narrow bayous, some no more than streams, to our advantage to hide the cargo coming off our ships. We stored the cargo in warehouses, some forty in total, scattered throughout Barataria and hidden away in the bayous where no one could find them. There were goods from all over the world, including the finest silks, furniture, clothing, tapestries, rugs, leather goods, china, crystal, whiskey, wine, and rum.

We also needed a marketplace in the bayou to sell these items. Sometimes we brought the market to New Orleans. But people knew to come to Barataria to buy their goods. The Barataria region is not all bayous, mind you. There are several small islands that we also utilized to great advantage. These became my home for years. They offer all one needs to survive. Some are covered by shells and shaded by chênières of oaks. On one of these islands, Jean built our base of operations, which we called the Grand Temple. This was a reference to our Freemasonry ideals.

Jean, Pierre, and I were all proud Freemasons. There were many of our brethren in Barataria. The structure that Jean built, he therefore named after King Solomon's Temple. The Bible says God told Solomon's father, King David, to construct it as a final resting place for the Ark of the Covenant, where the tablets bearing the Ten Commandments are kept. The ark was to be housed in the innermost room of the temple, known as the holy of holies. Solomon constructed his temple in Jerusalem, and Jean constructed his in Barataria, Louisiana. Freemasons are builders at their core. They build a better world by seeking out truth and working for the betterment of all people. It is fitting that my tomb will house this journal, a tomb built by my Mason brothers, a tomb that bears the Mason symbol on my nameplate, the nameplate behind which this journal is hidden. There is much about my Brotherhood that I cannot reveal. Yet the Masons are a part of this story. I will tell what parts I can when the time comes.

The Grand Temple that Jean built was not just a temple of Freemasonry. It was the place where we accepted our cargo and regularly held auctions. This was a secret spot. It could be accessed only by pirogue. We would spread word through the blacksmith shop in New Orleans about what would be for sale at the auction that weekend, and many would journey to Barataria, sometimes spending a night or two there. It was a grand party in the bayou. People came to buy what they needed and stayed for some raucous fun.

I would be remiss if I led the reader to believe that we lived rough in Barataria, even though we lived among some who were themselves rough and coarse. On the contrary, we lived in grand style there. Jean built a mansion on the island of Grand Terre. He entertained gentlemen of the finest sort in a manner that would rival the most lavish parties in New Orleans. He hosted feasts that lasted days, with tropical fruits, a variety of game, and perfectly prepared seafood straight from the Gulf, all served on magnificent silverware. The finest French and Spanish wines were offered in the most delicate crystal glasses. Jean was the consummate host. He was charming and full of grace, ever the brilliant conversationalist, brimming with wit and colorful tales. When the meal finally came to an end, Cuban cigars were offered alongside rare vintages of brandy and other liqueurs. His guests must have thought they had been transported to Paris for all the extravagance of his parties, yet they were in the bayous of Louisiana.

I cannot continue with my tale until I explain something about our actions in those days. It is something grave and shameful that I know Jean would disapprove of my leaving out. I can only ask the reader to forgive my omission, as my haste prevents me from rewriting my account correctly. I must explain that some of the "cargo" sold in Barataria and at auction in New Orleans was human. At that time, slaves from Africa were worth a fortune in the South.

They were so valuable as to be called "black ivory." Planters from around New Orleans required slave labor, and since 1808, it had become illegal to import them to America. Our ships were able to commandeer slavers as they traveled from the Guinea coast across the Atlantic. These captured ships with their miserable human cargo were brought to Barataria, where they were sold at some of these auctions.

Jean, Pierre, and I were all involved. I will not pretend we were not. I will not deny that we turned a blind eye to the suffering of these souls. We thought only of the profit they represented. It was not until later that we came to deeply regret our part in the heinous trade of human beings. Jean, before either Pierre or I, profoundly and bitterly regretted it. He convinced Pierre and me of the error of our ways. I cannot find the words to express how ashamed I am, and that is ultimately between the Lord and me. The story of how Jean came to know the horrors entailed in the selling of humans for profit will be told in due course in my account. The time is not right to tell it now.

New Orleans was booming in those days, and the people enjoyed luxury items. Our enterprise was making money hand over fist. Pierre stayed in New Orleans most of the time, minding the blacksmith shop and handling business matters there, while I remained in Barataria, living among the privateers in the bayous. I was happy to do it, as I had found my place there. I was given a great deal of responsibility by Jean, who found it necessary to split his time between Barataria and New Orleans.

I enjoyed my life in Barataria. We had created our own city, complete with all that we needed. We had fortifications, scouts everywhere to warn us of approaching danger, and more weaponry to protect ourselves than most armies possessed. Everyone knew we were there, but the government let us be, at least for a while. People came and bought our wares at auction, and Jean lorded over it all.

They called him "king of the pirates." I should not need to say that he despised this epithet. Yet the splendor in which he lived in his "kingdom" of Barataria made it a somewhat apt title.

In Barataria, we used to amuse ourselves with pranks, aided by a good bit of drink. I was known as the jokester of the island. I liked to scare the fellows, especially when they were new to the place. I would make dummies out of straw and hang them from the rafters of the barns or warehouses. At night, these straw men looked just like corpses swaying in the moonlight. More than once, a hardened privateer came screaming and running out of the building after seeing one.

One night, after more than a bit of carousing, I put gunpowder in Cook's pepper shaker. We all went to sleep and forgot about what I had done until the sound of a gun awakened us. We thought we were under attack! We woke up scrambling for our weapons (and our breeches). We could not find the source of the gunfire we had heard, but we saw Cook come running out of the kitchen, screaming "au secours!"

Then we remembered what I had done, and we could not breathe for all our laughing. Cook had shaken the pepper into some eggs he was heating in a cast-iron pan, causing a small explosion in the kitchen. He did not take kindly to that prank! He would have quit, but Jean paid his people well, and he was not hurt, so he stayed on. I do not believe he seasoned our food much after that. I suppose I cannot blame him.

Jean did not mind our good-natured larks. He liked a good laugh as much as anyone, and he could drink and carouse with the best of us. It never ceased to amaze me what a chameleon the man was. He would interact with a seaman one day and a gentleman the next.

There are many stories of Pierre, and especially Jean, in New Orleans. They had a wide circle of friends and were invited to the city's most coveted balls and parties. Jean was accepted into the highest ranks of New Orleans society. People did not think of him as a pirate any more than Jean thought of himself as such. Jean was a hero to them, even before he saved the city and the country from the British. New Orleans was too civilized for me in those days, but Jean fit right in. It was a place with people from all around the world due to its port. Jean could charm them all, especially the fairer sex. He could have his pick of them, and I must confess I saw him with many a different stunning beauty on his arm, white, quadroon, free woman of color. It did not matter to Jean. Beauty was beauty, and Jean appreciated it in all its feminine forms. New Orleans was not like most places. That sort of thing was accepted more so here. He took advantage of it until he met the one woman who would blind him to all others. I shall tell that story in time.

By 1812, we Lafitte brothers were on top of the world. We had built an enterprise, and it was thriving. We were helping the people of New Orleans, and they loved us for it. We had fortunes beyond our wildest imaginations. Jean had become one of the richest men in America.

But our enemies were circling. There were those in the government who wished to see us and our commune at Barataria destroyed. Jean was loyal to the Americans, the country he had chosen, even as they targeted him and all that he had built. America was also at war with Britain. The British were preparing to invade New Orleans, and with Jean's help, they could take the city and most likely win the war. With the Americans bearing down on him and the British courting him, offering him astronomical wealth if he would agree to help them, Jean had to decide where his loyalty lay, and his decision would affect the course of history.

Chapter Eight

New Orleans

September 1831

"It is quite a peaceful evening, is it not, Mr. Whitney?"

Tobias had been approaching his cottage, picking his way gingerly through the muddy street, when his neighbor's voice caught his attention.

"Yes, Madame Auclair, so it is," Tobias replied.

Mme. Auclair was a widow who lived with her daughter to the right of the Whitneys. Her home was the same brick-between-post structure as most in the neighborhood, but it was grander than the others. The plaster was painted a pleasing pale yellow, and the porch boasted intricate ironwork. The interior was brimming with imported French furniture, including a pianoforte in the parlor. The Creole lady did not get on particularly well with Mary Catherine. Tobias thought perhaps this was because they had little in common. Mary Catherine was of the opinion that it had more to do with Mme. Auclair being a snob.

"I do enjoy tending my flowers this time of year," she said.

Tobias looked at the pristine garden in front of her cottage and said, "Your zinnias are looking lovely."

"Why, thank you, Mr. Whitney. I am quite proud of them. Of course, I could just get Honoré to care for them, but I find it fulfilling to tend my own gardens."

Her remark reminded Tobias of Mary Catherine's complaint that the woman never passed up an excuse to mention that she had a housekeeper—a luxury that the Whitneys could not afford.

"And I must find a way to fill my days, after all," she added, reminding Tobias that Mary Catherine also found the constant flaunting of her status as a wealthy woman of leisure insufferable.

"Yes, well, you've done an excellent job with them," he said.

She smiled for a fleeting moment. Then her eyes landed on the Whitney cottage, and the smile withered into a scowl.

"Regrettably, it is not often that I can tend my garden in peaceful solitude. At least not when your brood is about, which they nearly always are this time of day. Where have they gone?"

"I've no idea," he replied, genuinely perplexed.

Tobias realized that though he was near his cottage, he could hear no noise emanating from within. This was an unusual occurrence. Mary Catherine and the boys were always home when he returned from the cemetery. The cottage was never this eerily quiet.

He wondered where they could have gone. Had Mary Catherine needed to run an errand? It would be most unlikely behavior for her at this time of the evening. Perhaps she had been called away for an emergency. But this seemed an improbable scenario as well. Tobias's parents were deceased, and he had no siblings, so there were no relatives on his branch of the family tree to require assistance. Mary Catherine's parents were also deceased. Her one sibling had married and moved to Memphis some time ago. Surely, if she had summoned her sister for help, Mary Catherine would have waited for Tobias to come home before departing. She would have to arrange transportation and work out many details. No doubt she would have taken pains to ensure the boys were well cared for in her absence.

She had always been one to fret over her children, but now that it was just the boys, she was even more consumed with their welfare. She was forever clucking over them like a mother hen, fussing over whether they had eaten enough and monitoring the rate and consistency of their bodily functions.

The woman knew no boundaries when it came to protecting her loved ones' health, but Tobias certainly could not blame her for that.

He knew she was as saddened by the loss of their children as he was, if not more so. He had returned home from the cemetery on too many occasions to find his wife rapidly wiping away tears and then promptly beginning to fuss about something or other to cover up her crying. She managed what he could not—to allow herself to grieve while still fully engaging with the world around her. She was the bedrock of their family, and Tobias was in awe of her strength.

What if something had happened to her? Whereas Connor and Shane resembled Tobias in coloring, build, and features, Kathleen and the twins took after Mary Catherine. If he lost her, he would truly feel as if there was no one left to remind him of what he once had.

What if something had happened to one of the boys? A panic jolted through Tobias as it always did when he thought something might be amiss with his family. If one of the boys was ill or injured, Mary Catherine might have needed to seek help. Perhaps the situation had grown so dire that she'd had no time to send word to him at the cemetery.

He barely registered that Mme. Auclair was still prattling on about how Mary Catherine was typically bellowing like a cow by this time of evening, while the boys carried on with banshee wails fit to wake the dead. His mind was otherwise occupied with terrible scenarios. It was unmanly of him to think this way, and he felt ashamed of his hypocrisy for mocking Mary Catherine's overprotectiveness and constant worrying when he was precisely the same. He simply concealed his disquietude, whereas Mary Catherine hid almost nothing.

Unfortunately, concealing his worrisome thoughts did not make them go away, and though he wished he could master them and live his life without dread and fear following him like a shadow, he could not. Therefore, with an unwelcome but familiar feeling of foreboding spreading through his limbs, he wished Mme. Auclair a pleasant evening and willed his leaden legs to ascend the front steps to his cottage door.

Suddenly, a new worry sent a wave of terror through him—what if the feeling of being watched in the cemetery had not been a figment of his imagination? What if a pirate, or other unsavory character, knew he had found the journal? If it contained information about the whereabouts of pirate treasure, as Tobias suspected, perhaps the rogue had come to his house to steal it. What if Mary Catherine or the boys had been about? What might have happened to them? With fingertips like ice, he awkwardly grasped the knob and entered. The scene that unfolded before him was nothing he could have imagined.

In the center of the front room, Mary Catherine sat in the wingback chair, next to the unlit fireplace. The boys were settled on the rug at her feet, looking up at her with rapt attention. There was no blood, and all three were breathing. They did not appear to be in any apparent distress. The oddest part was that Mary Catherine did not seem even mildly vexed.

They looked over at him when he entered and smiled. Tobias closed his eyes for a brief moment while he uttered a prayer of thanks. Then he opened them, taking in the cozy domestic scene before him with the reverence of a man setting a keepsake in his mind.

"Tobias!" exclaimed Mary Catherine as the boys jumped up and ran to him.

Tobias embraced his family and then asked the question that had been burning in his mind. "What is this? I thought I had entered the wrong cottage."

Mary Catherine giggled. Tobias could not recall her doing so in many months.

"I have been entertaining the boys with stories of Captain Lafitte."

"Have you now?"

"He was a pirate who—" Shane was cut off by his older brother.

"Not a pirate, a privateer!"

"Yes, a privateer," continued Shane. "He was just like Robin Hood, only he lived right here in New Orleans."

"But mostly Barataria," added Connor.

"And he had to pretend to be killed so that he would not hang, even though he fought with President Jackson and saved us all in the Battle of

New Orleans!"

"You weren't even born then," Connor interjected.

"Neither were you!" said Shane, punching his brother in the leg. This action precipitated retaliation from Connor, who promptly tackled him. Fortunately, the boys were already on the rug, so they rolled about with minimal damage done to their persons.

The boys' melee finally broke the spell of domestic bliss. Mary Catherine sprang out of her chair and began smacking the tangle of boy limbs with the dove-gray book that Tobias had just noticed was resting on her lap.

"I have never in all my days seen such ruffian behavior!" she declared. While generally not one to employ physical violence against her offspring, Mary Catherine sometimes needed to get a situation under control in a timely fashion. With boys bigger and much stronger than she, there were occasions when a whack proved almost as effective as her strident voice. It was then that she enlisted the help of whatever was on hand, usually a broom or dishrag, and set about clobbering what was nearest her. Sometimes it was one of the boys. More often, it was a bedpost, chair leg, or tabletop. To achieve maximum effect, she usually combined this with shouting. The result was a cacophony of noise with Mary Catherine yelling and the boys belly-laughing.

"Boys, stop this foolishness and get washed up for supper," said Tobias. "And then come help your mother with whatever she needs," he added for good measure. Tobias had found that it was always wise to appear as if one had a plan when it came to parenting.

The boys disengaged and bounded away, all youthful energy and laughter.

"How was your day, Tobias?" asked Mary Catherine as serenely as if he had just walked in on her knitting.

Later that evening, after supper was over and he had finished reading *The Last of the Mohicans* to the boys, Tobias found his thoughts drifting back to the exchange with his family upon his return from work that day. He searched for Mary Catherine and heard her milling about in the courtyard behind their house, completing her final tasks of the day. She entered the dining room looking perturbed, brushing feathers from her skirt and mumbling about "varmints" in the neighborhood.

"Kitten, how is it that the boys know of Lafitte's part in the Battle of New Orleans? I haven't read it in your translations. Did you work on it today?"

"Aye! And I've been waiting to tell you about it." Mary Catherine gave Tobias a preview of the upcoming pages of Dominique's journal.

"Remarkable, truly," mused Tobias. "So much adventure lived by one man. It hardly seems possible."

"And so much treasure gained," added Catherine with a mischievous twinkle in her eye.

"Treasure? Kitten, why did you not tell me this before? What treasure?"

Mary Catherine grinned slyly. "The mystery will unfold as you read it. Far be it from me to spoil your surprise."

"But—"

"No, Tobias. You must discover it for yourself."

"Then I shall begin reading your translations at once!" he said.

Mary Catherine held out the journal, but paused before releasing it into his hand. "I should warn you that the treasure may or may not be included in these pages. I must confess that I do not recall exactly when I first discovered it."

Tobias's brow furrowed. When he remained silent, she continued. "You see, I've read ahead."

"How far ahead exactly, Kitten?"

"I have read the journal in its entirety."

"You have?" Tobias was closer to losing patience with his wife than he had been in quite some time. "Well then? Out with it! Tell me what happens next!"

"You would not want me to do that."

"That is precisely what I want you to do."

Mary Catherine sighed and looked up at the heavens. He had seen that expression on many occasions and knew she was silently praying to God to give her the strength to deal with her husband.

"I want you to read the journal on your own. Read Dominique You's words for yourself. Let the secrets reveal themselves as he meant them to do."

Why was she being so purposefully abstruse? He breathed deeply, struggling to master his emotions so he could deliver his next remark in a calm, collected manner. "But Kitten, you have yet to finish translating the book. I cannot know how it ends until you do so."

Mary Catherine responded with a long-winded oration on the difficulties of translating the French language, concluding by questioning what exactly he would know about such matters. At least he thought she had concluded, but to his dismay, she went on.

"And all the while, I've got to keep the house running, and are you even aware that a coyote got into the courtyard and ate our best laying hen? Couldn't go next door and make a meal of one of the Auclairs' hens, now could he? She's enough to spare, but now I'll have fewer eggs to make breakfast with, not that you'd care. Oh no, you'd have me working day and night to translate these pages for you! And how do you expect me to do that and complete all my household duties with your incessant questions?"

Their mother's raised voice alerted the boys that others were up and about in the cottage, and that was all the impetus Shane required to leave his bed. The boy was one of those children who never stayed put throughout the night. Tobias had no idea how he managed to grow with so little sleep. He was like a cat, ever alert and able to awaken in a flash.

"Ma, Da! What's all the bother for?" he asked.

"Shane Whitney, what are you doing out of bed?"

Shane opened his mouth to respond, but Mary Catherine continued before he could answer.

"If I've told you once, I've told you a thousand times. You've no business traipsing about the house after I've put you to bed! You'll catch your death walking around in your bare feet and nightclothes!"

Shane was a bright boy, and as such, he did not point out to his mother that it was September in New Orleans and that he was far more likely to succumb to heatstroke than to catch a cold. Instead, he asked, "Are you talking of the treasure, Ma? The one you told Connor and me about today? Are you telling Da about it?"

Mary Catherine ushered her son through the dining room door, back toward his sleeping room. "No more of your blathering tonight, Shane. Time for bed."

Mary Catherine reentered the dining room and stood before Tobias, raising herself to her full five feet, and stared him down, though this required her looking up at him.

But Tobias stood his ground. "You told the boys? They know about the treasure, but you will not tell your husband?"

In an infuriatingly calm voice, Mary Catherine replied, "Tobias, they are children. They are bright, but they would struggle to read the translation. At least Shane would, and parts are not appropriate for young boys. I don't intend to fill their heads with thoughts of pirates."

"But you must have told them! They know about Lafitte and the Battle of New Orleans and the treasure as well!"

"Yes," replied Mary Catherine. "I told them a tale or two. That is all they need to know. And don't you dare ask them to tell you, Tobias Whitney. All will be made clear once you've read the rest of the journal."

"I am married to a sphinx! You've grown quite fond of speaking in riddles as of late, Kitten."

She smiled and patted his cheek. "So I have."

He suspected she was enjoying keeping him in suspense and lording her knowledge of the upcoming events in the journal over him. Yet as infuriating as this was, Tobias knew he could not ask the boys in secret to tell him what they knew. She would invariably discover what he had done, and it would only make her angrier. And making Mary Catherine angry was never a good idea. She had a way of repaying an offense that made the transgressor regret crossing her.

He recalled one incident that occurred when they were newly married. He had foolishly complained about a scorch mark on his shirt. She had not seemed unduly upset at the time, but after that, he had noticed a suspicious number of scorch marks on his clothing. Had she been burning his clothes every so often since then on purpose? He was not certain, but he could not discount the notion. If she were spiteful enough to abuse his shirts this way, she would surely not hesitate to take more time than necessary on the translation. It would be the ideal means by which to make him suffer. Tobias sighed. As much as he was loath to admit it, he must follow Mary Catherine's timeline.

He lit the lamp at the dining table and settled in to read the translations she had written that day. He stayed up quite late, until he had read every word she had transcribed. There was no talk of treasure, but he was not disheartened as he felt certain it would be coming soon. He readied himself for bed. Mary Catherine was already sleeping peacefully when he extinguished the lamp and with it the otherworldly shadows dancing across the cypress timber walls.

As he lay in bed, he thought about the disconcerting feeling he'd gotten in the cemetery today. Should he tell Mary Catherine about it? He didn't wish to frighten her. What if it truly had been his imagination? He decided to wait until he had proof. As he drifted into that space between consciousness and sleep, he imagined himself hunting for Lafitte's buried treasure. Would Mary Catherine help him search for it? She told him he must find it for himself. What could she have meant by this? *All would be made clear once he'd read the journal*—such an enticing mystery.

He contemplated that he should be angrier at Mary Catherine for being so enigmatic. Yet, truth be told, he enjoyed reading the journal in bits and pieces. With each day, he learned a little more about Lafitte and wondered when he would reveal the secrets of his treasure. For Tobias was sure there must be treasure. As curious as he was, he did not wish to rush through the adventure. Since finding the journal, he'd daydreamed about embarking on an adventure and going on a real-life treasure hunt. Maybe it would lead him to Barataria or even Galveston. He had never ventured beyond New Orleans in all his days.

What would he do with the treasure if he discovered it? Tobias found it hard to imagine how vast wealth would improve his life. He would enjoy purchasing gifts for Mary Catherine and the boys. Perhaps Mary Catherine could live a better life. If they were wealthy enough, she would never have to do a chore again. There would be no cooking, no cleaning, no mending of clothes. He wondered momentarily what she would have to fuss about and thought she might not be happy in such a situation. If given the choice, she would prefer to remain vexed than have nothing to complain about.

He did not require niceties, and he was utterly content in his cottage. He thought perhaps it would be good to add a half-story onto the cottage. Many in the neighborhood were a story and a half, with additional sleeping space upstairs, but the Whitneys' cottage was only one story. He and Mary Catherine used to wish for more space as a family of seven, but now that they had only the two boys, their home was adequate for their needs. Still, one never knew. He and Mary Catherine were not so old. Could there be more children to come? He could not believe he had even allowed his mind to ponder this. It was the first time such a notion had occurred to him in the past three years.

He shook these thoughts away and wondered again how the treasure might improve his life. The peculiar thing was that the more he thought about it, the more he realized he did not need the treasure. He was ripe to solve the mystery he felt sure the journal hid, but he was not convinced that some pirate treasure was the solution to his problems. He needed the mystery more than the treasure. He hungered for the adventure that it promised.

The only real benefit of finding the treasure was that it would allow him to leave his job at the cemetery and buy back his bookshop. Of course, Mssr. Loutrel would sell Chapter and Verse back to him even if he lacked the money for an outright payment. He had repeatedly told Tobias that a suitable arrangement could be made. It was time Tobias was honest about why he had stayed at the cemetery so long. It was time for him to return to the living and give himself a second chance.

Tobias wondered what Captain Lafitte had done with his second chance. He hoped the pirate had found peace, maybe even settled down and made a home for himself. Tobias doubted it. Lafitte always seemed to take tremendous risks and engage in daring exploits, yet his actions never brought him happiness. What would happen next to the intrepid Captain Lafitte? As he drifted off to sleep, the cryptic words of his wife echoed in his mind: "One thing I will promise you, Tobias Whitney, is that there is treasure hidden within this book. Of that you can be certain."

Chapter Nine

Mary Catherine Whitney's Translation of the Journal of Dominique You

The Battle of New Orleans

There are always those grasping individuals who cannot bear the success of others, who would deny a man his livelihood, even if that livelihood benefits others. W.C.C. Claiborne was that sort of man. In 1812, Mr. Claiborne was elected governor of Louisiana. At first, he had few issues with our enterprise until our company became too successful for his liking. He eventually grew bent on destroying our commune in Barataria and ridding New Orleans of the Lafittes.

Before then, we had little trouble with the authorities. All the governmental officials reaped the benefit of our smuggled goods. They readily accepted the "gifts" we gave them in exchange for allowing us to ply our trade in the city. Gov. Claiborne was undoubtedly among those officials who benefited. I believe he was jealous of my brother's success and fame among the citizens of New Orleans. Gov. Claiborne accused us of being pirates. We knew he wanted nothing more than to see us arrested as such. Though we were indicted for violations of US revenue laws, we were never indicted for piracy. Indeed, if they had just cause, they would have done so, but they did not. Jean had his own tribunal in Barataria to dispense justice when necessary. Our Barataria tribunal suffered no pirates. They tried and convicted pirates, sometimes deporting those found guilty. We always operated under letters of marque issued by countries with shared enemies of the United States, namely England and Spain.

Yet Gov. Claiborne would have us accused and convicted of piracy. He was intent on orchestrating our demise. There has never been a love between pirates and the governments of sovereign nations. I understand why this is so. I know of the countless atrocities committed by pirates against the innocent. I could tell stories that would curl your hair. I do not blame the law for wanting to curtail such rogues from plying their evil trade.

In the old days, pirates were hanged and their bodies left on display as a deterrent to others who might be tempted to follow a similar path. If the reader has witnessed a hanging, he knows the horrors of death on the gallows. When the condemned is pushed from the ladder at the top of the gallows, he dangles from the noose as he slowly strangles. His agony is on display for all to see. His tongue bulges. His eyes pop out of the sockets. He pisses his pants and empties his bowels. It is a humiliating end and one he deserves for all the crimes he has committed.

In the golden days of piracy, it was not enough to hang them. When the pirate was dead, his body was cut loose and taken down to the water, where it would be staked and left for three tides. Then he would be buried in an unmarked grave where no one would ever mourn him. If he were a notorious pirate or a captain, his corpse would be left to rot in an iron cage. This was the fate of Captain Kidd over a hundred years ago. His body was hanged in a cage by the River Thames. It remained there for two years as a warning to all passing ships.

I say this to explain how high the stakes were for us. Jean and Pierre were not ignorant men. They would not have flouted the law in that way. They steered clear of piracy. They did not wish to hang. There is no honor in being hanged. We were not afraid to die, but we wished for an honorable death. We would not have tempted fate by engaging in piracy. It was the most flagrant disrespect for the governor to accuse us of such. Gov. Claiborne was signing our death warrant by doing so.

Gov. Claiborne should have been concerned about the British threat. The war was raging, and America was ill-equipped to protect New Orleans from the invasion any sane man knew was coming. But instead of worrying about the British, Claiborne chose to focus on our enterprise. He sent men to storm Barataria. He had attempted to do so before, and he had been embarrassed in the process. Once, he'd sent men under the command of a captain who formerly worked for Lafitte, thinking he would know all the secrets of Barataria. But Barataria does not yield her secrets willingly. She did not do so then, nor does she now. Claiborne's men soon found themselves surrounded by Jean's forces. These men had come to kill Jean and burn down Barataria. And what did Jean do when he caught them dead to rights? He allowed them to return to New Orleans unharmed and presented them with gifts to give to the governor upon their return. In that moment, Jean showed his true character, but Claiborne chose not to see it. He would not relinquish his witch hunt. He would do all that he could to destroy Jean and the Baratarians.

The governor tried again to attack our commune at Barataria, and this time he had more success. Jean and Pierre were captured, along with many of the Baratarians. Jean and Pierre were able to post bail. They knew better than to show themselves for the hearing, but in failing to attend, they became wanted men. Claiborne was furious that Jean was so beloved among the people of New Orleans. The governor threatened the citizens, letting it be known that if they so much as spoke to the Lafittes, they would be arrested. He tried to make Jean and Pierre anathema. It did not work. Claiborne was an outsider. He did not know the regard people held for Jean and Pierre.

In November of 1813, Gov. Claiborne posted a five-hundred-dollar reward for the capture of Jean Lafitte—a veritable fortune. Had people viewed Jean as a criminal, they would have lined up to haul him in and collect the prize. But they did not. Jean was in New Orleans when the reward was posted. No one molested him. They did not see him as a criminal, and Jean knew this. He was not afraid of Claiborne's threats. In fact, the night Claiborne's wretched posters were being hung up all around the French Quarter, Jean was dining at a friend's home. Claiborne's wife was in attendance. She was filled with praise for the dashing man with whom she dined, declaring him the most remarkable man she had ever met. By daylight the next day, there were posters all over the French Quarter offering a one-thousand-dollar reward for the capture of Gov. W.C.C. Claiborne. I imagine the governor was fit to be tied when he saw those!

We continued to go about our business right under his nose, which only infuriated him further. We still held our auctions, but by the summer of 1814, Claiborne had enough and arrested Pierre in New Orleans. He was shackled and imprisoned in a lice-infested cell in the Cabildo. The heat and unhealthy miasmas of that cell affected his health, and he was never the same after his ordeal. Try as he might, Jean was not successful in getting Pierre released, and he remained in that wretched place until he could escape on the sixth of September. It was fortunate that the jailor guarding him was a Freemason. Masons are always willing to help one another. Pierre fled to Barataria, but there was a price on his head, and Gov. Claiborne was nipping at his heels.

It is now necessary for me to tell two disparate tales at once because they will converge like a crash of lightning. I shall do my best to adhere to the timeline as accurately as possible, to the best of my memory. A great many events were transpiring all at once. It was chaotic. The first was our persecution at the hands of the Americans, who, amidst the constant braying of that jackass Gov. Claiborne, were determined to destroy the Lafittes and our commune at Barataria. The second was the British government's repeated attempts to gain Jean's cooperation in their efforts to invade New Orleans. These occurred simultaneously.

Our troubles with our own government were such that after Pierre escaped his hellhole in the Cabildo, it was no longer safe for him or Jean to be in New Orleans. They were forced to abandon the blacksmith shop and their home there. That meant we were all in Barataria. Jean knew that the British were keen to attack. They sought control of the Port of New Orleans, which would grant them command of the lower Mississippi River Valley. To that end, the British had been testing the waters around our Barataria commune, trying to gain a foothold there. We were expert cannoneers, so we repelled their advances. They made several attempts, but we were able to hold them off. Had we Baratarians not kept them at bay, they would have invaded far sooner and, no doubt, successfully taken New Orleans. General Andrew Jackson had not yet arrived. We were the city's best hope for defense.

When the British realized they could not take Barataria by force, they changed tactics. Now they aimed to lure Jean with the promise of riches if he would allow them passage and guide them up the Mississippi, a feat he could have achieved as easily as taking a piss. When Jean did not immediately appear receptive to their offer, they eventually reached the sum of thirty thousand British pounds. Such an astronomical amount would have been enough to tempt many Americans to turn traitor to their country. Not Jean. He knew that if he allowed the British transit through his territory and aided their passage up the Mississippi River, it would result in defeat for the United States. He would not consider it.

The story of how they got word to Jean about their offer is worth telling. In September 1814, we spotted an English man-of-war, the *Sophia*, off our harbor. We were fired upon by the ship, yet immediately after, they hoisted the flag of truce. Jean's curiosity was piqued, and against the counsel of his men, he decided to get to the bottom of this odd behavior. He set out to meet the ship in one of our small boats. A yawl sent from the *Sophia* came to meet him. Jean should have feared for his life, but he was not such a man. Curiosity overcame fear with him.

The captain, a man named Lockyer, was aboard the yawl and did not recognize Jean, so he asked, "Where is Captain Lafitte? I wish to speak to him."

Jean replied, "Alas, the captain is not about. May I offer you my assistance?"

At this, Captain Lockyer handed a package to Jean, saying, "See that this is delivered to Captain Lafitte with all due haste."

Once again, Jean's curiosity got the best of him, and he said to the rival captain, "I am he whom ye seek."

It was then decided that the two men should meet to discuss the British offer. Jean escorted him to his home amidst grumblings from his men to "Shoot the rascals!" or "Hand them over to Claiborne to swing!" Jean would not hear of it. Instead, he was a gracious host, even though the British had been trying to invade our commune for some time now. Jean conducted the meeting with the British captain and led him to believe he would consider their offer. Jean had no intentions of doing so, but he needed to buy time for the Americans, so he played the British game. He asked for a fortnight to settle his affairs in Barataria, and he promised them an answer at that time.

Well before this encounter with the British, Jean had long been trying to convince Gov. Claiborne that a British attack was imminent and to offer his help. He had sent a letter to Claiborne, trying to prove to the hard-headed man that he was not the criminal Claiborne considered him to be.

He wrote to Claiborne, "I am the stray sheep, wishing to return to the sheepfold. If you were thoroughly acquainted with the nature of my offenses, I should appear to you much less guilty and still worthy to discharge the duties of a good citizen." But like most ignorant men, the governor was a stubborn cuss.

We had the weapons and supplies the Americans desperately needed to defend New Orleans, and we were eager to donate them to the cause, yet Claiborne, and in turn General Andrew Jackson, would not listen. Jean sent word several times, reiterating his willingness to help. He was rebuffed each time. The Americans thought Jean had ulterior motives for his offers. Mind you, Pierre was still imprisoned when he first tried to convince them, and Jean himself had a price on his head. They were not interested in what he could offer them. They should have been. Jean possessed knowledge of the land and the best places to build fortifications. He could contribute ammunition and skilled artillerymen. But no one wanted to accept the help of "pirates." Especially not General Jackson, even after he finally arrived in New Orleans.

The sight of the army he brought was shocking. They were dressed in tatters. They hardly had any guns. They were in desperate need of flints. Their ranks were made up of state militias from all over the land, Indians, and free people of color. So many spoke French that the general needed a translator to address them. We knew better than anyone else the number of British troops preparing to invade and the superiority of their weaponry. The Americans desperately needed us. We could have equipped an army of thirty thousand with the flints and gunpowder we had at our disposal. We continued to offer assistance.

Instead, the Americans attacked us ten days after Pierre escaped the Cabildo. On 16 September 1814, our commune was invaded by those we had offered to help. Jean and Pierre were able to hide in the bayous, but some of our men and I were arrested. It was now my fate to be imprisoned in the lice-ridden dungeon of the

Cabildo. We were not entirely unprepared for the attack, although we had assumed it would be by the British and not by our own countrymen.

Nevertheless, we'd seen the storm clouds brewing and knew it might be a possibility, so we'd hidden what we could. They confiscated a fortune in goods from the warehouses they managed to find, along with Jean's fleet of ships. What they could not steal from us, they burned to the ground.

What they did not know was that Jean would have burned everything to the ground himself, and in fact, he gave orders to his officers and me to do so if the British invaded. He knew that if the British discovered the warehouses, stocked with flints, powder, and other necessary supplies, they would undoubtedly have been victorious. New Orleans would have fallen into their hands. They would have been poised to seize the upper Mississippi River Valley. It would only have been a matter of time before the Americans lost the war.

Jean had no reason to help the Americans and everything to gain from aiding the British. All he had worked for had been destroyed by those he sought to save. He had nothing to show for his years of toil. He would have been a rich man had he accepted Britain's offer. He would be free to live his life. To refuse the British meant staying in America as a wanted man. His home and livelihood had been destroyed, his men had been arrested. What kind of man could resist such an offer? Jean was such a man. He was a patriot. He would not act as a traitor to his adopted country.

No man worked harder than Jean to defend New Orleans and its environs. He had to fight back enemies from both sides. He battled corrupt American politicians. He combated the British through force at first and then through a clever ruse to buy time from Captain Lockyer.

To that end, after he requested more time from the British captain, Jean went into the city, risking his freedom, and offered his services once more. He paid a visit to Gov. Claiborne, a man who had every intention of destroying him, at the man's home. Jean was hopeful that by now, the American government had realized their dire straits. Their enemy was closing in. They were ill-prepared to defend themselves. I was still held in captivity at this time. I know only what I have been told, but as the story goes, Jean entered Claiborne's house. The governor's wife, a great admirer of Jean, led him into her husband's study so the two could talk. Gov. Claiborne did not recognize Jean at first. Perhaps he was expecting my brother to have horns and a pointed tail. Jean drew two pistols he had concealed on his person, cocked them, and aimed them at Claiborne. Jean may have been the bravest man I know, but he was no fool.

"I am the pirate, Jean Lafitte." He introduced himself with the pejorative term the governor had often used to describe him. "I come to you, man to man, putting myself at great risk in doing so, and offering my services and those of my men to you in defense against the British. You have rebuffed me before. I shall not ask again."

Claiborne hesitated for only a moment before accepting the offer. Jean saluted him deferentially and left. And that is how we ended up fighting the Battle of New Orleans.

The Americans knew Jean could be of great help in planning the defense of New Orleans, so a meeting was arranged in December 1814 between him and General Jackson in a private room at the Absinthe House. Now the general, who had once called Jean a hellish banditti and refused him so many times, eagerly listened to all of Jean's counsel. Jean provided extensive knowledge of the area and the defense measures that should be taken, along with much-needed supplies and skilled artillerymen to fight. In return, the other Baratarians and I were freed from our imprisonment and received full pardons. It was now safe for us to move about New Orleans and prepare to defend her from the British.

The skirmishes began in late December and continued until 8 January 1815, the date people recognize as the Battle of New Orleans. We did not know then, but later, we found out that the war was already over and the Treaty of Ghent had been signed. The British were to cede any territory gained during the war and withdraw. Word had not gotten to either side about that yet, so we forged on. Bitter irony, is it not? All those lives lost for naught. But life is like cards. You play the hand you are dealt, and all we knew was that the British were coming for us, and by God, we were going to be ready.

The night before the battle on the eighth, the citizens of New Orleans, led by the Ursuline nuns, prayed for our victory. Those pious women placed a statue of Our Lady of Prompt Succor over their chapel door. They prayed through the night that our side would be victorious and our casualties would be few. Many people gathered to pray with them. I firmly believe in the power of prayer and that our resounding victory, outnumbered as we were, was due to their prayer for divine intercession.

I was placed in charge of a battery composed of the Baratarians' best gunners. General Jackson initially considered us rogue pirates, but he came to respect our bravery and skill in battle. I commanded two 24-pounders. The British were positioned directly across from us, staring us down with six 18-pounders. At one point, my arm was pierced by a shell fragment from British cannon fire. It hurt like hell, but I did not let it stop me. I decided the British must pay for my wound, so after my arm was bound, I directed our cannon to fire and knocked their gun carriage to pieces, taking down at least six of their men in the process.

Jean was integral to the American war effort. He directed where fortifications should be built and contributed flints, powder, weapons, and whatever else was needed by General Jackson for his motley crew. Jean's men were some of the best in Jackson's army. Though I proudly count myself among them, it would not be immodest to claim that the Baratarians were a significant part of why the Americans were victorious in that battle. I write only what was told to me by General Jackson himself.

The British commander, General Pakenham, brought over twelve thousand troops, whereas General Jackson commanded only about four thousand. Despite being outnumbered and outgunned, our side lost only seventy or so men. The British lost around two thousand men. Pakenham was killed during the Battle of New Orleans. I heard they shipped his body back to England in a rum barrel. It was a fitting way to go home after being beaten by a bunch of pirates, as I see it.

It is no small thing to kill a man, even in battle, and we killed many. Jean later remarked that seeing the bodies of all those British soldiers on the ground was a horrible sight. But you cannot wake the dead, and they were the enemy and the aggressor, so Jean turned his attention to the living. Alongside Gov. Claiborne, Jean assisted those angels upon this Earth, the Ursuline nuns, in caring for the wounded in the days after the battle.

If the reader will pardon an old man telling his war stories, I shall relate one amusing anecdote. One cold morning during our skirmishes with the British, my men had brewed some coffee. General Jackson came by during his inspections and caught a whiff of our brew.

"What is this heavenly aroma?" he asked.

"It's our mornin' brew," I told him.

"It smells far more enticing than the swill my troops are issued."

I may not be the smartest of the Lafitte boys, but I know a hint when I hear one, so I offered him some.

"This wouldn't be contraband, now would it?" he asked me.

I just smiled and kept my mouth shut. Our coffee may have been black as tar, and if the enemy did not know our position, the smell of it would have given us away for a mile, but it was a damn fine brew. For all his haughty talk of not wanting pirates or smugglers in his ranks, he sure accepted that tin cup full of coffee mighty quickly!

Now I do not wish to boast, but I counted General Jackson as a friend of mine after that battle. I believe my skills as an artilleryman impressed him. I was told sometime later that after he drank my coffee, he remarked that he wished he had fifty such guns on our line, with five hundred such devils as we Baratarians. I take that as great praise from the man who was just elected president of the United States.

He mentioned Jean and the Baratarians in his victory speech shortly after the battle. He said we showed uncommon gallantry and skill in the field. I cannot attest to the gallantry, but I do know we can shoot.

There was a grand celebration of the victory, including a parade, in which we, the Lafitte brothers, took part. Bands played "Marseillaise" and "The Star-Spangled Banner," bells pealed all over the city, and cannons fired. It was indeed one of the best days of our lives. Just a few months before, I had been imprisoned here, and now we were being celebrated. President Madison granted Jean and all of us Baratarians full pardons for past crimes in gratitude for our role in defending the city of New Orleans. We had gone from criminals to heroes in the eyes of the law.

The victory celebrations included fêtes and galas attended by the city's well-heeled citizens. I am far too much the crusty privateer to attend balls, but Jean did. He tells an amusing tale about one in particular. At that ball, he was introduced by a mutual acquaintance to General Coffee, a man who looked upon us Baratarians as his social inferiors. It did not matter that Jean had proven himself in battle. The man considered Jean beneath him. No matter that both were guests at this victory ball, hosted by army officers. General Coffee was hesitant to converse with Jean. Sensing his hesitation and the reason for it, Jean stared him down. He again introduced himself to the man, declaring loudly, so there could be no doubt as to Coffee's hearing it, "Lafitte. The pirate."

There may be no greater testament to his love for the people of New Orleans than Jean choosing to leave the city forever in the moment of his most significant victory, when he was held in the highest esteem. He wished to be remembered always as the city's favorite son. He would not tarnish his reputation. He had known for some time before the Battle of New Orleans that new adventures awaited him elsewhere. He had cast his gaze along the Texas coast.

Masons must build, and he was eager to construct a new enterprise in Galveston, where he could play a part in Mexico's struggle for freedom from Spain and obtain letters of marque so that he could once again take to the seas. He could never have been content on land. The sea would always call to him, no matter what happiness he thought he might find in New Orleans.

Chapter Ten

Mary Catherine Whitney's Translation of the Journal of Dominique You

Galveston and Campeche

After the Battle of New Orleans, Jean was a hero. Yet he had little to show for it. He hired lawyers to regain the property stolen from his warehouses in the raid on Barataria, as well as his confiscated fleet of ships. It was to no avail. The United States was not willing to return what was rightfully his. Jean was a privateer with no ships and scant wealth. He needed to remake himself. It had come time for Jean to forge a new path.

The sea always called to Jean, yet he needed a place on land to establish a base of operations if he were to rebuild his commercial enterprise. Barataria was no longer an option. Despite his new status as a war hero, he would have been under constant attack by the United States government. Instead, he and Pierre set their sights on a settlement along the coast of the Texas province called Galveston. There was not much there but salt marshes and mud flats. A French privateer had already occupied the island, but Jean aimed to take it over and build a new base there. It would be one to rival Barataria.

Galveston was attractive to Jean for several reasons. He and his men could operate out of there as legitimate privateers for the revolutionaries in Mexico. He would help them gain independence from Spain, thus doing some good for others with his privateering. Pirates are parasites, privateers are philanthropists.

Despite all that had happened to Jean and Pierre in New Orleans, despite having their enterprise raided, their commune burned to the ground, and their fleet of ships stolen by the government, the Lafitte men harbored nothing but love for New Orleans and her citizens. They still intended to help the people of that city buy the things they needed at a reasonable price. Galveston was close enough for them to do this, yet far enough away from the reach of the Americans.

I have said before that Jean was a patriot. His assistance in the Battle of New Orleans should have silenced all whispers to the contrary. This was not so. Some people thought him a pirate. Others thought him a spy for Spain. Some even thought him both. I have gone to great lengths to explain that he was not a pirate. Now I will explain that he was never a traitor to his adopted country. No matter what people might have said.

Like most rumors, this one started with a kernel of truth. Jean and Pierre were enlisted as secret agents for the Spanish crown. That much is true. They did it to raise the capital they needed to build a settlement on Galveston and start their new enterprise.

Jean got the idea that they could be paid by Spain in exchange for information from his earlier dealings in Barataria with Captain Lockyer. When Lockyer presented him with the British offer in return for his assistance against the Americans, Jean pretended to need time to consider the proposal. He led them to believe he would accept it. He was stalling. He never intended to accept their offer. He began to think that ruse worked quite well for him. Now he reckoned a similar deception might work on the Spanish. "It takes a special kind of fool to trust a pirate," he'd told me. And though he was not a pirate, the Spanish thought he was.

The Spanish truly were fools, yet they recognized that Jean could be of great use to them. They saw a man with a unique set of skills they could exploit for their benefit. So they made him an offer. He had no intentions of helping the Spanish, but he seized the opportunity nonetheless.

You must forgive me, reader, if I am vague when recounting this part of Jean's story. I have attempted to record my recollections of events to the best of my ability up to this point. I must confess that I will not do this now. When it comes to Jean and Pierre's business as agents for the Spanish government, I must proceed with caution for two reasons. Primarily, I was not involved in these dealings and know only what Jean and Pierre revealed to me. This was very little. I did not take offense. I knew they did so for my own protection and for theirs as well. The second reason for the scant details I shall record is that they were acting as double agents.

They accepted the Spanish offer, knowing they were duping Spain. They used their positions as secret agents to work against Spanish interests in the area, for the benefit of the United States. They were patriots. To think otherwise is ludicrous. They were playing a dangerous game, but they knew the risks. They were therefore very secretive about these events, as well they should have been. Discovery of their true intentions by the Spanish would have meant death for them. This is why they let people believe they were Spanish spies. It was safer for them to do so. This is how much they loved their country. They would remain silent as their name was smeared. Not defending themselves—just doing what they knew was right.

The money Jean and Pierre earned working for the Spanish allowed them to replenish their fleet of ships and build a new commune at Galveston, which they called Campeche.

"Spanish wealth built it, so a Spanish name we will give it," Jean wrote to me. I recall being astonished that he had managed such a dangerous coup. He called it "a pretty little spot to launch our campaign against the Spanish, bought and paid for by the enemy we hunt." I could almost hear him speaking the words, picture him throwing his head back in laughter at the irony of it all.

What he built there rivaled the commune in Barataria, including his own home. It was a lavish, bright-red house, which he named Maison Rouge. There would be no Spanish-named house for Jean!

When the Baratarians heard of his new settlement in Texas, they flocked there. He soon had nearly a thousand men. They were once again privateering, hauling in goods, and then shipping them to New Orleans to sell. It was as if Barataria moved a few days' sail west. Here he was governor. He kept order and dispensed justice when necessary. He made a fortune.

Jean had Campeche for only a short time, from 1817 until 1820. I was there for a while, captaining a schooner. Yet I knew my home was in New Orleans, so back there I went and remained for the rest of my days. Jean and I communicated when we could. Sometimes we would see each other in person. He was in New Orleans occasionally, gathering supplies when he needed them, though he did not come here as much as Pierre. We sent letters to each other through his most trusted men, who regularly made the trip to sell the wares they gained from their privateering ventures. To prevent our correspondence from being intercepted, we developed a secret code for communicating with each other. We were the only ones who could make sense of it. We continued to use this code for the remainder of our lives.

Pierre spent most of his time in New Orleans, conducting business on behalf of their Galveston enterprise, often from Maspero's Coffee House in the Vieux Carré. Pierre set up a home in New Orleans and had children. He lived a very different life in those days than Jean. I would have liked them both to have settled in New Orleans permanently, but Jean still had too many enemies here.

Those who would paint Jean as a pirate were aided by traitors in his midst. One in particular worked against Jean at every turn to ruin his reputation and make him the object of scrutiny by the United States government. I speak of Grambo. I cannot say if Grambo was his Christian or family name. No one knew him by any other. You may recall the tale I told of Grambo. He was the cuss who challenged Jean's authority and forced Jean's hand so that he had to shoot one of Grambo's men to make an example of him.

The Baratarians who followed Jean to Galveston were mostly a good sort. They were privateers, and some were plain old smugglers, but they did not mean any harm. Yet there is always one bad apple spoiling the bunch. That was Grambo. Grambo fancied himself a Captain Jean Lafitte, though he was not fit to shine Jean's boots. He was a privateer who ran a small fleet of ships. He did what Jean did, but on a much smaller scale. He was not the only one. There were many privateers in Barataria and Galveston who had their own ships and their own men, but who worked for Jean's enterprise.

Yet Grambo thought he was more than he was. He did not like to think he was under Jean's command. But if you lived in Campeche, you were subject to Jean's laws. With a lesser man as governor, this could have been unfair. There might have been corruption, misdeeds, even cruelty. But Jean's laws were just, as was his enforcement of them. They were in place to keep order and benefit all who called Campeche home.

Grambo hung over Campeche like a black cloud. Jean was ever waiting for thunder and lightning to explode from him. He had been difficult in Barataria, but in Galveston, he was worse. He was older now. He knew he could not sail the seas, wreaking his havoc, for much longer. Yet he still needed more treasure. He was a man running out of time. He was a man who had no patience to begin with. He was a dangerous man.

Grambo was a pirate. There is no denying it. Hell, Grambo

himself refused to call himself and his men privateers. He knew what he was. He was the cruelest, meanest man I ever knew. And I've known some devils.

He surely looked like a demon, I can tell you. He had many wounds from pirating, plus the brawling he did, just for a lark. He was missing one eye. Naught remained but a gaping, blackened socket, crusted over where the eye had once been. That was not the worst of it. He had a hole in his neck from where a bayonet had gone straight through it. He still had pieces of musket ball in his shoulder and was missing a calf. His face, arms, and legs were full of angry scars. Yet he lived. He wore a permanent scowl on his deformed face. He was only happy when he was inflicting pain and misery on others.

His men followed him, not out of respect but out of fear. I asked a deckhand on one of his ships why he did not leave Grambo's fleet for another ship. He told me, "I'd rather swing in New Orleans than desert Grambo. His justice will make a man beg for the gallows." He knew because he had seen Grambo inflict punishment on his men. He always punished an offender in front of his men as a warning.

And he did worse to the poor souls on the ships he captured. I do not know the strength of the reader's stomach, so I will only say a Grambo death was long and it was painful. Death was welcome when it finally came for its victims. And hundreds of them died at his hands. He would brag about the number of people he killed. I do not doubt that he told the truth about how many there were. It might have been the only truthful thing he ever said. When Grambo captured a ship, he thought nothing of killing the entire crew, regardless of whether or not they surrendered. The killing was his favorite part. It was his sport.

If you sailed for Grambo, there was something wrong with you. No man could say before signing up to work on one of his ships that he did not know the nature of the man. He once scalded a ship's cook to death for burning the bread. When one of the crew looked askew at him for doing this, he shot him in the head. That is the kind of man he was.

Jean would have liked to be rid of him, but Grambo came to Campeche not long after Jean set up there. He followed the Lafittes around because he wished to profit from their skills. He had neither Pierre's acumen in business nor Jean's way with his men. He was like a bad cough. Jean could not seem to shake him. He should have shot Grambo in the heart all that time ago in Barataria instead of his man. That mistake would come back to haunt him.

If Grambo wasn't the devil himself, many of us thought he'd sold his soul to Satan because he had more lives than a cat. He had been accused of piracy and murder, but he never swung for it. We thought he would be hanged in New Orleans once, but his lawyer got him freed, and he was right back to piracy.

Jean's strictest policy for his privateers was that they were not to attack American ships. They were after Spanish spoils. This was mainly because Jean was a patriot, but there was also a practical reason. The Americans were finally putting together a decent navy. They were starting to patrol the waters we plied. Jean did not wish to give them reason to harass him at Campeche. He was somewhat safe there, as it was disputed territory, but he did not like to churn up trouble.

Grambo cared not a whit what flag a ship sailed. They were all ripe for the picking as far as he was concerned. One of his men captained a ship that attacked an American vessel. When Jean got word of it, he was furious. His tribunal found Grambo's man guilty and hanged him. Jean confiscated his ship in accordance with his laws. Grambo knew the laws and the consequences of breaking them. Yet he could not accept that his captain had been executed and his ship seized. He would not tolerate it.

Jean should have dealt with him right then and there. He had no reason to execute Grambo, as he did not captain the ship, but

Grambo was ultimately in charge of his men. To my mind, that made him guilty. But Jean was not one to think like that.

Grambo was furious. He swore to Jean that he would make him pay. He said to him, "You have taken something dear from me, and I will take the same from you!" Grambo held no human dear to him. I know he referred to the ship. It set him back a good bit to lose it. He already hated my brother from back in the Barataria days, and now he seethed with fury once again.

Jean knew he could defend himself from the likes of Grambo. He thought he had nothing to fear from the miserable pirate. How wrong he was. Grambo ended up feigning his death, not long before Jean did. He wished to escape the law. It was Grambo's "death," I believe, that gave my brother the idea to do the same thing. I shall tell that story in due time.

To make matters worse, Jean was beginning to feel his control as governor over Campeche slipping away. Grambo had been instigating insurrection among the men. He appealed to their greed. As much of a nasty cur as he could be, he had learned, I suspect from Jean, how to turn a phrase. He spoke to the men in a way they could understand and led them to believe they could fare better without Jean as their leader.

By 1818, Jean was once again a wealthy man. Yet his life was not peaceful, nor was his future assured. The US Revenue Collectors and the Port of New Orleans officials grew weary of him flouting customs laws. They had hoped they were rid of him when he vacated Barataria. The Americans were closely watching Campeche. Jean once again felt the noose around his neck. He was falling out of favor with both the United States and Spain. Mexico was no friend to him either. He'd taken on more than any man could handle, and it was all about to come crashing down around him.

I wrote earlier that Campeche rivaled Barataria. This is true regarding the riches that passed through it and the splendor of

Jean's house. Yet for all its men and the wealth it produced, Campeche was never Barataria. It was a mirage. It could not last. The United States would not allow it. Each year that passed in Galveston was one too many. I kept waiting to hear that they had left the place. It was part of why I returned to New Orleans when I did, though it was true that I missed my home and was eager to go back there.

And then disaster struck. In September 1818, a fearsome hurricane destroyed Campeche. "It sounded like the gates of hell had been opened on Galveston," Jean wrote to me. "The winds snapped trees like matchsticks and picked up whole buildings, throwing them back down yards away. The tidal wave that crashed into the island brought water so deep that men could only escape by climbing as high up the sturdiest trees they could find, where they clung to them for dear life or risked getting swept away in the torrential waves that flowed across the island. Some of my men tethered themselves to the trees to keep safe when their grip gave way."

When the fearsome storm finally ended, hardly a building stood at Campeche. Maison Rouge was in tatters, yet it remained standing. Jean had survived by grounding his ship in sand and riding out the storm on it.

Jean was once again forced to start anew. He should have left. But to Jean, anything seemed possible. Despite the odds stacked against him, he began to rebuild. All men have their faults, and Jean's fault was that he could not see the world changing around him. He thought that with enough determination, he could accomplish whatever he set out to do. Yet the days of privateering in the Gulf were over. He could not see this. The seas, which had always seemed so vast as to be immeasurable, were shrinking.

The United States was cracking down on piracy. The Gulf was increasingly patrolled by the US Navy, which did not distinguish between privateers and pirates. It was no longer the frontier it had once been. In August 1818, one of Jean's ships, *Le Brave*, sailed under Captain Desfarges, took the *Filomena*, a Spanish schooner bound from Pensacola to Havana. On the way back to Galveston, Captain Desfarges was detained by two American revenue cutters, the *Alabama* and the *Louisiana*, that had been patrolling those waters. Though Captain Desfarges was able to produce his letters of marque, which authorized him as a Lafitte privateer operating out of Galveston, he and his crew were indicted by a United States grand jury for piracy. The authorities meant to make an example out of the Desfarges crew. They did not care whether they had papers or not.

Their hanging was a spectacle. It occurred in New Orleans on 24 May 1820. I have written before that hanging is not an honorable death, and Captain Desfarges did not wish for his life to end in that way. He requested a pistol so that he could shoot himself. When his request was denied, he threw himself into the water, hoping to drown. He was retaken by the authorities and forced to the gallows where he was hanged.

Hanging may not be an honorable death, but it is an appropriate punishment for piracy. Jean had to hang men before for piracy. However, such treatment should be reserved for those who truly are engaged in that heinous act.

The final straw for Jean at Campeche was the Americans learning about another attack on a United States vessel. This time, Grambo himself was the transgressor. He had attacked a small American trading schooner. He boarded the ship and remained on board as it returned to Campeche. He treated the captain well and assured him he would come to no harm. Grambo could play the gentleman when he so desired, but he was a wolf in sheep's clothing. He dined with the man, bringing the finest wine and Cuban cigars from his own ship, and entertained the captain for several days. As they neared Campeche, they enjoyed cognacs together after a fine meal.

Grambo looked the captain dead in the eye and said, "Your

company has been most amusing, but I shall kill you now."

The captain thought Grambo was joking and laughed, not the least bit concerned. Grambo enjoyed toying with his prey, like a cat with a mouse. He stood up from the table, calmly set his glass down, pulled out some rope, and proceeded to bind the man's hands. He marched his prisoner to the starboard side, where he tied the other end of the rope to the railing. With the help of a few of his men, Grambo tossed the unfortunate captain over the side. He was dragged to his death in the water.

Grambo later told his crew he was fond of the captain. He did not need to kill the man, but he knew doing so would cause trouble for Jean. That was his reason for capturing an American ship. Murdering the captain would enrage the Americans and send them after Jean and his Galveston settlement. And Grambo was correct. Now Jean had a reason to hang Grambo. He had flagrantly violated the laws of Campeche. But Grambo was a slippery sort. He knew better than to return. He let his crew face justice in Campeche while he and a few others sailed the trading schooner elsewhere, I know not where. He never returned to Campeche. He likely sensed the end was near. If he must move on, he would destroy Lafitte in the process. I wish he had perished. I wish Jean had never crossed paths with him again. His story will continue later.

Grambo's men did not cease their treachery simply because Grambo stayed away from Campeche. He still commanded them. They did not confine their terror to the seas. They sailed their armed vessels inland, up rivers and bayous, to wreak havoc on the innocent. His men would blacken their faces and break into people's homes. They would bind the terrified families with ropes and take anything of value. Though they tried to disguise themselves, people knew they were part of the Campeche crew. Grambo wanted it that way. He wanted Jean's feet held to the fire. No matter that Jean had not authorized such things. No matter that he was appalled by them. I wish Grambo had led these men in person, but he was too savvy, or perhaps more likely, too lazy to commit these heinous acts. He put his men up to it and let them suffer the consequences, all the while safely hiding himself, I know not where.

When Jean learned what these men were doing, he brought them to justice. He would have been right to kill them on the spot. Yet that was not the kind of man Jean was. He convened a trial with three judges and thirteen jurors to determine their guilt or innocence. The court found them guilty and sentenced them to death. The captain was hanged from a gibbet on a prominent point of the island where passing ships could see. The others he banished from the island. Their sort was not welcome in Jean's enterprise. He would have been within his rights to execute them all. Yet Jean showed leniency when dispensing justice.

I ask the reader to consider the tale I have just related. If Jean were a pirate, would he have done this? Would he not have been content to share in the spoils? He was the governor of Campeche. All authority ultimately rested upon his shoulders. He chose to stop illegal and immoral behavior in his ranks, regardless of the cost to him.

Jean was disgusted with the behavior of Grambo's men. He did not wish to be seen as one of them. He was done with Campeche. He was done with Galveston. To that end, he sent word to the United States government that he was willing to clear out Campeche and leave Galveston voluntarily. He offered to do this at his own expense. All he asked for in return was a permit of safe conduct for his vessels.

The United States sent representatives to Campeche to discuss this plan with Jean. Ever the patriot, he entertained these men. These were people who would hang him as a pirate if given the chance. Yet he hosted an elaborate feast for them as he explained how he would use his own resources to once again destroy what he had built. The Americans were so impressed by his hospitality and gentlemanly demeanor that one man reported to his superiors, "Captain Lafitte may have some vices, but his virtues far outweigh them." Truer words were never spoken of my brother.

In keeping with his word, in 1820, Jean burned Campeche to the ground. He boarded his ship, the *Pride*, and sailed away from yet another place he would have made his home. He would once again have to chart a new course, his future more uncertain than ever.

Chapter Eleven

New Orleans

September 1831

Tobias got up from his chair at the dining table with the ink-stained tablecloth and opened the door to the courtyard, hoping to coax a cross breeze through the cottage, though he feared the air was too still for any such measure of relief. He pulled his cotton shirt away from his chest and let it fall back into place. The air stirred by this movement against his perspiration was as close to a breeze as he would get on his warm, sticky evening. September in New Orleans is not a harbinger of autumn, as it is in many places. It remains hot and is the height of storm season. There is, in short, little to recommend September as a month.

The newspaper on the table read "Yellow Jack Seen About the City." Tobias had witnessed a slight uptick in burials lately, though the death toll had not been terrible so far. But he had concluded that it mattered not a whit how many died in a particular season. If one's family members were among the victims, that made it the worst year for yellow fever. And to Tobias, there would be no worse year than 1828. He should go back to the dark place inside himself now. He should force himself to replay the details in his mind of that terrible time. And yet, he did not wish to do so.

Instead, he picked up the dove-gray journal. Ever since Mary Catherine had teased him with the promise of treasure within its pages, he devoured each new installment with increasing anticipation. He had to admit he was surprised when Dominique You failed to mention treasure hidden in Barataria. He thought the mystery might have been solved when Captain Lafitte made a new home in Galveston. Yet he had just finished that section, and there was still not a whisper of treasure. Where could he have hidden it? Surely, he would not have abandoned it at either of those places. Even if he intended to return later to retrieve it, would it not have been a tremendous risk to leave it in the first place? What if someone else stumbled upon it? What if the terrain changed, and he could no longer find his hiding spot? What if he needed it in a hurry and could not return to wherever he had hidden it?

Tobias knew the savvy Captain Lafitte would have considered these possibilities. But he could not understand why Dominique You had gone to all the trouble to write and hide this journal if not to reveal some profound secrets. Perhaps the journal's purpose really was to tell Lafitte's story. After all, that was the claim Dominique You made right from the beginning. But Mary Catherine had assured him there was treasure in the journal. She would not have made that statement unless it were true.

And why, if the journal was nothing more than an account of Lafitte's life, did he continue to feel that he was being watched, particularly at the cemetery? Just today he'd been taking a break, sitting on his favorite bench and reading aloud *The Last of the Mohicans*, when the hairs on the back of his neck stood on end. Why had he suddenly felt that he was not alone? Surely it couldn't be the likes of Grambo, hoping to follow Tobias to the captain's long-lost treasure. The thought sent a shiver down his spine. He really did need to stop imagining himself as part of an adventure tale.

Mary Catherine entered the stifling dining room, fanning herself. "So late and still so hot, even Satan's sweating."

"I'm pleased you're still up, Kitten. I was just reading your translations."

"Enjoying them, are you? I should hope they are worth the strain to my eyes. I'll not be able to see the nose on my face by morning."

"I've just read where Captain Lafitte has left Galveston, yet there's been no word of the treasure."

Mary Catherine continued fanning her face, her countenance giving nothing away.

"Surely there will be word of it soon?" He posed this statement as a question.

"Well, I suppose Dominique You will get to it in good time," she replied.

"But perhaps you could just—"

"No, I could not." After a pause, she added, "The next part is Captain Lafitte's involvement with Napoleon Bonaparte, so perhaps that will shed some light on things." She patted him affectionately on his shoulder and headed off to their sweltering sleeping room.

Mary Catherine Whitney's Translation of the Journal of Dominique You

The Emperor Napoleon

Now I must pause my narrative to assure the reader that while many will consider the tale I am about to tell the most fantastical of all the adventures contained in this volume, I give the reader my word that every bit of it is true and accurate. If I record any detail in error, it is an honest mistake. I must make such a statement because what I am about to describe will defy most people's imagination. Very few know these facts. I commit these events to writing only because everyone involved will have passed by the time this journal is discovered, and all must understand the true nature of Captain Jean Lafitte. Jean was to sail across the sea on a mission to rescue Napoleon. And I was to accompany him.

The timing of these events overlaps with Jean's living in the French Quarter and Barataria after the Battle of New Orleans, through his time in Galveston, and for some months beyond. I must begin by reiterating that, although the Lafitte brothers have love in our hearts for our adopted country, we will always harbor a love for France as well. There is room for both. We are French by birth, even if we have not lived there since our youth. We all fought for Napoleon. We were honored to do so. We believe in his cause of freedom and equality.

People still dared to disparage Jean as a pirate after he fought valiantly in the Battle of New Orleans. They accused him of being a spy when he acted as a double agent for the United States. Understanding the events I am about to relate is essential to understanding just how loyal Jean was to the two countries he loved most.

In May 1814, Napoleon suffered a defeat in his Russian campaign and was exiled to the island of Elba. We Lafitte brothers were crushed by this news but believed he would regain his throne as emperor. We wanted nothing more than to witness his triumphant return to power. We spoke of it often with our fellow Frenchmen in New Orleans. The reader must understand how French New Orleans was and still is.

French culture was so deeply entrenched in the city that the first mayor elected by the citizens after Louisiana entered the union was a Frenchman from the Savoy region. His name was Nicolas Girod. He was elected to that position in 1812. Mssr. Girod spoke only French. He was not interested in learning English, despite being the mayor of an American city. Americans had only recently begun pouring into New Orleans after the Louisiana Purchase, so his attitude was not unusual at the time.

Mssr. Girod was an outstanding mayor, reelected to a second term in 1814. He saw the city through the Battle of New Orleans. He helped General Jackson organize local men into militias and garner supplies for the fighting. He made many civic improvements and was an esteemed philanthropist.

When his brother died, he left Mssr. Girod a property at the corner of Rue St. Louis and Rue Chartres. He used the inheritance for his grand scheme. He would renovate it into a townhouse opulent enough to house the Emperor Napoleon himself. All that was left was to rescue him and bring him to New Orleans. Who was his best hope to perform such a daring feat? Who better to return the Terror of Europe to his throne than the Terror of the Gulf?

Mssr. Girod went to the blacksmith shop and began talking to Pierre and Jean about his idea to send a rescue mission to Elba Island. A Lafitte never runs from danger nor turns down a chance to go adventuring, so naturally, they were interested. They began making plans in the weeks that followed. Their plans were disrupted by the joyous news that the emperor had escaped his exile and would return to his throne. Word spread through New Orleans like a fever. We eagerly awaited the emperor's next move.

But alas, fortune is a fickle mistress. Napoleon was defeated at Waterloo on 18 June 1815 and again exiled, this time to St. Helena. St. Helena is a more remote island. Napoleon's captors were taking no chances. I imagine he was the most heavily guarded prisoner in the world, in the most remote prison in the world.

Mssr. Girod resigned as mayor that year and redoubled his efforts to rescue Napoleon. But by 1815, Jean and Pierre were making plans to leave New Orleans. They arranged for me to meet with Mssr. Girod at the blacksmith shop. We did not wish to have our confidential business overheard. I shall relate our conversation as best as I remember it. I recall the excitement I felt upon seeing the esteemed gentleman enter the narrow wooden door of the shop. He locked eyes with me, then glanced about, no doubt to ensure we were alone. I ushered him over to a table near the back and offered him a chair. After we exchanged pleasantries, I listened to his passionate plea.

"You, Dominique, must lead the planning!" he insisted with a shake of his head so forceful it freed several unruly gray curls that bounced about his round face.

"But why me?" I asked.

"I need a Lafitte to lead this mission. Jean and Pierre will do what they can, but you are here. I need someone in New Orleans to help plan and strategize—someone with a sharp mind, a steady hand, and loyalty beyond question. This mission is far more complex than what we'd been planning when the emperor was on Elba."

I wasn't so sure about the "steady hand," and certainly not about the "sharp mind," but I was loyal. I could not resist helping him.

Jean and I would be the ones to sail the rescue expedition. Mssr. Girod was supplying us with a two-hundred-ton schooner called *La Séraphine*. He busied himself outfitting the schooner and completing and furnishing the home for Napoleon. Both had to be accommodations fit for an emperor. This mission was laid out over many a year. The planning occurred during my time in New Orleans, when Jean was in Galveston. He might have been miles away from us, yet he was doing his part for the Bonapartists there.

There were groups of exiled supporters of Napoleon in America who set up colonies to await the emperor's rescue. One of these was the Vine and Olive Colony in Alabama. There was another group comprised of some of the same people who traveled to Texas in early 1818. They came armed to the hilt. Yet they had few survival skills. There was much infighting. They lacked leadership. They were doomed to failure.

Every group trying to survive in a frontier needs someone who knows how to keep order. Someone they will obey and respect. A ship is no different. Without a strong, just captain, chaos reigns. Whether on land or at sea, Jean was such a leader. This is why he could take over the operation at Barataria and make it successful, even though many a man harbored the same ambition. This is why he could start again in Galveston and build a new enterprise. The men came because they knew he was a good leader. They stayed because he proved himself with each passing day.

When the Bonapartists first landed in Galveston, near Campeche, they were standoffish with Jean. They thought they were better than a bunch of pirates and smugglers. That is how they saw us. Yet Jean saved them right from the start. He assisted them. He gave them supplies and his hospitality when they needed shelter.

They built an encampment called Champ d'Asile on the Trinity River. I believe they thought Napoleon would return to power, and they would go back to France. They might have thought we or someone else would rescue him and bring him back to America. If that happened, they intended to form a new land with Napoleon as their leader. They figured they could invade New Spain and establish a colony there. The emperor could gather support and eventually continue his campaigns in Europe. That might have been the plan, but it did not work out that way. Indians attacked them. The Spanish were sending troops their way. They were low on food and supplies.

They had already retreated to Galveston and were living right by Campeche when the hurricane hit in September 1818. Jean was their savior. Maison Rouge, battered though it was, still stood. He sheltered them there and kept them alive with his supplies. When they wanted to get to New Orleans, he used his resources to transport them. He did all this while in dire straits, if the reader recalls my account of Jean's hardships during this time.

Even as I was planning the Napoleon rescue mission, Jean was assisting Napoleon's supporters. I knew he would be ready when the time came to do his duty. It did not matter what else he was juggling. He was a patriot and a Freemason. Duty was everything to him.

Our plan to liberate the emperor was intricate yet straightforward. Mssr. Girod would outfit the schooner. It was a small, fast boat. Precisely what was needed. Jean and I would sail *La Séraphine* near St. Helena. We would rendezvous with another vessel there and make the remainder of the journey in that vessel, which I shall describe in time. Once again, I must ask the reader to forgive the imprecision of my account. My vagueness is intentional. Powerful men and powerful forces were backing our expedition. Mssr. Girod was merely the conduit through which their orders passed.

I have no doubt they will be gone from this Earth by the time this journal is found. Yet I promised them that their part in this plot would not be revealed. A Mason keeps his promises. I make some references to the others involved so that the reader can understand the time and resources invested in planning this mission. We were never going to sail up to St. Helena, overpower some guards, nab the emperor, and secret him away to our ship. We were many things, Jean and I. Yet we were never fools. Neither of us wished to die. Though dying in the service of great men is an honorable death.

We knew from well-informed sources that Napoleon was not in good health. Jean and I aimed to permit him to die a free man. Despite what the Bonapartists thought about his returning and leading an army, we knew such a thing would not come to pass. They did not have the information we did. It would not have mattered if they had. They were fools when it came to their beloved leader. They could not see the truth. Perhaps they chose not to see it.

St. Helena was a much different island prison than Elba. St. Helena lies in the South Atlantic. It is some twelve hundred miles off the coast of Africa. There is nothing else around it. The nearest landmass is Ascension Island, an equally desolate place some eight hundred miles to its northwest. Even if one were to approach the island, it is a forbidding volcanic mass with sheer cliff walls. The island was guarded by three thousand men, armed with five hundred cannon. There were four vessels on continuous patrol of the coastline.

Napoleon was housed at Longwood, a structure situated in the most desolate area of the island's interior. One hundred twenty-five men guarded him in the daytime and seventy-two at night. It was the most impregnable place on God's Earth. And exceptionally well-guarded to boot. And Jean and I were going there to free him.

By the summer of 1821, our plans were complete. Jean had arrived in the city in disguise. We waited to receive word from Mssr. Girod that we would sail.

I was gleeful as a boy at Christmas when it finally came time to reveal the details of the plan to Jean. I wished to savor the rare moment when I led him on an adventure. I explained that we had no hope of arriving at the island undetected. St. Helena has only a few landing spots and no secure anchorages. The patrolling vessels would have spotted us. Had we managed to slip by them, one of the guards on the island would no doubt have seen us before we could have made landfall. We would need a miracle to infiltrate the island. Luckily, we had one.

"And exactly how do you propose we access this island unseen? Have you discovered a way for us to become invisible?" he'd asked with that amused smirk on his face. Jean knew I would never have summoned him to the city without a solid plan in place.

"Indeed I have!" I answered him.

We had at our disposal a remarkable vessel, the likes of which I had never seen before. It was an underwater vessel. A small one at that. When first I saw it, I exclaimed, "I'll not ride in the belly of that porpoise!" For that is what it looked like to me. It was but thirty feet long. It had an inner chamber no more than ten square feet. It was lined with cork to protect its occupants, of which there could be no more than three. Jean and I were to be its crew, and Emperor Napoleon was to be our passenger. It was propelled by sails when it rode the surface like a ship. It could also be submerged underwater and propelled by oars. It did not sink to the bottom as one would imagine. It moved through the water undetected above. It was the closest thing to invisible a man could get.

In all my days, I have never dreamed of such a vessel. But an

American inventor had. His name is Robert Fulton. He has built such underwater vessels before. He did not build ours. We had someone else do this for us. I shall not disclose his name or the details of his life. I shall only say he worked with Fulton and knew of his plans. With the help of an engineer, he created a customized version for our purposes. He was well compensated to do so. Jean and I got to christen this remarkable vessel. We named it *Lelantos* after the god of invisibility and stealth. We felt that was a fitting name.

When I showed Jean the blueprints of this wondrous vessel and explained what we were to do, he leaned back in his chair, propped his feet up on the table, and crossed his arms. I awaited his words with no small impatience. Would he reject the plan? Deem it ridiculous and chastise me for summoning him to a city where danger surrounded him? He let the silence stretch like a hangman's rope, then he laughed. It was a deep, throaty sound, devoid of anger, overflowing with my brother's unique zest for life.

After he composed himself, he said, "Pulled off a Daedalus trick, did you?"

"Aye, but with sails instead of wings." I was proud to acknowledge his mythological reference. I lacked the education he and Pierre had, but I remembered hearing the story of the tinkerer who built the Labrynth for old King Minos, then had to escape the tower with his son by fashioning wings out of feathers and flying to freedom. I remember, because Jean told me the story, as a lesson against pride.

"Just stick to the plan, and see that you don't pull off an Icarus trick, mind you!" I added, referencing Daedalus's son, Icarus, who flew too close to the sun and melted the wax of his wings, leading to his watery death in the sea below.

This evoked another hearty fit of laughter from my brother, who knew good and well that his own pride and sense of daring, if left unchecked, might well lead to our doom. "Fair warning, brother! Now, carry on. I find myself eager to hear more of the impossible feats with which you have tasked us."

As I mentioned earlier, our plan was simple yet intricate. Many parts must happen seamlessly for us to be successful. Jean and I would sail *La Séraphine* across the Atlantic. She was a swift vessel, as speed was of the essence. We would rendezvous with others closer to St. Helena, under cover of darkness. From there, Jean and I were to board the *Lelantos*. At that point, we would be on our own. We were to approach the island underwater. We would not be spotted by the patrols or guards, as there would be nothing for them to see. We knew anchoring near St. Helena would be dangerous. To that end, extra cork fenders were attached to the *Lelantos* to prevent it from being bashed to bits along the volcanic rock of the cliffs.

Jean and I were to exit the vessel with our supplies. I was to remain on the rocks while Jean effected his escape with the emperor. To accomplish this, we needed to unload a bosun's chair from the vessel, which had been modified with a standing footboard attached to the back and a large quantity of twine. He was to climb to the summit of the cliffs. It would take great skill and courage to scale those sheer rocks. I warned him not to look down, no matter how tempting it was.

Once on top, he would attach an iron bolt to the rocks and deposit a block there. This would be his escape back down to our vessel once he had the emperor with him. From there, he must make his way to Longwood and enter the home undetected. No small feat, I assure you! Yet, it was not nearly so fearsome as what he had to accomplish to arrive at this point.

We had been furnished with a great deal of information about the guards who watched over Napoleon and their customs. We felt assured that Jean could enter and escort the emperor into the darkness of night without being halted. We were certain that the emperor would accompany Jean with all due haste. Many had plans to rescue him, but no one else came close to being able to execute their plans. We were different because of the influence of those who backed us. Their reach was far and wide. To that end, I can assure the reader that the emperor would not be taken aback by the sight of Captain Lafitte crossing the threshold of Longwood in the dead of night. One might say he would be expecting the visit.

Once back at the spot where he had inserted the iron bolt, Jean was to tie one end of the twine to the iron bolt and throw down the rest of the twine to me at the bottom of the cliff. He would then haul up the bosun's chair, place the emperor upon it, and step onto the standing footboard. Then he would lower the emperor and himself down the side of the cliff with the block weighing down the other side to keep their descent steady.

Once on the ground, the three of us would board the *Lelantos* and be off before we could be detected. We would rendezvous with the crew we had left on *La Séraphine* and switch places. They would reclaim the *Lelantos*, and the three of us would board *La Séraphine*. We would make all haste across the Atlantic and return to New Orleans, establishing the emperor in his home in the Vieux Carré.

Our plan was devised by men much more skilled than I and possessing the means to bring it to fruition. I do not doubt that, as daring and risky as it was, ours was a solid plan. We would have successfully rescued Napoleon and brought him to New Orleans.

I will not soon forget the evening Mssr. Girod arrived at the blacksmith shop. The former governor was practically incoherent. "Il est mort! Il est mort!" was all we could get from the man until he calmed down. Our mission had to be aborted. Emperor Napoleon Bonaparte was dead. Our dream of granting him freedom to live out the rest of his days was not to be. He took his last breath as a prisoner, exiled on a godforsaken island in the middle of the ocean. We had failed. Not because we had not planned well. We had failed because we had not acted swiftly enough.

Failing to rescue Napoleon and bring him back to New Orleans was one of the greatest disappointments of Jean's life, and of mine as well. Napoleon's rescue was not meant to be. Yet Jean did not know then that he was still destined to execute a rescue mission that would impact many lives. There were others in need of a savior. Jean would be that savior.

Chapter Twelve

New Orleans

October 1831

Tobias sat on his favorite bench in St. Louis Cemetery No. 2, feeling the late-afternoon sun on his face, its warmth not overwhelming but pleasing. The humidity had finally begun to loosen its grip on the throat of the city. *Perhaps the summer is nearly over*, he thought. He recalled how Guthrie used to make it a habit to mark the seasons in part by the flowers family and friends brought to adorn their loved ones' resting places.

"When ya start seein' marigolds and zinnias laid out on the tombs, sure as a cat's got whiskers, fall is here!" he would say. Tobias looked at the yellow, orange, and rusty red blooms mourners had left on the tombs around him. *Yes, autumn was approaching*.

He pulled out his book but paused before reading. He was contemplating Captain Lafitte's daring rescue attempt of Emperor Napoleon. The journal implied that the Freemasons played a significant role in the plans. Tobias had read about the Brotherhood before and knew them to be a secretive and powerful group. He looked around, searching the grounds for any visitors, as had become his habit of late. A few mourners had stopped by earlier in the day, but there was no one about at the moment. Could it be the Freemasons who had been watching him? The journal was not supposed to be read until fifty years after it was written. Were they angry that he had found it before the intended time? Did Dominique You reveal the identities of men still alive? Men who would take violent action to protect their secrets? He wasn't sure if the idea that a Freemason was watching him made him more apprehensive than imagining it to be Grambo or one of his men, but he was certain he was being watched.

At least he was fairly certain. He still had no evidence. The sensation discomfited him, but he reasoned that if the person had ill intentions, harm would already have come to him. It had been weeks—or more accurately, years—since he first had the sensation of being watched in the cemetery. He suspected he was only being observed, at least for the moment. When he embarked on the treasure hunt, which he hoped would be in the near future, he must be exceedingly careful.

He would soon need to confide in Mary Catherine. Soon, but not quite yet. He had been practicing glancing around quickly every so often, and he was hoping to catch a glimpse of the watcher. He wanted to be able to tell Mary Catherine after he'd solved the mystery of the spy's identity, especially since his reliance on her translations meant she would inevitably solve the mystery of Lafitte's treasure before he could do so.

He expected that she would finish the translations in short order. She was working on them every day, although her pace had settled down. Tobias was fairly certain this was not retaliation for his actions toward her. They both knew she could not keep up the frenetic pace of translating she had first employed.

"Tobias Whitney, you've got me working harder than a one-legged man in a footrace," she'd complained just the week before.

Tobias reasoned that Mary Catherine's slower pace might be influenced by the fact that she was no longer burning with curiosity about the treasure, as she had already finished reading the journal, though he dared not voice this thought. Mary Catherine continued her uncharacteristic reticence about the journal's outcome. He had not tried to coax information out of her since their last conversation on the subject in September. As riveting as he found the rescue mission of Napoleon, there was not the slightest hint of treasure in that part, nor in the parts she had translated for him after that. He found this quite curious and more than a bit puzzling.

Nonetheless, he had noticed a shift in the installments he was reading lately. They were becoming more adventurous and even more exciting. A nagging suspicion that had flickered in the back of his mind since Mary Catherine had first begun translating the words of Dominique You was growing into a steady flame of doubt. How closely was Mary Catherine adhering to the words on the page? Was she editorializing? Or was Dominique You becoming a better storyteller as he progressed? He'd implied early on that he lacked a proper, formal education. How was he telling such a gripping tale—one that Tobias could not stop thinking about?

Indeed, the story had of late invaded his dreams. It was a welcome respite from the ones he'd grown accustomed to. When he'd gone to sleep these past few nights, he'd entered a world of corsairs on the high seas and daring rescue plots. Just last night, he had dreamed it was he who carefully lowered the bosun chair, a trusting and grateful Emperor Napoleon beside him. It had been an exhilarating adventure.

Still, the dreams only confirmed his suspicions that the journal translations that inspired them were beginning to resemble one of the adventure stories he so loved reading to the boys, and he wished to know why. He had broached the subject with Mary Catherine just the day before, interrupting her as she finished washing linens in the outbuilding that housed the kitchen and laundry areas of the Whitney household.

"Do you think I have time to go spinning yarns for your amusement when I've a whole book to translate for you?" She'd paused in her washing, putting her wet, soapy hands on her hips in a truculent manner, glowering at him.

"Of course not, Kitten. It's only that I wondered if perhaps you were embellishing a bit."

"Embellishing? What with all these chores, wrangling those sons of yours, and that one always skulking around, trying to pry into every single bit of my business?" She gestured through the open door to the weathered cypress picket fence that separated their property from the Auclair home. Tobias followed her angry gaze and noticed that Mme. Auclair was indeed just on the other side of the fence, trying to pretend she was not listening to their conversation.

"I've had my fill of the lot of you!" Mary Catherine insisted.

"It's just that I know how clever you are. I thought it might be easy for you to improve on the skills of a less adept writer, so I thought I'd inquire."

"Well, you asked. Now, if you want your supper sometime today, I'd thank you to let me finish up." She brushed past him with the pail of rinse water from the laundry. She marched out of the kitchen door and dumped the water over the fence, directly onto Mme. Auclair, who sputtered in fury.

"Mon Dieu! Mais t'es folle?!"

Mary Catherine feigned a shocked look. "Why, Mme. Auclair, no, I'm not crazy. I didn't see you there. What a coincidence that you would be leaning over my fence right when I need to empty my laundry pail."

Tobias had quickly made his way back to the house from the kitchen before either of the feuding women noticed him.

Now, sitting on the bench in the cemetery, he mused that he should have realized confronting Mary Catherine when she was feeling frazzled had not been the wisest decision. He looked down at his scorched shirt, fingering the dark mark that marred the fabric. No, asking Mary Catherine hadn't gone well.

He had decided, after yesterday's incident, that he must keep his word and not press the boys to yield any particulars about what their mother had disclosed to them regarding the journal. He had resigned himself to accepting the story in installments. What other option did he have? He was running out of shirts.

Besides, Captain Lafitte's tale was having the most amazing effect on him. If he received nothing else from the journal except relief from the dread of autumn that had gripped him since his children were taken that terrible October three years before, it would be more than enough. What a precious gift, indeed.

He still thought of them often. Every single day. Multiple times. He had been thinking about them as he pulled *The Last of the Mohicans* out of his pocket just a few moments before. The memory of his lost children for the past three years had been a searing pain in his heart that eclipsed all else. The pain was still there, certainly, but its intensity no longer crowded out all other emotions.

In the six weeks since he had discovered Dominique You's journal, much had changed, even though his life appeared the same. He went to work each day and returned to care for his family, as a good man should. Yet his life was not the same. Not at all. He was brimming with excitement as day after day, Mary Catherine wrote her translations and presented them when he returned home from the cemetery. The journal's installments kept him engaged in the story and gave him something to ponder while he went about his work. Knowing he would have a new excerpt to read each day made him look forward to waking up in the mornings. He could hardly wait to learn what would happen next. Such enthusiasm had been lacking in his life for some time.

Had Mary Catherine known he needed the contents of the journal to unfold slowly? He could not dismiss the idea. That woman knew him better than he knew himself sometimes. He doubted that had he been capable of reading the journal himself, without her doling out pieces to him as she saw fit, the benefit to his mood would have been as marked. He was so consumed with unlocking the mysteries within that he knew he would have read through to the end immediately. As satisfying as that might have been in the moment, it would have robbed him of the delicious anticipation he enjoyed each day. It was precisely the tonic he needed to cure his apathy and world-weariness. How had she known? One thought kept circling his mind: Was Mary Catherine a genius? An angel? A witch? More than likely, she was a combination of the three.

Tobias, therefore, had mixed emotions about Mary Catherine's progress on the translation. She was near the conclusion of her task. Tobias was reasonably sure she would give him the last of it soon. Perhaps even tonight. That thought brought a tingle of exhilaration but also a twang of regret that he would no longer have this mystery to solve. It had been the most gripping fun. The tale of Lafitte's life after the world thought him dead was remarkable. Tobias could hardly believe it. Yet there it was, written by

Dominique You himself.

Tobias wondered if Mary Catherine was at this very moment in the cottage putting the finishing touches on her translation. The dove-gray volume looked a bit worse for wear after the use it had received since Tobias purchased it from Chapter and Verse. It did not help that Mary Catherine's rough handling, countless ink drippings, and smeared writing marred the cover and pages alike. He would not complain, as it would do no good and would probably only result in more retaliatory scorch marks on his shirts. He needed to keep his wife happy, he thought with a sigh, or risk having no decent clothing to wear. Besides, she was exceedingly cautious with Dominique You's original journal, treating it almost reverently and strictly forbidding the boys to go near it. Tobias was grateful for his wife's caution in this regard, though he suspected it had more to do with the journal's key to a pirate treasure than her respect for the written language.

The sun was hanging low in the cloudless sky, indicating that it was nearly time for Tobias to leave for the day. With one last wistful look at the tomb before him, he rose from his favorite bench and left the cemetery.

When he returned to his cottage, he pulled at the edge of a piece of the plaster that was wearing away on the facade, exposing some of the earthen-colored brickwork beneath.

"Good evening, Mr. Whitney," Mme. Auclair's frosty tone let him know she would not soon forget the row she'd had with his wife.

"Good evening to you, Mme. Auclair." He had walked right past her, not noticing her bent over her flower garden. The cooler fall weather meant Mme. Auclair would spend more time in her front garden, cultivating her fall-blooming flowers. It would mean interacting with her nearly every time he left the cottage for the foreseeable future. *Perhaps living in the cold North would not be so bad,* Tobias mused.

"It's not like you to be remiss about your home's maintenance," she pointed out.

"No, I shall make this repair soon."

"I'm surprised you've left it this long," she pressed.

"I have been a bit distracted as of late."

"I can certainly see why, what with that untamed brood of yours always up to mischief. And I don't only mean your sons," she said, crossing her arms and straightening herself up to her full height.

"Well, have a nice evening, Mme. Auclair," Tobias said as he moved to open the door to his cottage.

"I suppose you are aware that your wife accosted me yesterday," she said before he could make his escape.

"I am terribly sorry, Mme. Auclair. I'm certain it was an innocent mistake on her part," he soothed.

"Hrumph!" Mme. Auclair grunted. "There's nothing innocent about that one, I can assure you. And speaking of Mrs. Whitney, she's quite the gadabout-town these days, is she not?" Mme. Auclair's lips pressed into a thin, disapproving line. "Not that I'm complaining, mind you. I am quite enjoying the solitude in the neighborhood. I feel far safer on my own property when she is gone. I just wonder when she'll have time to get to her chores if she is never about." She looked pointedly at the front door of the Whitney cottage, which needed a good scrubbing.

"I hope your evening is pleasant," Tobias said, tipping his cap to her and opening the cottage door. He was pleased to note that the quiet interior no longer stirred the same unease in the pit of his stomach that it had the last time Mme. Auclair had drawn his attention to it. Perhaps he was becoming slightly better at not fearing the worst. With a mix of curiosity and mild concern, he took in the scene in the front room of his home.

There had been some odd sights greeting him upon his return from work, but this might have been the strangest of them all. Mary Catherine was nowhere to be seen, but the boys were sitting on the rug, near the unlit fireplace, reading from a book. More specifically, Connor was reading aloud to Shane, who seemed enthralled by the tale. The boys were not scuffling. Tobias wondered if their mother had recently scolded them, and they were attempting to make amends. Had he missed the fracas and come in just in time for the calm after the storm?

The boys greeted him with their usual warmth and fervor.

"What's going on here?" inquired Tobias.

"I'm reading about Robin Hood to Shane," answered Connor, as if this was something they did regularly, which it most certainly was not. Tobias did not have time to question the boys further because just then, Mary Catherine, who had heard her husband enter the cottage, poked her head out of the dining room.

"Tobias! Just in time. I'm almost ready to give you the last of the translations. I can finish up if you don't mind supper being late."

Tobias settled himself in the wingback chair in the front room, tapping his boot nervously against the wooden floor, and listening to Connor read aloud to his brother about the heroic deeds and spine-tingling adventures of Robin Hood as he righted wrongs and distributed his bounty to those in need. The boys had been enthralled with Robin Hood since they heard the story of Captain Lafitte, as told in Dominique You's journal. Their love of adventure stories was one of the things they had in common with their father. Tobias had to admit that he was more than a little proud of Connor's reading skills as well as the boys' love of books. It was in their blood, after all. Their grandfather had opened a bookshop, and their father had run it, at least for a time.

No, thought Tobias with a resolve that had been building within him for the past few weeks, not *for a time*. The bookshop was not the Whitneys' past. It was their future.

Mary Catherine broke off Tobias's reverie with her triumphant entrance from the dining room. "It is done!"

Tobias had long imagined this moment. He thought he would whoop with joy. Instead, he looked into her green eyes, searching for information. "All will be made clear, as you say?"

"As clear as day," replied Mary Catherine.

Mary Catherine and the boys remained blessedly quiet while Tobias read her translations. He had excused himself from supper to finish the journal. His wife had not objected.

Tobias's eyes flew across the pages of Mary Catherine's journal. The ink was still damp and smudging, but Tobias paid no mind to the mess he was making, so intent was he to learn the secrets that had been kept from him all these weeks. He found himself growing frustrated. Why had he not learned of the treasure yet? The end was drawing near. Before he knew it, he had reached the final page of the volume. It was over. He knew all. Or did he?

Dominique You had answered so many questions, yet one burning question remained. Tobias still did not understand where the treasure was hidden. He felt sheepish. Clearly, Mary Catherine had understood something in the journal that he did not. Was a key piece of information literally lost in her translation? She had been so confident he would find it. How could he face her knowing he had failed to grasp the riddle concealed in the text?

Mary Catherine was busying herself with dusting and tidying up the cottage, but he could feel her eyes constantly upon him as he read, as if appraising his cognizance of the mystery before him. Did she sense that he could not follow the clues? For a few agonizing moments, he pretended that he was still reading. However, he knew he could not fool her for long, as there was very little writing on the final page.

He decided to face the truth. "Well?" asked Mary Catherine, looking at him expectantly.

* * *

Tobias rushed through the muddy streets, not worrying about the state of his shoes, until he reached Chapter and Verse. He would be hard-pressed to make it there before the shop closed for the day.

After finishing the book, he felt frustrated that he could not decipher the clues to the treasure and embarrassed that he had missed what his wife had so clearly seen. When he had been forced to admit his failings to her, she had gotten quite upset with him. A Mary Catherine tirade of impressively monumental proportions ensued. She had been madder than a wet hen, but her scathing diatribe had been worth it. All of the pieces suddenly fell into place. Tobias finally knew what he had to do.

He made it to the shop with hardly a moment to spare. Mssr. Loutrel was coming through the door, having closed up for the day.

"Mssr. Loutrel!" called Tobias as he rushed over to the man in a most unseemly fashion. "You must let me in. I have some purchases to make. It's of the utmost importance!"

"Certainly, Mr. Whitney. Do come in. Everyone is in good health, I presume? Mrs. Whitney and the boys are well?"

"Yes, yes, we are all fine. Please forgive my abrupt behavior. I was worried I might arrive too late and you would be gone," explained Tobias between gasps. He was quite out of breath after his brisk walk.

"You've caught me in the nick of time." Mssr. Loutrel opened the door to the shop, and both men stepped inside. Tobias was aware that in his haste, he had not taken care with his steps upon the street, and now he was concerned that he was tracking a suspicious-smelling substance into Chapter and Verse. The aroma of his boots was far too reminiscent of the deposits left by horses traveling the streets to leave him in denial of what that substance might be. He apologized for this lapse before telling Mssr. Loutrel what supplies he required.

While Mssr. Loutrel gathered the requested items, Tobias made his usual perusal of the shop. He found it easy to focus on the smell of leather rather than the smell of horse dung. After working in the cemetery for so long, he had become accustomed to blocking out unpleasant odors. It was also helpful that he adored the scent of leather. He had grown up finding it intoxicating.

Now that he considered it, there was not a smell in the shop he failed to find appealing. The ink had a unique tang, and the paper all around him had an array of musky but pleasing scents. Most of the paper in Chapter and Verse, from the writing paper to the books, was made from rags beaten to pulp. The fragrance was earthy and reminded him of a forest filled with mushrooms, and although he had never been in such a forest, he imagined this must be what it smelled like. When Mssr. Loutrel returned with the parcel, Tobias added one more item, a gross of steel pens. He felt he had earned them.

"So, Mr. Whitney, you'll be keeping busy with all this, will you?"

Tobias knew Mssr. Loutrel was eager to learn why his actions were so out of character, but he would have to keep the old gentleman in suspense.

"I will, Mssr. Loutrel. Of that you can be assured," was his only reply.

Mssr. Loutrel was well-mannered to a fault, but he could not help pressing Tobias on the usual subject between them.

"Mr. Whitney, the doctor tells me my gout will only worsen. Stocking the shop requires picking up boxes, and then I must arrange all the wares just so. It is not something I can continue to do, much as I love the work." He allowed that thought to sink in for a moment before continuing. "I am afraid I will not be able to carry on much longer. By the end of the year, I will most likely have to make other arrangements for the shop."

He looked hopefully at Tobias. When Tobias did not offer him the usual array of excuses, Mssr. Loutrel continued. "I certainly would like to have it return to the Whitney family. A man like me, who has no children of his own and no one to leave a shop to, begins thinking of others as family. Mr. Whitney, forgive me for being so bold, but you are the closest thing to a son I have in this world. This shop should be yours again."

Tobias was taken aback by Mssr. Loutrel's uncharacteristically intimate words. Truth be told, he had come to think of the man as a father, since his own had passed away some time ago. He swallowed a growing lump in his throat. He hoped his voice would not crack from the emotion he was feeling. "Mssr. Loutrel, I am deeply touched. It was never my intention to step aside while you suffer. Perhaps I could help you after work here at the shop, lifting boxes and such."

"Does that mean you are not ready to buy back the shop?" asked Mssr. Loutrel, unable to mask the disappointment in his voice.

"I am not ready presently. There is something I must do first. It is of the utmost importance. After that..." Tobias let the words linger for a moment to steel his resolve and ensure he meant them before he spoke. He would not give this kind man false hope. "Yes. I do believe I will then come back to Chapter and Verse."

Mssr. Loutrel lifted a gnarled hand, placed it on Tobias's shoulder, and gave it a squeeze. It was a gesture made all the more poignant when Tobias realized the discomfort it must have caused the man.

As Tobias left the shop, he felt hope surge within him. He was moving forward with his life. He was rejoining the living. It felt good. Was it the confidence he had gained from learning the mystery of the book that finally propelled him to take his first steps toward his future after he had remained stagnant for so long?

The mystery. It was not as evident as he thought it might be. Had he expected Dominique You to state where the treasure was buried or mark the spot with an "X"? Tobias silently reprimanded himself. Such naivete! Yet it did become obvious once Mary Catherine had explained it to him. She was a brilliant, if not patient, woman. He recalled the moment when it all crystallized for him. In a fit of frustration over Tobias's inability to grasp the clue that was right in front of him, Mary Catherine threw the dove-gray volume at him, shouting, "The treasure is the book!"

Chapter Thirteen

Mary Catherine Whitney's Translation of the Journal of Dominique You

Jean's Life after Death

Every Robin Hood needs a Little John, and I suppose I was Jean's. I was his second-in-command. I'd been his companion for many years. He was my younger brother, yet I would have followed him anywhere. He had an air of authority and a surety of manner that made people want to listen. Most were happy for him to lead. It came naturally to him. Yet after he burned Campeche to the ground, he knew not how to command himself, let alone others. He was a ship without a captain. I knew he had lost himself in those days. Yet I did not know how to help him find his way.

He could no longer bear the burden of his sullied reputation. He was constantly maligned. He met enemies at every turn. "The wolves were ever circling," he used to say of his Barataria and Galveston days. He was disillusioned. Most would think a privateer, a man as hard as Captain Lafitte, would not care what those around him think. Most privateers no doubt would not. Jean did. He cared because he had not committed the acts his enemies accused him of. Decent people believed these false rumors and spurious stories spread about him. For a man as devoted to his country and the ideals of Freemasonry as Jean was, such slander struck a nearly fatal blow. He thought his days of being Robin Hood of the Bayou were over. He did not realize that many still thought him a hero. He did not realize he had more to give.

One thing was clear. He would never be able to sail the seas again. He would have been accused of piracy and hanged. No matter that he never committed such a heinous crime. There had been too many people claiming to be Captain Lafitte or claiming to be sanctioned by him when they committed despicable acts. Grambo was the worst offender. Yet there were countless others. Nary a pirate in the Gulf did not claim to be Captain Lafitte when he boarded a ship. No, it was far too dangerous for him to continue privateering. Even Jean could see this. And he was a man who thought anything was possible.

After he sailed away from Galveston in his ship, the *Pride*, he wandered about. He was a man without a home. I have few details to share about this time because Jean did not share them with me. Our correspondence was scarce during these years. Even after, when we saw more of each other, he did not like to speak of them. "The lost days," he called them. I believe he felt alone in the world. He was yearning for a home. He had no prospects for one.

Pierre was no better off. He left New Orleans after Captain Desfarges and his crew were hanged. His reputation had been sullied every bit as much as Jean's. Pierre was not keen to wander about the Gulf. He was like me in that sense. We all three had been seafarers for much of our lives, but Pierre and I did well on land. Better than Jean did. I stayed in New Orleans. I had distanced myself enough from the events in Campeche and made a home for myself. I opened a tavern and got by. I grew land legs and planted them here.

Pierre tried to make a home for himself on Isla de Mujeres. He quickly became beloved by the people there. They still tell stories of his kindness and generosity. He helped not only the inhabitants of the island but also the hapless sailors who found themselves marooned there. Yet I do not believe he ever felt at home on Isla de Mujeres. He contracted a fever and died in 1821. Jean was due to meet him there soon after. I believe Jean blamed himself for not arriving sooner, so he could have been with Pierre at the time of his death. I know I wish I could have been with him. Yet it was not meant to be.

Jean was even more adrift after Pierre died. The two had been as close as brothers could be. Jean was hunted like a pirate for his privateering activities. The authorities did not care whether his actions were legal or not. He was arrested twice in 1822 in Cuba and jailed in Porto Principe. After a few weeks, he'd had enough and pretended to be ill. He was transferred to a hospital where he made quick work of their security and escaped, leaving his handcuffs hanging from the door. He always did have flair, my brother. The second arrest happened just a few months later. The Americans arrested him this time but turned him over to the Cuban authorities—the same ones who jailed him before. Jean escaped again. My brother is a slippery sort, that is for certain. He is a man with many enemies, as I have said. Yet he has many friends as well. It is good to have friends when one is unjustly arrested and jailed. Friends can help set things to rights.

By now, he was privateering for Great Columbia, as I described when first I began this journal. He was searching for a way out of that life because he sensed his good fortune was running out. Though he operated under legitimate letters of marque, the papers in New Orleans painted him as a criminal. How quickly they forgot all he had done for them. When word of his escape from his unjust imprisonment got around, the *New Orleans Courier* called him a monster who had shed too much innocent blood. They expressed their regret that he had escaped the sword of justice! The very people who owed this man their liberty clamored for his blood. Is it any wonder Jean felt disillusioned? Betrayed?

Jean learned that Grambo had faked his death the year prior.

Grambo was many things. Cruel and ugly are the two that first come to mind. Grambo liked to think he was clever. Yet if brains were whiskey, he wouldn't get a thimbleful. He was wily, though, I must admit. I cannot recall how many times he was accused of murder. Yet he never went to the gallows. The world would have been a better place had swung years before. The authorities were harassing my brother while Grambo was free to terrorize and plunder. Makes a man wonder where the justice is in this world.

Yet even Grambo saw that things could not last for him. He decided life would be easier if people thought he was dead. Or so I assume. I never talked to Grambo unless necessary. I did not wish to know what was in his black heart. He got a friend to place his obituary in a Charleston newspaper. I should say accomplice, not friend. I never knew Grambo to have a friend, rotten scut that he was. We all knew he was not dead. We figured we were not that lucky, and some of the fellows from Barataria ran into him later. Regardless, I believe that put the idea in Jean's head that he might be better off if the world thought he was dead. No doubt that was the only good that came from knowing Grambo.

It is here that Jean's story ends as far as the world is concerned, in the first days of February 1823. Jean may have survived that battle aboard the *Santander*, but he had one foot in the grave and the other on the gallows. He could never live as Jean Lafitte again. Pierre was dead. He had no home. It was not safe for him to sail the seas. He was at his lowest point.

There were a million places Jean could have gone to make a new life for himself. Any country or city in the world would do. He could speak French, English, Italian, and Spanish. He could blend in with people. He was charismatic. He could have found a place to call home. Yet he did not wish to do that. He did not wish to start anew. There are only so many times a man can remake himself. I believe Jean had reached his limit.

So he came back to Louisiana. I know that seems incomprehensible. Why would he risk being recognized? I asked him that myself on more than one occasion, but Jean was not one to share his thoughts. The most he ever said on the subject was that he figured he had an inkling of how the Emperor Napoleon must have felt, forced to live out his remaining days on St. Helena.

"I 'died' to give myself another chance to live, but a life exiled from home is not a life worth living," he told me once.

He knew he could not go back to New Orleans. That was out of the question, even for him. But he could settle close by. And that's just what he did. He had spent so much time in Barataria that the bayous of Louisiana were just as much a home to him as the city of New Orleans. So he returned to Louisiana to start again, and this time, he settled in the bayous right outside the city. He could not have gone so far south as Barataria. There were still too many down that way who would have recognized him.

He did not intend to live there for long. It was a place to go while he figured out what he should do for the rest of his life. He had money. He had time. He just needed a plan. And who would think of looking for him there? It was a mad place for him to hide. That is precisely why he chose it. That is precisely why it worked. Until it no longer worked.

The area surrounding New Orleans is nary the same place as the city at all. I suppose that is true in many places. It is especially true in the bayous. In the city, you are on dry land for the most part. There's the river, of course, and the lake is nearby. Yet the city is built on solid ground. If you venture out just a bit, things change. There are bayous all around and swampy areas accessible only by pirogue. There are small footpaths that lead through mazes of cypress forests and marshland buzzing with mosquito swarms so thick you must part them with your Bowie knife. The ground beneath your feet never feels solid. It shifts and slides underfoot, threatening to give way to the murky black water that surrounds everything in the bayou.

The people live differently out there than they do in the city. They do things for themselves mostly. They may occasionally come into the city. Some do not at all. A man could live on his own out there and have all he needs. Some do not wish to mingle with civilization. Some need to hide out. Others just prefer not to be bothered.

The bayous outside New Orleans were good places if you were any of those kinds of people. A person could cut cypress trees and sell the logs to mill owners. He could grow beans or corn. He could fish or hunt or trap and have all the food he needed. He could go to New Orleans and sell whatever he had left over in the markets there. Or he could wait for the traveling merchants to come and sell him what he required. They barter a lot out there, too. Where one has fresh eggs, the other might have fish, and so forth. The communities are very close-knit. They do not care for outsiders. Yet if you are one of them, you are accepted.

Everything out there revolves around the water. People travel by boat. Houses are built on stilts to keep them dry. For a man like Jean, who loved the water, this was to his liking. It may not have been the seas, but it would do. He had decided he was willing to make some sacrifices to have a home. That was one he was willing to make.

I confess I was happy to have him there. It was closer than I ever thought I would be to him. We could get word to one another without much trouble. He did not come to New Orleans for fear of being recognized. Yet I could go to him.

He did not need to worry about money. He had plenty to live on, and there is always treasure to be found if you know where to look. He was not far from his old haunt in Barataria, mind you. Still, he needed to be cautious. It would not do to flaunt his wealth. He was content to live simply in this place. That is how the others lived there, anyway.

Most of his neighbors spoke French, just like Jean, or French-

Creole patois, which was not too hard to understand if you had some French. Many folks there had come to Louisiana after the revolution in Saint-Domingue, where Jean grew up, if you recall. Most were not white. The white folks had settled in the city by and large, save for the Acadians and a few Irish or German immigrants. A lot of his neighbors out in the bayous were free people of color, mulattos, quadroons, and the like. Not all, but a lot of them. This suited Jean just fine. When you've sailed as long as he had, you are used to being around people different from you. And he had memories of Haiti in common with them.

For their part, they accepted him. Everyone lived there together, mostly in peace. No one cared who you were or where you came from. It was not their business. That is just how they were. I do not mean to say it was easy for him to join their community. It was not at first. Yet he had a way with people. It helped that he had the means to be generous to all.

I suspect some of them knew who he really was. He was not naive. He figured if he had not been turned in when Claiborne offered a hefty reward for his capture, when he was right there in the Vieux Carré, right under Claiborne's nose, no one out in the bayou would bother with him if they did figure out who he was. There is no reward for a dead man's capture. He figured most would keep his secret if they put the pieces together. He was still a hero to many. Yet he had enemies who he knew would relish the thought of him hanging. He needed to hide from them. He did not wish to give those people the satisfaction.

He did not use his real name, of course. He chose a new one. He was Mssr. Robin du Bois, a wink to a Robin Hood alias or something of that sort. I was never the type to stick my nose in a book, but I do believe it was a fitting name for him to assume. He indeed was the Robin Hood of the Bayou in his days there.

Jean lived in the bayou long enough to know the people around him and to think of them as family, though anyone could see they were not blood relations. When you first look at a man, you see the color of his skin. Then maybe you notice how he is dressed. Is he a gentleman, a working man, or a beggar? After you know someone for a while, you still see those things. Yet maybe you see other things, too. Maybe you see the scar on his finger from when he cut it on the fishing net. Maybe you see the wrinkles around his eyes when he smiles. Perhaps that does not make sense. Perhaps that is just me. I think it was Jean, too. He was not like them, and they were not like him. And that was of no real consequence.

I believe he could have been happy there. He could have put his wandering days behind him. He could finally know the peace of a home. I have no doubt he was lonely, though. I have always been content to live by myself. But Jean liked feminine companionship. He had enjoyed the company of lovely, refined ladies. There were not too many of them hanging about in the bayous. Yet it only takes one, and sure enough, leave it to Jean to find her.

Her name was Olivia. She lived in the bayou not far from Jean. She was a young mulatto woman. Her mother had been a slave on a sugar plantation in Saint-Domingue. She fled to New Orleans after the slave revolts. Her father was a white man, a merchant living in Port-au-Prince, as they call it now. Her parents met on the boat that brought them to safety in New Orleans. They spent some time together. Then her father left to live in the city while her mother stayed in the bayou. Olivia was born in those bayous. She lived there all her life. She had little formal education, yet she was clever. A woman without wit could not have held Jean's attention for too long.

He had seen her from time to time before they formally made each other's acquaintance. Though formality in the bayou is a world away from what it is in New Orleans. He once told me she was the most beautiful woman he had ever seen. This was a woman living in the swamps. It was not as if she had all the trappings that women used to make themselves up. She had a natural beauty that attracted Jean to her. Like a moth to the flame, you might say.

He talked to her for the first time in the bayous one day when he was pulling a crab line. If the reader has never caught crabs, the process is simple. You tie a piece of fish or a chicken neck or whatever is about to one end of a rope or twine and tie the other end to the dock. If there is no dock, you still have no worries. You can tie it to a stick and stake it into sand or grass or mud. Then you wait for the crabs to start nibbling. When you see the bubbles rising to the surface, and the line begins to go taut, you have a crab. To catch it, you have to slowly and gently pull in the line. If you have someone to scoop for you, this next part is easy. When you pull the line near the surface, just close enough to be able to see the crab but not enough to spook it, the other person scoops it up in a net. You keep on doing this until you have all the crabs you want. The bayou will just keep giving them to you. Jean was able to pull the line and scoop for himself. He had done it enough times.

This particular time, he was standing on a pier while pulling the line. As he tells it, he was slowly stepping backwards to bring the crab near the surface so he could scoop it.

"Something caught my eye down the shoreline, and when I looked over, I'd have sworn I saw an angel," he told me. It turned out to be Olivia.

"She was in the bayou, bathing, with not a stitch of clothing on." Jean always chuckled at that part of the story, no doubt replaying the memory in his head. Jean was surprised by the sight before him. What man would not be? He lost track of what he was doing. "I backed up clear off the pier and landed in the bayou with a splash! Olivia heard the commotion and looked my way. She was not the least bit embarrassed to be caught at such a disadvantage. She continued her bathing, like no one else was around, even though she knew I was watching her."

My brother, the Terror of the Gulf, found himself entirely without words in her presence.

"I felt like a stuttering school boy. I climbed out of the water, drenched as a drowned rat, my hat dripping bayou water into my face. But I was determined to match her composure."

He drew himself up to his full six-foot height and, mustering all the dignity he could, apologized for disturbing her bathing. She just looked at him with an amused smirk and asked if he would like to join her.

Olivia was not like most women. She did not like to play games. She knew exactly who Jean was, and I do not mean Mssr. Du Bois. I suspect she had been interested in making his acquaintance for some time before that. Although my brother has never said so, it would not surprise me to learn that she knew he was there when she disrobed and began bathing in the bayou. It is of no consequence. Olivia knew how to get what she wanted. She wanted Jean. She got him. He was glad for it. They hardly left each other's side after that day in the bayou. Two more compatible souls could not be found. Perhaps it was the time in his life. Perhaps it was his loneliness. I do not know, but he fell under her spell. Jean had finally found what was missing in his life. He had found Olivia.

Chapter Fourteen

Mary Catherine Whitney's Translation of the Journal of Dominique You

Olivia

Jean and Olivia lived together as husband and wife for five years, from 1824 until 1829. I must apologize to the reader for not disclosing her surname. I cannot give what I do not have. Jean never told me what it was. Nor did Olivia. I do not know if they were trying to be coy or secretive. I did not think to ask. She was Olivia, plain and simple. That was all I needed to know. They were never formally married, of course. It did not matter a whit to them if the law or the church blessed their union. It was enough that they wished to be together.

I first met Olivia when I came to visit Jean. He had not told me she was living there. I climbed the many steps to reach his house. Bayou dwellers must rise above the water. The problem is, the water does not stay put. It rises when it will. Houses on piers were the only way to live dry out there. She was standing on the porch, tending to her hanging pots of ferns. Pretty green color and full, they were. Jean never had such adornments in his house before she came to live with him.

She greeted me as if I should know exactly who she was. As if she and Jean had been together their whole lives. "Hello, Dominique. I shall fetch Robin," she said.

I admit I was taken aback. I had to think for a moment whether I had met her, and it had slipped my mind. Yet it was not possible to forget Olivia. She was a stunning presence. A tall woman, she could nearly look Jean straight in the eye. She was solidly built, yet her movements were lithe. She had dark brown skin and tight curls that bobbed as she moved. Her most arresting feature was her eyes. They were the most mesmerizing shade of gray I have ever seen on a person. I found it difficult to look away when she turned those bewitching eyes on me. She had a manner of looking at you as if she saw right through to your soul. I always felt I could hide nothing from Olivia. She saw it all.

On this day, when first I met her, she sauntered into the house and returned shortly with Jean. He welcomed me warmly. He was always glad to see me. I was always equally glad. He inclined his head toward Olivia and said, "I see you've met Olivia."

No other explanation was forthcoming. I did not like to press. Jean could be secretive about his life. I accepted the scant information he gave me. I tried not to be greedy. I pretended this was the usual manner of conducting introductions.

We had a pleasant visit after that. Olivia was charming and witty. I enjoyed her company very much. And I enjoyed who Jean was when he was with her. He seemed relaxed around her. It was as if he had been searching for a part of himself his whole life. Now that he had found it, he could be at ease. When he was with Olivia, he no longer seemed like a man in hiding, like a man waiting for his enemies to pounce. I thought this was an excellent sign of things to come for him. Now he could finally be happy. I know now that he should have been more on guard. If only we could see the future. Sadly, we are doomed to stumble through life. We hope we can see far enough ahead to avoid danger. It has been my experience that we usually cannot.

On that first visit, when I met Olivia, I noticed that she used a particular inflection when referring to Jean as "Robin." It was as if she were part of the ruse. I suspect she knew his true identity, whether or not he ever told her. You could not hide secrets from Olivia. I wonder if she called him Robin or Jean when they were alone. I suppose I shall never know. When I left Jean's home that afternoon, Olivia gave me a gris-gris bag she had made. Olivia practiced Voodoo. She was very skilled at it. The gris-gris bag was a special one to ward off evil. She filled her gris-gris bags with herbs, roots, stones, and always a fava bean for luck. She stuffed them so tightly that Jean used to joke they could stop a musket ball. When she handed me mine that day, I laughed and asked if she had made one for Jean. He was the one who needed it. Her demeanor turned deadly serious in that moment.

She leaned in so close I caught the faint scent of jasmine in her hair. She whispered, "He does need one. As do I. Evil is all around us."

I did not want to ask what she meant by that. I accepted the bag and went on my way.

Jean was finally a happy man. He had all that he required. These years of his life passed peacefully. I visited him when I could. I saw his contentment for myself. Jean and Olivia were usually pleased with just each other's company. Jean had acquaintances in the bayou, but few close friends. He needed to keep it that way. When a man is hiding, that is for the best. The exception was a neighbor Jean had befriended.

His name was Virgil. I remember his surname because it was Freedman. At first, I thought that was a lark because of his past. Virgil used to be a slave back in Saint-Domingue. He was freed after the rebellion, and he took to the seas. He found his way to New Orleans and settled out in the bayous when he was done with the sea. I think that is why Jean was drawn to him. They could talk about life aboard ship and their adventures. Virgil was not a privateer, as far as I know. Jean told me he was a second mate for a merchant brig. When he left Saint-Domingue, he needed a surname, and since he had just been emancipated, he took the name Freedman. He was not the only freed slave to do so. Some take the name Freeman instead. I imagine it is because they are proud of their freedom. They wish to wear it like a badge of honor. I do not blame them. I imagine I would want to do the same.

Virgil and Jean spent most of their time together fishing or catching crabs. I met Virgil several times on my visits to see Jean. He was generally about, especially when Olivia was away. He was an easy man to be around. Taciturn in an amiable sort of way. They got on well since Jean was not one for many words either. Virgil had dark skin and eyes. His build was stocky like mine. His shoulders were broad and muscular. You could tell he was a strong man. Working aboard a ship for years builds such strength.

Jean was content to remain safely tucked away in the bayou, but Olivia was another story. I mentioned she was smart. She was also a quick study. She had learned the practice of Voodoo from her mother, who had an interest in it back in Saint-Domingue. Lots of slaves there practiced Voodoo. Lots of them also practice in New Orleans. It is not just slaves, either. Plenty of free folks do as well, mostly free people of color.

Voodoo in New Orleans was brought here by African slaves, some by way of Haiti. It is different here because so many folks are Catholics. Here, Voodoo mixes the two. When she got to Louisiana, Olivia's mother found others who practiced. They would meet in the bayous at night and teach each other what they knew. Olivia learned much about Voodoo right there in the bayou by her home.

Olivia was younger than Jean. She would never have been content to live out her days in the bayou without seeing a little more of the world. She had too much to offer. She would come to New Orleans from time to time to learn about and practice

Voodoo. It is not the sort of thing a person picks up in a lesson or two. There are intricacies I do not pretend to know. She would go to Congo Square on Sundays. I learned of the place from her stories. It is where slaves and free people of color gather. Besides practicing Voodoo, there is singing, dancing, and drumming. Sunday was the day for Congo Square because the Code Noir gives slaves that day to rest or tend their gardens.

Because Congo Square is the only place blacks are allowed to congregate, all the major New Orleans Voodoo practitioners gather there. Dr. John, or Bayou John, as some call him, was the reigning Voodoo king. He is a freed slave who tells fortunes and has magic and healing powers. He is so popular around New Orleans that whites and blacks pay him for his prophecies. He still rides around the Vieux Carré in a carriage pulled by white horses. It is always quite a sight. He taught Olivia all his skills. He saw the potential in her.

There were powerful Voodoo queens there as well that Olivia could learn from. The old quadroon from Saint-Domingue, Sanité Dédé, was the first, and then she was overtaken by Marie Salopé. Marie liked to teach the younger girls about Voodoo. She, too, recognized the gifts Olivia possessed. One other girl around Olivia's age had almost as much potential. Her name is Marie Laveau. Olivia and Marie had much in common. Olivia was a mulatto, and Marie was a free woman of color, but they both came from women who had been slaves. Olivia's mother and Marie's grandmother. They were both taught the ways of Voodoo by the reigning Voodoo royalty.

I am a man who has found God. I was scared of Olivia and her Voodoo ways when I first met her. I wanted nothing to do with such things. Yet Olivia was also a Catholic. Many of the others who practiced were, too. Marie Laveau, who goes by the name the Widow Paris now that her husband is gone, is a devout Catholic. She was baptized at the Cathedral of St. Louis and attends mass there. In New Orleans, you can be a practicing Catholic and a Voodoo practitioner. People who are not from here do not realize this. They think Voodoo is a dark art. It can be. I do not pretend to know much about it. I only know what Olivia has told me. All I can say with certainty is that Olivia was not a priestess of the dark arts. Olivia was a ray of light.

I mention all this so that the reader can understand her potential. She would have been famous in New Orleans. She would have surpassed Marie Salopé as the Voodoo queen here. I wonder sometimes how Jean would have felt about that. I think he would have been proud. Had she lived.

I do not believe in Voodoo or magic. Yet Olivia was convincing. She could charm people just like Jean could. If Jean could have shown his face in New Orleans, the two of them would have glittered like stars. They would have had no rivals in the city. Yet that was not meant to be. None of it was meant to be.

It was during his time with Olivia that Jean changed his thinking about things. Olivia abhorred violence of any kind. She would make healing potions or love potions or gris-gris bags to ward off evil, like the one she gave me the day I met her. She would never have used her powers to hurt anyone. When she went to New Orleans, she would join Marie Laveau in doing charitable works. They would tend to the sick around the city. They went to the Cabildo and offered solace to the prisoners there. She was the kind of woman who made a man want to be better. I believe Jean thought about his life and the things he had done. He was a good man, mind you. I have recounted many of his acts of kindness in this journal. He treated his men fairly. Even in his privateering days, he avoided violence when possible.

Yet there were things in his past he was ashamed of. I have mentioned his most shameful one before. He was involved in the selling of human lives. Pierre and I were, too. I believe he would have come to regret what he had done on his own. His enemies had chased him for so many years. His thoughts were of survival. He was always trying to stay one step ahead. There was no time to look back. There was no time for retrospection. What was done was done. Until he slowed down. Until he had time to think.

Olivia told him stories about her mother's time as a slave. She had been a cook in Saint-Domingue. Her mother had told Olivia stories about what happened to the ones who tried to escape. Horrible stories, they were. Her mother had come over from Africa on a slaver. She told Olivia about the conditions on board. They were chained in the hold of the ship for days. Many did not make it. Her mother talked about what it had meant to have her freedom—what it was like when she was denied it. It was a freedom she did not think she would ever have. It was a freedom so many did not have. Olivia told all this to Jean.

Jean had brought that misery to people. Maybe he did not kidnap them. Maybe he did not chain them in the hold of the ship. Yet he arranged for them to be bought and sold. He knew in his heart he was every bit as guilty as the rest involved. I believe the guilt would have festered. It would have robbed him of the peace he had finally found in the bayou with Olivia. He was the kind of man who had to make things right. Anything less would have been unacceptable.

Yet what could one man do? He was a man in hiding at that. He needed to protect his identity to protect his safety. He had few options. I knew he deeply regretted his actions. He told me as much. It was impossible to spend time around Olivia, to hear her stories about her mother's people, and not be moved. Olivia could tell stories that made you think you were there. You would swear they were your own memories. She had a magic about her when it came to that. I wish she could have written this account of my brother's life. She could have done him justice in a way I cannot.

I do not know what action Jean had planned to take to right the wrongs he had done in his life. Perhaps he had no plan at all. Perhaps he only had a desire to do something without a clear notion of what that might be. Sometimes, possessing the will to do something is enough. When the opportunity arises, you will surely grab hold of it. Perhaps that is what he was waiting for.

As it happened, the impetus for him to avenge the wrongs committed in his past punched him in the face. He could not ignore it. He probably thought he deserved it. Yet no man deserved what happened to Jean. That is a tale I shall have to tell soon enough.

In the meantime, I must relate the actions of the unfortunate Grambo. The year was now 1829, and Grambo had been "dead" for eight or so years. Since then, his life had not been to his liking. Grambo could never tow the mark. Rules did not apply to him. He wanted everything without working for anything. He always thought people owed him just because he was Grambo. Just because he wanted it. Grambo had no head for business. He had been arrested several times in those eight years for everything from petty theft to bigamy. I have no doubt he committed far worse crimes, but was not caught. He would never learn from his mistakes, nor would he ever regret making them. There was no remorse with that man. He only knew how to take.

I am certain he spent most of the eight years he was "dead" hunting for treasure. He was convinced Jean still had a fortune hidden around Barataria and Galveston. I know because when Jean left both places, Grambo would stay and slink around, hoping to find a cache. He never did, but that did not mean he thought there was no treasure to be found. He just figured he had not yet uncovered it. He always assumed Jean lived like a king, no matter where he was. That he shat in a solid gold privy. Jean had enough to live the rest of his days in comfort, but not the treasure Grambo was angling for.

Then Grambo somehow got it in his mind that Jean was still alive. No doubt he heard whispers. I believe the old crew from Barataria and Galveston knew the score. Those aboard the *General*

Santander did, of course.

No one loves to spin a yarn more than a sailor. And no matter how well-intentioned they may be, once they've had a bit of the grog, their tongues start wagging. I should know. I serve sailors in my tavern all the time. The more they drink, the more they talk. The more they talk, the more they lie. Unless they are lying to begin with. Then they start telling the truth. I suspect that is what happened in this case. One of them who knew Jean was alive must have happened upon Grambo and gone out carousing with him. The truth must have come out. *Secrets cannot stay buried forever.*

That brings me to November of 1829. I was working in my tavern when an old mate from my privateering days walked in. I had not seen him in many years. I greeted him warmly and expected him to do the same. Instead, he looked like he had just seen a ghost. I soon found out he had. Or a visit from the devil is more like it.

"I come to warn you, Dominique. Evil is about."

"Evil is always about! This is New Orleans!" I attempted to lighten the dark mood. He would not be deterred.

"Not this kind of evil. Not the kind Grambo brings."

The sound of the man's name after so many years sent a chill through me, and I am not a man to scare easily. But my fear was not for myself. It was for my brother.

"He came to Barataria lookin' for the captain. Keeps sayin' he knows he's alive, and he wants his share of the treasure he's been hidin.'"

My old mate had confirmed my worst fear.

"I figure if anybody knows where he is, it'll be you. So I came here quick as I could. Captain Lafitte is a good man. If he's still breathing, he deserves better than to be caught unawares by Grambo."

I knew I must get word to my brother. If Grambo were able to track him down, nothing would ever be as it was before. Grambo would wreck what peace he had found like a bullet through a bottle of whiskey. I did not want that for him. I did not want him to have to leave the bayou. I did not want him to have to leave Olivia. I knew she would not want to go away with him. The bayou was her home, and she was poised to become Voodoo royalty in due time. She would not have been happy to follow Jean into hiding. I knew he would never ask her to. Always going from place to place, always looking over her shoulder, as he had done for so many years. If Grambo found him, he would have to leave Louisiana forever. He would have to leave Olivia forever.

There was only one way out for Jean. He had to get to Grambo first. I do not condone killing a man. Yet there are times when doing so is for the greater good. I believed this was one of those times. If Jean killed Grambo, he would be safe again. His life could continue the way it was. The world would be a better place without Grambo. Of that I was convinced.

I dashed off a letter to Jean, using our secret code, warning him of the danger. I dared not go to him in person for fear that Grambo might be watching me. I dared not post the letter. Time was of the essence. Instead, I enlisted a trusted friend to deliver it to Jean under the cover of darkness. I felt like I was playing at spying. I knew how Jean had felt when he had pretended to spy for Spain.

Jean received my letter late that night. He began preparing to track down his old enemy. Grambo would not have risked staying around New Orleans. Even he was not stupid enough to walk about the streets of the city when he was supposed to be dead. If he had been to Barataria, he was staying somewhere near there while he looked for Jean and the treasure he suspected was hidden there. Who knew how long he would remain? He might leave if he didn't find anyone to tell him Jean's whereabouts. And that would be even worse. Jean would always wonder if Grambo was coming back. He would never have peace.

Jean figured if he could find Grambo first, he could end this once and for all. So Grambo was searching for Jean, and now Jean was searching for Grambo. They were two dead men seeking each other out. Only one of them could live.

What Jean did was right. He could have made no other decision, given the circumstances, given what he knew. It did not matter how many times I told him this later. He would not listen to me. He blamed himself for what happened next. There are no words I could speak to convince him otherwise. No matter what I said to him, we both knew he had fallen into the trap of thinking he could see far enough ahead to avoid the danger. Maybe if Bayou John had prophesied for him, he would have been warned. Maybe not.

Chapter Fifteen

New Orleans

December 1831

Tobias sat on his bench in St. Louis No. 2, but he was not alone. "I need to get the pins and needles out of my legs for a moment. We've been at it for some time now," he said, rising from the bench. "I suppose I should be heading home anyway," Mary Catherine said. "I need to get supper on. Besides, I've kept you from your duties long enough, and I know you detest shirking them."

"Aye, but it can't be helped, can it? Not with all the planning to be done. Though I admit I'm pleased to be working along with you now, and not waiting on your translations."

"Waiting on my translations? I nearly expired from the effort of producing those translations in a timely fashion! It wasn't an easy feat, I can tell you, not with the likes of you always breathing down my neck!"

"But it was worth it, wasn't it?" he asked with a smile. "Once you figured out the mystery!"

"I suppose so, but now you've got me toiling away once again!"

"Aye, but now we can labor as a team and make twice the progress." Tobias had been amazed by what they had accomplished in a short time. Each day, they seemed to discover a new angle. Everything slowly but steadily fell into place.

Since there were not enough evening hours to complete their task, Mary Catherine came to the cemetery during the day so they could work even more. As a result, it was becoming increasingly difficult for Tobias to find time to read aloud on his bench, but he somehow managed, progressing all the way through *The Last of the Mohicans* and beginning again. The shortened reading sessions were regrettable, but worth it. He told himself he would have curtailed his reading anyway this time of year, as the weather was getting cooler and could be dreary at times. At least the falling temperatures ameliorated the stench, which Mary Catherine greatly appreciated.

He observed her carefully in these meetings, eager to discern if she sensed eyes upon her, as he did. But she had mentioned nothing so far. He decided it was time to broach the subject. "Kitten, I have been feeling as if someone is watching me when I go about my duties in the cemetery. Do you not feel it as well?"

Mary Catherine looked around at the orderly rows of tombs. "Considering there are hundreds of dearly departed occupying this space with you, I hardly find that an unusual sensation."

"It's not a specter I suspect is watching me. I think it may be someone who knows I discovered Dominique You's journal."

Mary Catherine considered this. "How would someone know you found it?"

"They might have known, or at least suspected it was hidden in You's tomb. They might have been keeping watch to ensure it was not disturbed. Then, when I found it, they might have begun watching me to see what I would do next."

"You mean to see if you went treasure hunting?"

"Precisely."

"And who do you suppose might be watching you?"

"It could be a pirate who knew Captain Lafitte, or maybe even a Freemason."

"What an absurd notion! I can assure you that I've not seen many a pirate around the cemetery," Mary Catherine said. "And it was the Freemasons who hid the book in the tomb, remember?"

"Aye, but Dominique You made them swear they would not read it, or so he wrote in the first pages of his journal. Perhaps one of the Brotherhood got curious, and when I discovered it, he decided to watch me to see if I found the treasure."

Mary Catherine drummed her fingers on the arm of the bench, lost in thought. Finally, she said, "Tobias Whitney, I think you've read one too many adventure tales for your own good. I've been here for days, and I've not so much as felt a squirrel's eyes on me. This place is playing tricks on your mind. I've told you a thousand times, it's unhealthy to spend your days in a cemetery!"

Tobias thought that perhaps his wife was correct. His imagination must be playing tricks on him. If he really were being watched, surely he would have spotted someone by now. And besides, things had changed drastically since he'd finished reading the translation of the journal. It was time for him to focus on their new project.

Tobias was glad he had finally told Mary Catherine, though he was not surprised by her reaction. She had never been keen to set foot in St. Louis Cemetery No. 2. She did not find the peace within its walls that he did. The fact that she overcame her misgivings to work with him here was a testament to her dedication to the project.

He'd always assumed her reluctance to visit him stemmed from the usual things people found distasteful about cemeteries. Yet he had come to realize that what she disliked most about it was that it took him away from her and the boys, more so than a place of employment should. It was the space to which he had retreated after the death of his children. Even when he left St. Louis Cemetery No. 2, a part of him remained here. He was beginning to understand that she was correct. It was time for him to leave this place behind and return to Chapter and Verse.

Tobias had made many trips as of late to the bookstore for the supplies they required. Poor Mssr. Loutrel was all atwitter, but Tobias merely told him he would reveal all when the time was right. He had become quite fond of speaking in riddles and realized why Mary Catherine had done so, vexing as it had been at the time. Mssr. Loutrel, for his part, stopped asking questions about Tobias's significantly increased need for writing paper and pens and instead focused on turning over the shop to Tobias. This momentous event would occur by the end of the year. Tobias was still unsure how he would afford to buy back Chapter and Verse, but Mssr. Loutrel was working on a plan to have Tobias repay him slowly. Tobias found himself delighted by the prospect. In the meantime, Connor and Shane spent their afternoons helping Mssr. Loutrel at the shop.

Tobias felt as if a veil was lifted from his eyes, and he could see everything more clearly now. It was strange how the truth could be right in front of a person yet wholly concealed. Solving the mystery of Dominique's journal, finally comprehending what had been in plain sight the entire time, had a spillover effect on the rest of his family. He and Mary Catherine were busy well into the evening. They did not wish to neglect the boys, so after some discussion, they decided to include them in their special project. This decision was precipitated by a scuffle one night, when they were trying to work amid the boys' roughhousing in the next room.

"Connor! Shane! Stop your shenanigans this instant!" Mary Catherine had gone from deep concentration over her writing paper to yelling loud enough to shake the shutters in an alarmingly brief moment. Tobias barely had time to look up from his papers before she popped up from her chair, her skirts nearly toppling the inkpot in her haste to move away from the table and enter the parlor where the boys had begun wrestling each other and knocking over the wingback chair in the process.

"The Lord did not set me upon this Earth to have my work interrupted by such foolishness, do you hear?"

By the time Tobias had scooted the inkpot closer to the center of the table and joined the family in the next room, her face had already turned that bright shade of red that indicated her temper was flaring, and her hands were placed defiantly on her hips. If he did not diffuse the situation soon, she would ramp up even more, and there was just too much work that needed doing for such a delay.

"Kitten," he quickly interjected, "Perhaps we should discuss the possibility of including the boys in our work." He looked at her, his eyebrows raised expectantly. While she considered this, he made short work of collaring both the boys and holding them at arm's length from each other to minimize the amount of bodily harm they could inflict.

"We'll give ya a hand!" Connor said.

"We won't fight, promise!" Shane assured them.

"Not a single scrap, devil take us if we're lyin'!" Connor added.

"The devil would hand you right back, he would, after seeing all the trouble you two get up to!" Mary Catherine said.

After some discussion, Tobias and Mary Catherine deemed it wise to allow the boys to assist them. They were burning through more oil than Tobias cared to think about, but it could not be helped. After supper, the four of them huddled around the dining room table, with a glowing lamp in the center and writing paper and steel pens scattered all about. Tobias had put his foot down regarding what he felt were the superior merits of this new technology. Mary Catherine acquiesced. She was pleased that he was expressing a passionate opinion about the bookshop's offerings after displaying such apathy for the past few years.

The boys were thrilled to be included in such important grown-up business. They took the work seriously and were on their best behavior, speaking only when necessary and positioning themselves on either side of the table so they would not be tempted to elbow or kick one another. Initially, their parents assigned them only minor tasks. After proving themselves as valuable resources, Tobias and Mary Catherine allowed them to participate to a greater extent. The Whitneys worked tirelessly. Before they knew it, they had finished.

* * *

Carey & Lea Publishing
Philadelphia, Pennsylvania

Mr. Tobias Whitney
New Orleans, Louisiana

24th April 1832

To Mr. Tobias Whitney:

Dear Sir,

I trust this letter finds you and your family in good health. On behalf of the Carey & Lea Publishing House, I wish to express our gratitude for your submission of the manuscript entitled The Amazing Adventures of the Life and Death of the Pirate Jean Lafitte, Terror of the Gulf. We found the tale most entertaining and were particularly taken with the remarkable exploits of the gentleman privateer. As you correctly note in your query, this novel will undoubtedly appeal to the same readers who enjoyed Mr. Cooper's The Last of the Mohicans: A Narrative of 1757. We are confident that your work will capture the imagination of our adventure-loving audience.

It is with great pleasure that I extend to you an offer for the publication of your book. Please find the accompanying documents, which contain the terms and particulars of our agreement.

We eagerly anticipate the opportunity to collaborate with you on this exciting project.

Yours, &c.,

Henry C. Carey

Carey & Lea Publishing House

Tobias's hand shook as he read the letter for the third time in as many minutes. Could it be? Could this actually be happening? The excitement and jubilation bubbled up, and he let out a whoop of joy, not caring that the patrons in Chapter and Verse might think him mad. After regaining his composure and apologizing to the startled folks in the shop, his first thought was that he must get home to tell Mary Catherine the news.

He had eagerly awaited a response from this publisher for some time, checking daily with the postmaster in hopes of receiving a letter. When he made one of his daily trips this morning, he was almost shocked to see a piece of mail addressed to him. He had endured so much waiting, and here it finally was. But what news did it hold? It seemed too thick to be a simple rejection. Surely, that could be accomplished with a single sheet of writing paper. Yet Tobias did not wish to raise his hopes if they were merely to be dashed.

He'd felt guilty as he headed back toward Chapter and Verse after picking up the letter. He knew he should go straight home and open it in Mary Catherine's presence. After all, she had worked on the project as much as he had, and of course, she had translated the source upon which their tale was based. But Mssr. Loutrel had been kind enough to watch the shop for him while he made his daily visit to St. Louis Cemetery No. 2, and he had already added time to detour to the postmaster. He told himself this was the reason he should hurry back to the shop and open the letter there.

Yet if he was honest with himself, he must admit that he was hoping beyond all hope that this letter was a publication offer for the book he and Mary Catherine had written, with the help of the boys. He wanted to be the one to share the good news with them. It would make him feel like a hero to bring them such joy and excitement. And although Tobias did not consider himself a superstitious man, opening the letter in Chapter and Verse, a place teeming with excellent books, seemed like it might bring luck.

"Mssr. Loutrel!" Tobias spotted the man arranging an already perfectly placed volume on a shelf in the shop. "Mssr. Loutrel, I am sorry to impose upon you twice in a day, but I must return home."

Mssr. Loutrel had made it his habit to come to the store most days. Now that the strain of running it by himself had been lifted from his shoulders, he enjoyed visiting with people, and he enjoyed Tobias's company. Unless his gout was particularly troublesome, he could still be found pottering around Chapter and Verse, polishing the shelves or straightening stacks of books.

"Of course! Take all the time you need."

Bless Mssr. Loutrel, thought Tobias. He still had not told the older gentleman about his book, and with the outburst he had just witnessed, Mssr. Loutrel must think Tobias a complete loon. Ah, well, he would know all soon. But Tobias must tell Mary Catherine first.

Tobias allowed his senses to take in the glorious spring day as he walked to his cottage. The magnolias were in bloom, their heady fragrance wafting through the streets, partially masking the habitual, less pleasant scents. The azaleas bathed the city in a riot of color: pinks, lavenders, and whites, each more alluring than the last. The birdsong of cardinals and blue jays sounded particularly agreeable to Tobias's ears. A warm breeze felt pleasing against his cheek. The world was ripe with possibilities and new adventures.

He ascended the cottage stoop in two bounding steps, hardly noticing the freshly scrubbed door and newly plastered facade. He knew the boys would not be about this time of day, and he was glad for that. He wanted this moment alone with Mary Catherine. He found the cottage empty. This did not surprise him. On such a lovely day, Mary Catherine would perform as many outdoor chores as possible. When he entered the courtyard and still saw no sign of her, he knew she must be in the detached kitchen building on the periphery of the property. Sure enough, when he walked into that room, he witnessed a most unusual sight. Mary Catherine was doing her ironing.

She had the board upon the table and one flat iron in her hand, the handle covered in a thick cloth to protect her from the heat. A second iron was in the fire, ready to be swapped out when the one she was using cooled. Tobias was nonplussed. He had always thought Mary Catherine was careless with her iron. How else could he explain the numerous scorch marks on his clothing? Yet there she was, hunched over one of his shirts, meticulously ironing it with the most excellent care and precision. On the table next to her were some sandpaper and beeswax, both recently put to use, by the looks of them. That could only mean she had maintained her tools by smoothing the irons with sandpaper and applying beeswax to ensure they did not stick to the cloth.

Perhaps she was better at ironing than she had led him to believe. If this were true, then the scorch marks had been deliberate, which he had always suspected. The fact that he had nary a scorch mark on his clothing since he had begun working in the shop again told him all he needed to know about where he stood with Mary Catherine. And he could not help but feel the news he was about to deliver would place him even higher in her regard.

"Kitten, we did it!"

Mary Catherine spun around at the sound of her husband's voice. "Saints above! You nearly scared the life out of me! What were you thinking, sneaking up like that?"

Tobias rushed over to her, gathered her in his arms, and kissed her.

"Tobias Whitney!" she exclaimed. "What in heaven's name has gotten into you?"

"The letter we've been waiting for has just arrived! We did it! Our adventure tale is to be published!"

Mary Catherine went uncharacteristically silent. She stared at the paper he waved at her. Finally, she gathered her wits enough to speak. "We did it?"

"Aye, we did it!'

Mme. Auclair must have thought there was a coyote loose in the courtyard for all the gleeful exclamations that ensued. Tobias and Mary Catherine did not give it a thought, even when Mme. Auclair peeked over the picket fence, her expression pinched with disapproval.

"Such racket, mon Dieu! I might as well live next to a fishmonger and his wife," she exclaimed.

"Now Mme. Auclair, that's uncalled for," Tobias said.

Mary Catherine placed a hand on his arm to stop him. "Don't fret, Tobias. God bless her, the poor dear can't help herself—her tongue runs faster than her good sense."

The Whitneys left Mme. Auclair sputtering in a fine French rage. Mary Catherine retrieved her iron, which she had dropped upon her husband's shirt when she'd been startled by his unexpected midday visit. Tobias did not care in the least that the scorch mark was beyond mending. It was a small price to pay for bringing such joy to his wife.

Tobias eventually returned to the shop to finish the day's work. He and Mary Catherine agreed to share the good news with the boys that evening. Tobias was struggling to concentrate on his daily tasks at the bookshop. He found himself continually glancing over at the shelves of books, all smelling of new leather, so full of the promise of adventure, just as his life was now.

He could hardly wrap his mind around the notion that his book would be on these very shelves in due time.

The decision to approach Carey & Lea Publishing with their book had been an obvious one for Tobias. He had carried around his tattered copy of *The Last of the Mohicans* for the last four years, after all. He knew that the company's founder was an Irishman now living in America, much like Tobias himself. Who better to publish the tale written by his family than the company responsible for bringing the Whitneys joy for years?

The Last of the Mohicans was more than just entertainment for Tobias and his children. When he read the book aloud to them, he left his world and entered another. At first, this world was new to him. It was exotic and thrilling, with danger around every corner. It was as if he were one of the characters at the heart of the action. Over time, his feelings about the book changed. Instead of new and exciting, it felt familiar and comfortable. Within its pages, he found peace. While he knew that for most readers the pirate tale he and his family had written would be a diverting adventure, he hoped it might grant another struggling soul a temporary respite from the world.

The idea to send the manuscript to Carey & Lea Publishing had been his, but it was Mary Catherine who'd realized the value of what Tobias had found in Dominique You's nameplate. He was still unsure when exactly she had decided they must write an adventure book based on the incredible tale, but he would never forget the moment the idea crystallized in his mind. It was that fateful day last October when he'd been so frustrated. He'd read all the translations, but he still hadn't found the treasure his wife assured him was hidden within the pages of the journal. She'd thrown the dove-gray volume at him, calling him daft and insisting that the treasure was the book. When he had looked at her, dumbfounded, as her words slowly sank in, she had scooped up the volume from the floor where it landed at his feet.

She'd flipped maniacally through the pages of her messy handwriting, shoving one page after the next into his face, insisting, "It is here! And here! And here! The treasure lies in every page of the book! The *book* is the treasure!"

He'd finally understood. They'd begun planning right then and there how to transform Mary Catherine's translations into an adventure tale along the lines of the ones Tobias and the boys loved so dearly. Since women authors were a novelty, they decided the author should be known simply as T. M. Whitney, combining their initials into a single name.

In the weeks that followed, Tobias's own transformation had been complete. He'd finally resigned from his post as sexton at St. Louis Cemetery No. 2, leaving it in the hands of a capable man he felt would do an excellent job. He made arrangements with Mssr. Loutrel to buy back the shop, and he performed the deferred maintenance on his cottage.

He also found himself more engaged in his home life. When Mary Catherine railed against the boys, Tobias no longer remained a bystander, watching the events unfold. Depending upon the grievousness of the boys' offense, he would either diffuse his wife's anger and de-escalate the situation or jump right into the fray and fuss at them alongside her. He knew she did not require his help, but he sensed she appreciated the support. The boys seemed pleased with their father's increased attention, although Tobias suspected they missed the fun of provoking their mother without much interference from him.

Perhaps the most significant change in him, the one that made him feel certain he would be alright, had happened thanks to Mary Catherine. He had come to suspect that Mary Catherine had been prodding him out of his stupor these past few years, coaxing him back into their world. And since yelling was her way, this was how she tried to elicit a reaction from him. There was one incident just a few weeks prior that made him confident beyond a doubt that she was orchestrating his return.

Mary Catherine had been in rare form, even for her. She had just finished an impressive diatribe against the boys, and when Tobias had little to say on the matter, she had turned her attention to him. He was subjected to a ten-minute harangue that included a litany of all the tasks that needed to be done in the cottage, insisting that he, right this minute, fix the unsteady leg on the dining table. Tobias was weary from the day, but would have responded with a placating remark in the past and succumbed to her demands. Not this night.

He decided to test his theory. He looked down into her flashing green eyes and stated firmly, "No, Kitten. I would prefer not to."

He then settled himself into the wingback chair, crossed one leg casually over the other, and smiled serenely at the boys. They were dumbfounded. They glanced from their mother to their father, waiting for the inevitable explosion they were sure would ensue. Mary Catherine threw back her shoulders, turned on her heel, and uttered an indignant harrumph. As she turned to leave the room, she looked over her shoulder and whispered words so softly they could barely be heard, "Welcome back, Tobias."

Chapter Sixteen

Excerpt from
The Amazing Adventures of
the Life and Death of the Pirate Jean Lafitte,
Terror of the Gulf
By T. M. Whitney

Chapter XXXIV

(In which Captain Lafitte pays a visit to an old friend)

Convinced he must do all within his power to halt that odious beast of a man, Grambo, our intrepid Captain Lafitte made haste in his pirogue to the swampy marshes of Barataria. Such a journey should have taken at least a week, but Captain Lafitte knew the pirate's path. The shortcuts he'd used during his Barataria smuggling days shortened the trip to two days. This was fortunate, as time was of the essence. His very life depended upon finding Grambo before anyone alerted the man that Captain Lafitte was searching for him.

Captain Lafitte was still beloved amongst the people in this part of the world. He had friends he could call upon who would honor his need for secrecy. He was a good leader to his band of men in Barataria and a good neighbor to those around their commune. Still, he must choose wisely when deciding whom to approach for news. He knew that Grambo had been around, prodding, no doubt threatening people to disclose what they knew of his whereabouts.

He'd settled upon Mr. Beaufort, an elderly man who'd lived in Barataria all his life. He owned a general store on Grand Isle. He saw and talked to people each day. He had always harbored a fondness for Captain Lafitte. He would tell him the truth.

It was as dark as pitch outside. The moon was new. The store was closed for the day, but Captain Lafitte knew Mr. Beaufort slept in a room behind the tiny store. The store looked as decrepit as he remembered it. Its weathered boards were warped in places, and a few were missing altogether. He stepped cautiously onto the uneven wooden planks of the covered front porch to minimize their creaking. He navigated the crates standing on end, serving as makeshift seating for customers and loiterers to escape the burning sun during daylight hours. He breathed in the briny air. The smell of salt water, wet vegetation, and drying fish held all the comfort of home. But he had no time to reminisce about his Barataria days. He must complete the task at hand.

He surreptitiously entered the building. He was adept at letting himself into places where entrance was barred to most, though Mr. Beaufort's door would not have deterred the least competent criminal. All around him was fishing gear—spools of fishing line, hand-made fish hooks, cane poles and bobbers, cast nets, and crab traps. He needed to wait for his eyes to adjust to the low light. Should he make one false step, jars of molasses, tins of lard, and other such items would come crashing down from the over-stacked shelves, and the ensuing ruckus would surely wake others. He must conduct his business with Mr. Beaufort in secret. It was imperative that no one knew he had been here. Mr. Beaufort's safety would be compromised if word reached Grambo that he had talked to Captain Lafitte. He did not wish to bring harm upon this kindly man.

When he could discern shapes in the darkness, Captain Lafitte cautiously picked his way through the store, weaving around barrels filled with pickles and salt pork and snaking through piles of fabric bolts stacked precariously on either side of the narrow aisles. Even with his deliberate progression, it did not take long to traverse the space. The store was no larger than a sitting room. He arrived at the door to Mr. Beaufort's sleeping quarters. He must be sure to wake the man without startling him unduly. Captain Lafitte approached the cot where Mr. Beaufort peacefully slumbered. He pushed aside the mosquito netting. He could barely make out the man's white hair against the pillow. The rhythmic rise and fall of Mr. Beaufort's chest assured Captain Lafitte that he had not been disturbed by his entrance.

Captain Lafitte leaned close to the sleeping man and roused him with a gentle shake to his thin arm. Mr. Beaufort awakened. The captain addressed him fondly.

"Hello, Mr. Beaufort. 'Tis I, Jean Lafitte, come back from the dead."

Mr. Beaufort was not startled like a man should be when faced with a ghost waking him from his slumber. He was an even-keeled sort of man. This was another reason the captain chose him.

"My stars, if it isn't Captain Jean Lafitte! I always knew you weren't dead."

"Not yet, Mr. Beaufort. My time will come, no doubt, but not tonight."

The captain would have liked to visit with his old friend. It had been years since they had seen one another. Yet he knew that he did not have the time for such frivolities. He must soon be on his way. Speed was of the essence if he was to ensure the secrecy of their meeting.

"Mr. Beaufort, I must find Grambo. I understand he has been inquiring as to my whereabouts."

Mr. Beaufort nodded his head of wild, white hair. Captain Lafitte could barely discern the movement in the dim moonlight.

"That he has. He's been askin' all around for you, though demanding information might be a better way to put it." Mr.

Beaufort shuddered at the memory. "I'm fortunate he came here first. I told him the truth, that I'd not seen hide nor hair of you since you were reported dead. He took me at my word. His temper soured the more folks kept quiet. Young Henry Broussard did not care for his questioning and told him so. Grambo beat him near to death, I tell you. Knocked out most of his teeth in the front, and he can't see for all the swelling 'round his eyes. It'll be a good, long while 'fore he's up and about again. Don't know how he'll get his fishin' done. His papa passed last year, and his mama depends on him."

These words spoken by his old friend sent a dagger through the captain's heart. He had thought his "death" would save him. He had not meant it to come at another's expense. He would have liked to inquire further about the brave Henry Broussard, but he could not spare the time. He had to know all Mr. Beaufort could tell him about Grambo's whereabouts.

"Is Grambo still asking questions about me? Is he still in Barataria?"

"I believe we're finally rid of him," Mr. Beaufort said, his voice edged with relief. "He's been braggin' to anyone who'll listen about the fortune he's soon to collect. Last I heard, he's meeting a group fresh off a slaver and bringin' them to market in New Orleans."

Captain Lafitte understood at once what Grambo was planning. He knew well the law prohibiting the importation of slaves into Louisiana. To bypass it, pirates would often seize slave ships, carrying them to hidden harbors outside Louisiana—places beyond the reach of U.S. authorities, far from the eyes of legitimate port officials. Once there, slave runners would smuggle the captives across land into the state.

The runners would then turn the slaves over to the authorities, claiming to have "rescued" them from illegal traders, and collect a reward. The slaves would be auctioned, and the runners would buy them back with the reward money, securing a legal title to sell them at a substantial profit.

It was a vile, if quasi-legal, scheme. Captain Lafitte knew it well—had even been part of it himself when he was privateering in Galveston. The thought made him flush with shame. He wondered for a fleeting moment if he was any better than Grambo. But he forced the thought aside, steeling his resolve. He had to be better—for himself—for Olivia.

Captain Lafitte required no further explanation from Mr. Beaufort. He knew exactly what must be done. Mr. Beaufort, plainly relieved to have aided his old friend, offered a weary smile.

"I wanted to get word to you—to warn you of Grambo—but I wasn't sure you were still alive. And if you were, I'd no notion where to find you."

"It's just as well," Lafitte replied. "Doing so might have put you in danger."

He clasped the man's hand and offered his thanks with genuine warmth. From his coat, he drew several gold coins—no small sum—and left them with Beaufort, asking that they be used for the care of Henry Broussard and his mother. Then, without another word, the captain slipped from the shop as quietly as he'd entered, vanishing into the night like a specter.

✳ ✳ ✳

Chapter XXXV

(In which the evil Grambo does his worst and is hexed)

Captain Lafitte knew where to search for Grambo. He was determined to stop him from committing this act and whatever evil would come if his reign of terror were left unchecked. Yet Captain Lafitte did not know all that Grambo had planned. He did not know Grambo had one final score to settle with his old

175

captain.

Grambo was more successful in his search for information about Captain Lafitte than Mr. Beaufort was aware. The man had been truthful with the captain. He told him all he knew about Grambo, but he did not realize that Grambo had discovered the captain's alias. He did not know to warn the captain what Grambo had planned for him.

After Grambo's unpleasant visits with Mr. Beaufort and Henry Broussard, he crossed paths with another who pirated with him during his Barataria days. This man had sailed for Grambo, and anyone who sailed for Grambo was cut from the same ruthless cloth. He thought nothing of betraying Captain Lafitte. *Never trust a pirate!* The man was still loyal to Grambo. Perhaps he was fearful of him. Anyone with sense would be.

"Dominique You's been slippin' outta the city, headin' into the bayous," he'd told Grambo.

"Maybe he's got a woman out there, " Grambo speculated.

"Nah, not Dominique. He's half dead, he is. Got the gout or somethin' or other. He wouldn't be gettin' up to such sport."

"Then he wouldn't be making the trip at all unless it meant something."

"Aye. And I got a fair guess who he's goin' to see."

Grambo fixed him with a challenging stare.

The pirate leaned in, eager to share the information his captain desired. "There's a man livin' out there now, but he weren't born to no swamp. Folks say he's mighty generous with his neighbors, so they don't go askin' questions 'bout him. Don't work a day, but always got plenty to spread 'round."

Grambo's voice was low, laced with menace. "What's his name?"

The pirate grinned, pleased with himself. "Robin du Bois, Captain. That's what they call him."

Grambo mulled this over. The more he thought about it, the more confident he was that he had discovered Captain Jean

Lafitte's alias. It would be simplicity itself to locate him now.

A man's name is his treasure, as pirates are wont to say. Captain Jean Lafitte did not wish to share his, but secrets can't stay buried forever. Grambo intended to steal the captain's treasure. He did not realize that by discovering his name, he had already done just that.

Grambo, shrewd as he was, was not clever. He did not realize the significance of what he had uncovered about his nemesis. He only considered that now he would be able to find the gold and precious jewels he was certain the captain had hidden nearby. He salivated over the prospect of stealing from the captain. He had vowed many years ago to take from Lafitte what was most dear to him, just as the captain had done to Grambo when he seized his ships and hanged his crew back at Campeche.

Grambo headed off in his skiff toward the bayou where Robin du Bois lived. He was determined to discover where Lafitte had hidden his treasure. He was prepared to do this by any means necessary. Grambo was a rogue who did not mind extracting information from others using the most despicable means. He rather enjoyed doing so. He was untouched by the usual warmth or pity men feel for each other. It should pain a person to witness another suffer. It did not pain Grambo in the least.

He relished the thought of killing Lafitte. It would bring him great pleasure. He had harbored a deep hatred for the man since Lafitte first came to Barataria. Barataria had been a haven for pirates and smugglers since anyone could remember. They were never united. They operated separately, each looking out only for himself. D*** the others!

Then the Lafitte brothers came along. They were nothing but middlemen at first, moving the spoils the pirates brought in from their ships and selling them at the markets in New Orleans. It was a job a monkey could do. Yet, before Grambo realized what was happening, the Lafittes had become indispensable to the

Baratarians. Then, Jean Lafitte began organizing them into a single enterprise. He had the pirates coming to him to liquidate their treasures so they could go a-pirating all the sooner. They liked the convenience of the services Jean and Pierre offered. They sold their freedom to the Lafittes for it.

Once Jean had established his authority in Barataria, there was nothing Grambo could do about it. Jean was no different from him, Grambo thought bitterly. Both men were pirates. Yet Jean had made himself a leader among pirates, and Grambo hated him for it. He was not the type of man to bow down before a leader. There was something about authority in all its forms that riled Grambo. He did not care for law or order. He wanted what he wanted, whenever he wanted it. Captain Jean Lafitte had been a thorn in his side for years now. *That ends tonight*, Grambo thought as he guided the skiff to the dock outside of Du Bois's house.

Meanwhile, inside the raised home, amidst the cypress trees and the ceaseless croaking of frogs in the marshes, the lovely Olivia could not find sleep. She was unsettled. She sometimes had a feeling about things that she found difficult to describe. This evening, she felt a sense of foreboding. She thought perhaps something might be wrong with Robin, or Jean. She thought of him as Jean, but she was careful never to address him by that name. She rose from her bed and stepped over to her Voodoo altar. She reached for a gris-gris bag she had made to protect her from evil. She had given one to Jean as well. Years ago, she had given a similar one to Dominique You.

She slipped the bag into the pocket of her nightdress and gazed out the window. Darkness cloaked the world beyond, revealing little. There was nothing to indicate danger was near, yet the hairs on the back of her neck were standing on end. She wondered if perhaps it was her imagination, except that now the frogs had ceased croaking. They would not do so unless something had spooked them: something, or someone.

Olivia was a brave woman. She would not be frightened in her own home. She knew she had nothing to fear from her neighbors. They were good people who meant her no harm. Everyone around the bayou adored Olivia. They appreciated her charitable works. She served as a traiteur to the sick. There were no doctors out here. Healing fell to women, usually the old ones, who relied on remedies passed down through generations. Such women were well-versed in the healing properties of the local plants and herbs. Olivia was young to be a traiteur, but she was skilled nonetheless. She combined her knowledge of natural remedies with her potent Voodoo healing potions. She cured many of the bayou folks, and they cherished her for it. Why, then, did she sense the presence of another in her home? It was an evil presence, of that she was certain. She picked up the oil lamp from her altar and prepared to walk through the house, checking for intruders. As she turned away from the table, she was scarcely surprised to see a man standing there.

"Evenin', ma'am," Grambo drawled, his grin lewd and full of yellowed teeth. Before Olivia could react, he lunged and was upon her. He clamped a hand over her mouth to stifle her screams. He removed the clasp knife from his belt and held the gleaming blade before her eyes.

Grambo was disappointed that Captain Lafitte was not in his home, but he knew he would find him in due time. Instead, he had discovered something else he could take from him, or someone else. Grambo was delighted at the thought. He was chagrined that the girl did not look more frightened when he appeared in her sleeping quarters, as he relished seeing fear in a person's eyes. She seemed preternaturally calm, as if she knew what would happen and was resigned to her fate. He would force her to tell him where Lafitte was. Then he would have the satisfaction of informing the captain of what he had done.

"Tell me what I want to know, and I won't have to hurt you, love," he whispered, tightening his grip as she fought violently to break free.

He had not anticipated such resistance. She was strong for a woman, and she was fierce. Grambo was stronger, and he knew he could overpower her. She fought to twist free, grunting with the effort, kicking and thrashing like a wild animal trapped in a snare. In the ensuing struggle, she knocked them both to the ground.

She saw an opportunity to escape! She tried to leap to her feet just as he moved to grab her again, and they collided with such force that it knocked the breath from her. Olivia landed on her back, and Grambo fell on top of her, the knife in his hand plunging deep into her chest. Her vision faded, and the world around her darkened.

Grambo was shocked. He hadn't meant to kill her—not yet—but he saw the life drain from her eyes and knew she was nearly done. Her breath came in shallow gasps, her chest barely rose, but her lips trembled, struggling to form words. He could scarcely make them out, but the venom in her voice was unmistakable. She was cursing him—her last breath filled with hate. Now it was Grambo who felt the hairs on the back of his neck prickling, as if unseen forces were closing in.

* * *

Chapter XXXVI

(In which Captain Lafitte makes a bitter discovery)

Captain Lafitte made the trip back in record time. It was night when his pirogue approached the dock outside his bayou house. He'd been using an oil lamp to navigate the stygian darkness. The new moon was not doing its part to light his way. He did not fear these bayous at night, however. He had been traversing them for years. They were as familiar to him in the dark as they were during the day.

He must go after Grambo. He needed to plan his next move. He had been mulling it over the entire trip back and had started formulating a plan.

He contemplated what he should tell Olivia. He did not enjoy keeping secrets from her. He considered that perhaps it was time to reveal his true identity. He suspected she already knew, though they never discussed it. Something in her inflection of "Robin" made him certain she did not believe it to be his name. She spoke the name like a question, as if she was challenging him to tell her the truth. Tonight, he would do just that.

Yes, he thought, *it is time to tell Olivia everything.* He felt he could trust her with his life, and this was good because sharing his secret with her meant he was doing just that. He trusted very few people. Once Pierre was gone, only Dominique was left. Then along came Olivia. She had brought him happiness. She had turned this place into a home. Now it was his turn to offer her something just as rare, the truth of who he was, and the trust that came with it. She had earned this gift, after all. With his mind made up, he was eager to return to his house and confide in her. It would not be long now. He was but a few minutes away.

* * *

This was not how Grambo envisioned his trip to Captain Lafitte's home would end. He came here thinking he would catch the captain by surprise. He would find out where the treasure was hidden and then kill the man. He would have both his revenge and the treasure. Coming upon that stunning woman in Lafitte's home had been a surprise, though not an unwelcome one. He could still find out where Lafitte's treasure was hidden and exact his revenge on him by killing her.

Afterwards, he'd planned to hide in Lafitte's house and wait for the captain to return. He'd get to witness Lafitte discovering the body of the woman and revel in his suffering. Then he would murder Lafitte and steal the treasure.

The treasure would make his life in hiding more comfortable. For eight long years, he had struggled to find his way. He was a ghost among the living. He was tired of settling for a life he did not want. He deserved better. He desired to be a wealthy man. Captain Lafitte's treasure would make him one.

That plan had changed suddenly. He had not expected the woman to resist him. She should not have fought back. He had not meant to stab her. He felt no remorse for taking her life, but now he had no information about where Lafitte might have hidden his treasure. This was most unfortunate, but it was not the worst of his problems. He was sure she was a Voodoo priestess.

He'd spied the altar in the bedroom. It was a simple wooden table, draped in white linen and stained with candle drippings, pushed against the far wall. He'd guessed its purpose the moment he saw the ceramic bowl, darkened by the ashes of paper offerings, a few of which remained, petitions penned with careful hands. Nearby were pouches of herbs tied tightly with string, an assortment of feathers, and brightly colored beads.

He had found the scene before him slightly unnerving, but then the woman had turned around, and he no longer had time to dwell on who she might be. He had rushed her, and the terrible struggle had ensued. It had all gone wrong so quickly, and then he had delivered the unintentional death blow, his knife plunging straight into her heart.

Grambo had killed many people with his clasp knife. He was deadly accurate. He did not mind watching them die. In fact, he found the process fascinating. Yet never before had one of his victims hexed him. He knew beyond a shadow of a doubt that this was what she had done. For the first time in his miserable life, Grambo was scared. He believed in the power of Voodoo. He knew he was cursed. He knew he was doomed. All he could think about was getting as far away from the house as quickly as possible. He raced back to the dock and was off in his skiff in a flash. He would have to come back to deal with Captain Lafitte. It would have to be after he sold the slaves. He had run out of time.

* * *

Captain Lafitte walked up the steps to his home. He did not realize anything was amiss. He did not know his life would never be the same when he opened the door. When he first saw her, he thought perhaps he was imagining the scene before him.

"Olivia?" The voice coming from him sounded so very different than his own. He barely recognized it. Could that really be her lying on the floor? It seemed as if she was staring directly at him, yet her eyes did not blink. And then there was the blood. It should not be there, pooling around her still form, as unmoving as she. When the pieces all came together to form the horrible picture, when his conscious mind caught up to the shock of the scene before him, Captain Lafitte did a most uncharacteristic thing. The Terror of the Gulf dropped to his knees and wept uncontrollably.

Chapter Seventeen

Excerpt from
<u>The Amazing Adventures of</u>
<u>the Life and Death of the Pirate Jean Lafitte,</u>
<u>Terror of the Gulf</u>
By T. M. Whitney

Chapter XXXVII

(In which Captain Lafitte plans his revenge upon Grambo)

In the days that followed, our intrepid Captain Jean Lafitte was undone. He had felt lost before. He had thought he must find a new place for himself, but this time was different. Horribly different. Olivia's murder had wholly unmanned him. Grambo had succeeded in taking that which Lafitte most valued. He should have used this knowledge to fuel his desire for revenge upon Grambo. He certainly would have expected to want to do this. He hated Grambo. He felt the fires of a thousand flames raging in his chest when he thought of what the man had done to Olivia.

Yet the desire for revenge and the ability to rouse oneself from overpowering, all-encompassing grief are two disparate things. As much as he would have liked to kill Grambo, there were dark moments in those days when Captain Lafitte thought it would be easier to end his own life. He would be free of the pain. To that end, he lost himself in drink. The nights were the hardest to endure, so he found that he could sleep most of the day if he drank most of the night. He wondered if it might be easier not to live at all. He was so very tired. Tired of fighting, tired of trying to find a home and the solace that comes with it, only to have it ripped from him time and time again.

Dominique You tried all that he could to console his despondent brother. His words were meaningless, he could tell, yet he had to speak them nonetheless. He must try to help Lafitte, for he feared his brother would not find his way back from the darkness that surrounded him. Virgil Freedman also tried, yet his efforts were no more successful than those of Dominique You. As the days slipped away, so did Captain Lafitte. They feared they would lose him soon.

It was Virgil who finally brought Captain Lafitte out of his stupor. He was sitting on Lafitte's porch, amidst the lovely hanging ferns Olivia had cared for. He had taken to coming over every day to sit with him in the evenings when Lafitte finally arose from sleeping off the previous night's imbibing. Virgil knew what had happened to Olivia because Dominique You told him. Dominique You himself had to wrench the awful story from Lafitte, but neither of them had discussed it in the week since her murder. Yet on this day, Virgil decided to broach the subject. He figured it could not make matters worse. He was growing exceedingly concerned about his friend Robin, or Jean, as he now knew him.

Dominique You had told him that part as well. Virgil was shocked upon first learning that his fishing friend was a notorious pirate, but Virgil was not a man whose feathers stayed ruffled for long. He felt honored and humbled to be entrusted with such a monumental secret. Dominique told him that Lafitte would have to leave the bayou now that Grambo knew his alias. It was no longer safe for him to stay here. Grambo would be back. Dominique was sure of that. Dominique had been planning to help Lafitte relocate, although he had not shared the details with Virgil. He told Virgil it was for his own safety.

Virgil knew Lafitte would be leaving soon. He would never see him again. This saddened Virgil as he had grown accustomed to spending time with Lafitte. He would miss sharing stories about life on the sea. Funny how "Robin" had told him so many stories, yet he had not hinted at his true identity. Virgil would never have guessed the man had been a privateer. He thought he was just a sailor, same as Virgil.

Now they sat side by side on the wooden rockers on Lafitte's porch, Virgil occupying Olivia's chair. The silence between them was pierced only by the trill of cicadas and the soft rustling of grasses stirred by a passing breeze—a harbinger of the rain to come, as sure as the distant rumble of thunder.

"Where you s'pose Grambo's at right now?" It was a bold and unforgivably direct question for Virgil to ask Lafitte, but he could no longer bear the silence. He needed his friend to stop drowning in a rum bottle and return to him. He hoped his question would be the push Lafitte needed. Virgil realized he'd quite possibly overstepped, and in doing so, might prompt an explosion from the man sitting next to him on the porch, the man he now knew was an exceptionally dangerous one. But Virgil had decided to take the risk.

"I know precisely where he is," came Lafitte's reply. It was delivered calmly, devoid of emotion.

This was not what Virgil wanted from him, so he pressed on. "Well then, seems to me you'd best go find him. Seems to me you have some business to settle with him 'fore you leave this place."

At first, Virgil was concerned that Captain Lafitte had not heard him, as he offered no response. Yet after an eternity of waiting, Lafitte rewarded Virgil's patience with a slight inclination of his head and the words, "I believe I might just do that."

The simple statement from Captain Lafitte affected an almost complete change in the man. He began talking to Virgil, at first in that very slow, disconnected manner that had been his way since

Olivia's death, but then more quickly, urgently, and passionately. He told Virgil about Grambo's scheme to turn in the stolen slaves, buy them at auction, and then resell them.

"Maybe we oughta find him 'fore he turns those folks over to the authorities," Virgil said, the thought of it stirring something hot inside him. He blinked, then realized what he'd said—he'd offered to go along on the hunt.

Captain Lafitte had been warming to the idea of finding Grambo, settling old debts, and vanishing once again. He had not, however, thought to do so with an accomplice. "I imagine I should," he replied, his gaze still fixed on the horizon where the water slowly faded into the sky.

"You'd do better with me at your back," Virgil said, his voice steady but firm.

"I don't believe I invited you along."

"I don't believe I'm waitin' for an invitation," Virgil shot back, his usual quiet reserve replaced with stubborn insistence.

"I don't need another man's blood on my hands, Virgil."

"Look at you, already countin' me dead—when it's more likely I'm the one who's gonna be pullin' your sorry hide outta the fire."

Captain Lafitte couldn't hide a smirk. Virgil Freedman always could amuse him.

"Why are you so eager to meet your maker, Virgil? This isn't your fight."

Virgil sighed a slow, weary sigh. "Thing is, Robin, I been thinkin' 'bout life lately. Livin' out here—it's near enough to paradise. I got what I always wanted. Just fish my days away in peace, with no man layin' claim on me. But them others—the ones about to be sold? They ain't got that. And it don't sit right."

The two continued rocking in their chairs as the setting sun cast long shadows through the cypress, the low rumble of thunder rolling in across the bayou.

"Well, I guess maybe this is your fight, then," Captain Lafitte said.

Virgil nodded. There was nothing more to say. They were partners now.

Captain Lafitte, Virgil Freedman, and Dominique You spent their time plotting in the days that followed. Dominique You thought the plan was pure madness, if not suicide. Still, when he found he could not talk sense into either of them, he relented and agreed to help. His first task was to ferret out the information they needed to find Grambo. Dominique You's tavern, so close to one of the country's busiest ports, provided a wealth of information from sailors whose lips were loosened with grog. Dominique found out that a ship had brought its human cargo to Galveston. Dominique You was certain the slave runner who would be transporting these people to authorities in the Louisiana interior was Grambo.

Lafitte knew the route Grambo would take. It was the same one that slave runners had used during his Campeche days. He and Virgil would be able to intercept Grambo. His dilemma now was what happened after that. Captain Lafitte was focused on exacting revenge on Grambo, but Virgil's concern for the slaves had gotten him thinking. What would Olivia want him to do? He had been ashamed of his actions for some time, but he had not known how to make amends. Now he had the opportunity.

Yet even if he and Virgil could free them, then what? They could not just let these people loose in Louisiana, or in Texas, for that matter. They would not be safe. There were maroon settlements in the bayous, but those groups of runaway slaves had to distance themselves from civilization. It was a rough life. They lived in fear. They had to hide out for the rest of their days. Captain Lafitte knew what that was like. He did not wish that life for anyone else.

When the answer came to him, it was so simple he was surprised he had not thought of it earlier. He immediately enlisted his brother's help once again to execute the remainder of his plans. Time was of the essence. He and Virgil had only two more days to get to Grambo. With Dominique You's help and a great deal of luck, they might just make it.

Chapter XXXVIII

(In which Captain Lafitte attempts a daring rescue)

Captain Lafitte and Virgil Freedman had concealed themselves in the foliage around a copse of water oaks for many hours. Patience was an essential component of a successful ambush. They were willing to bide their time. They were finally rewarded by the sound of many feet moving along the path that cut through this otherwise wild terrain. As the sounds grew louder, they knew Grambo was drawing near. The time had come. Lafitte had estimated that besides Grambo, there would be no more than three additional men acting as guards. He was pleased to discover there was only one other man besides Grambo. Grambo was short on both friends and the inclination for sharing, Lafitte mused.

He and Virgil waited until the two were just past them, then leaped out onto the path behind them in a surprise attack. A struggle ensued! Neither Virgil nor Lafitte dared shoot the men for fear of striking the innocent prisoners. Instead, Virgil approached the guard from behind, knocking the man's pistol from his hand. Virgil fought the guard with valor. Ultimately, Virgil overpowered him, driving a blade into his side and felling him for good. Lafitte had noticed that Virgil was well acquainted with the use of a pistol and a cutlass from his days on the sea. He had proven himself so adept that Lafitte began to wonder if Virgil had not perhaps worked as a privateer, after all.

Lafitte had little time to ponder Virgil's past because, as Virgil was battling the guard, Lafitte came face-to-face with Grambo. He had to be cautious to avoid injuring the prisoners, just as Virgil had. Yet he knew that Grambo was a fearsome foe and that he would have no similar concerns about chivalry in battle nor harming the innocent. Lafitte tried to knock the pistol from his hand as Virgil had done, but Grambo anticipated the move. The vile man took aim and fired directly at Captain Lafitte!

There should have been the roar of the pistol firing. Lafitte should be lying lifeless on the ground. Yet there was no deafening sound. There was no fatal shot to fell the captain. Grambo's pistol had jammed! Both men were momentarily shocked by the turn of events, but Lafitte regained his wits more quickly than his opponent. He wrestled the pistol away from him and threw it into the bushes on the side of the path so that Grambo would not have another opportunity to do him harm.

"You never were one to keep your firearms in working order," declared Lafitte as calmly as if he were reprimanding a school boy about a missed assignment.

This only infuriated Grambo. He lunged for the captain. Captain Lafitte fought him off. It seemed the captain would be victorious when suddenly everything changed.

* * *

Grambo was shocked that Lafitte had found him. He realized he should not have boasted around Barataria about his slave-running plans. His loose lips might be the end of him. He'd figured there was a possibility they might be intercepted along the path, but he'd not expected it to be so soon, nor had he expected it to be Lafitte himself. Nevertheless, Grambo had been on alert this entire journey because he knew better than to underestimate the captain. Though it pained him to admit it, he had not heard the captain's approach. He was amazed at how completely Lafitte had bested him.

He understood the reason for this. It mortified and terrified him simultaneously. That woman had cursed him, and he was doomed.

As much as he would prefer to think this was not the case, that he was skilled enough and strong enough to overcome a hex, he could not convince himself of this. In his black heart, he believed, and so it was the truth. His only hope was to kill Captain Lafitte before the curse ended him.

These thoughts flew through Grambo's mind in the first few seconds of the battle between the two. After his gun failed to end their confrontation, and Lafitte gained the upper hand, Grambo thought he was doomed. Then he remembered his clasp knife, folded into his waistband. While he tried to fight off the captain, he retrieved the knife, and before the captain could even discern the movement from his opponent's hand, Grambo plunged the knife into Lafitte's chest.

Lafitte was struck! Grambo's clasp knife had sunk into Lafitte's waistcoat. Instantly, blood began soaking through. Lafitte feared the end was near. He waited for his vision to dim, for his strength to fail him as the life ebbed from his body.

Meanwhile, the ever-loyal Virgil had dispatched his foe and had come to Lafitte's aid just in time to witness Grambo's treachery. Virgil fought Grambo, wounding him in the arm. But Grambo got away from him before Virgil could deliver the death blow that Grambo so richly deserved.

Seeing that his guard was dead, knowing he was wounded, knowing he was cursed, shook Grambo to his core. He wanted to kill Captain Lafitte. He could not understand why the man was not already dead. There he was, lying on the ground, yet still breathing. Had his knife not pierced the man's heart? Had the captain actually died all those years ago? Could he have been battling a ghost this entire time? Such thoughts would never have entered Grambo's mind before the woman's hex, but now he felt unsettled and vulnerable. It was a feeling he had never experienced before, and he despised it. It was torture for a man like Grambo to know fear, to believe for the first time that he was not the strongest nor the deadliest. So Grambo took the coward's way out and ran for the woods, disappearing into the trees.

"Robin—you been hit?" Virgil dropped to his knees next to his friend's prone figure and ripped open Lafitte's coat to assess the extent of the damage inflicted by Grambo's wicked blade. "I'll be damned," he breathed, the shock coursing through his body.

He could scarcely believe his eyes. While the blade had indeed pierced Lafitte's skin, it was not a fatal blow. The blade had been arrested from doing its worst. An object had stopped the blade's progression to the man's heart, saving the captain's life. Virgil removed the object to examine it. "Never in my days could I have imagined this!"

He showed it to Captain Lafitte, whose eyes registered a similar look of shock and disbelief. It was the gris-gris bag that Olivia had made for him. Lafitte had kept it in the left breast pocket of his coat, close to his heart, ever since she was taken from him. Olivia had saved Lafitte's life. She had given the captain a chance to finish what he had started. Now it was up to him to enact the next part of his plan.

Chapter XXXIX

(In which Captain Lafitte sails the seas once more)

Captain Lafitte and Virgil looked at the motley crew before them. There were two dozen souls. Most were men, but there were a few women. There were no young children, but there were several older boys. They looked shocked at the sudden turn of events. There was a moment of tense stasis when Lafitte and Virgil thought the prisoners might try to flee, but the sight of Virgil must have calmed them at least enough to want to know more about these men who had come from nowhere and dispatched their captors.

Captain Lafitte and Virgil had agreed that it would be best for Virgil to explain who they were and reassure them of their intentions. They only hoped they would be able to communicate with the group. They knew not what languages or dialects they spoke. They were relieved to learn that some of the prisoners spoke English. A woman named Louisa became the spokesman for the group. She was able to translate for those who could not understand Virgil.

Captain Lafitte could have been a wealthy man had he turned the slaves over to the authorities and accepted the reward. He would have done so in the past and given it no thought. Yet this was not his plan. He had quite another idea in mind.

Virgil communicated to the group what was to be done as they began the journey back to the bayous. There was much to accomplish during this time. With Louisa's help, they were able to explain what they needed from the group. The plan would not work without their assistance.

Dominique You had been an integral component of this part of the plan, though he had spent his time back in New Orleans. In addition to gathering information about the timing and location of Grambo's slave running, he had followed his brother's orders and procured the necessary equipment. He found it amazing how quickly and secretively such tasks could be completed when money ceased to be an object. It also helped that he and Lafitte still had friends they could rely on when asked for assistance, particularly when it came to ships.

Captain Lafitte had requested his brother purchase a brig swiftly and discreetly. Dominique You paid an exorbitant price, but he needed the vessel, and he needed it quickly. Fitting it out as a privateer vessel had been more challenging. It should have taken far longer, but since he was willing to hire unlimited labor and supplies and was not particular about where those men or supplies came from, such things were accomplished in a significantly shorter amount of time than would have been the case had he employed traditional means. Fortunately for Lafitte's purposes,

Dominique You did not oppose operating outside of the law. He considered himself an upstanding citizen after giving up his life of privateering, but he told himself that sometimes it was permissible to bend the rules for the greater good.

Still, Dominique had deep reservations about the plan, especially the final part.

"This is madness, Jean," he'd told his brother when Captain Lafitte had first explained his plan. "Nothing but suicide, that's what it is."

"You fret like an old woman. Just do as I ask, and all shall be well," Jean replied in the insouciant tone that Dominique found maddening at times.

"Don't see how, not with the risk you're taking."

The hard set of Lafitte's jaw told Dominique all he needed to know—his mind was made up, and there'd be no budging it. Dominique sighed, "You know I'll do it. But I sure as hell don't have to like it."

Lafitte's shoulders relaxed, just a touch. "That's why you're a good man, Dominique."

"Then at least let me come with you," Dominique said.

"No."

He's a mule-headed old sea dog, thought Dominique. But aloud, he said, "Come now, brother—it'd be like old times. The Lafitte boys take to the seas for one last hurrah!" As soon as Dominique uttered the words, he longed to take them back. He hadn't spoken of his failing health, and though Jean surely knew, it was something better left unsaid.

Lafitte said quietly, "Your place is in New Orleans."

That gentler tone, rare from Lafitte, hit Dominique square in the chest. He cleared his throat, blinking hard. "I may not be in sailing shape, but I'd still like to be of some use to you."

"You are doing more than I should ever have asked of you. That brig will be my salvation." Lafitte's enigmatic words were the last he spoke on the subject. And Dominique knew better than to question him further.

Dominique You had the ship ready to go, stocked with weapons and provisions, and awaiting its captain in a discreet port in Barataria, when the group, led by Captain Lafitte and Virgil Freedman, arrived. Dominique You had christened the ship the *Freedman* in honor of the help Virgil had given his brother. It was an apt name for the coming mission.

Lafitte and Virgil were both expert seamen. Combined with the rudimentary training they had given the prisoners on the journey to Barataria, they had a crew of two very competent officers and a group of mates who, while not skilled, were more than eager to do as instructed. It would be enough if they were lucky.

And so it was that our intrepid Captain Lafitte found himself once more sailing the seas, smelling the salt air, feeling the wind on his face, and commanding a crew. He had not realized how much he had missed seafaring life. Yet this journey was different. He was not searching the waters with his glass for ships to plunder. He was the target, having to carefully avoid enemy vessels, ever ready to defend his ship and passengers should the need arise. He hoped it would not. He hoped his voyage would be charmed and that all aboard the *Freedman* could safely make the trip from Barataria Bay to Tamaulipas. For this is where his passengers would disembark. Slavery had been declared illegal in Mexico. If Captain Lafitte could get them there, they would be free.

Chapter Eighteen

Excerpt from

<u>The Amazing Adventures of</u>
<u>the Life and Death of the Pirate Jean Lafitte,</u>
<u>Terror of the Gulf</u>
By T. M. Whitney

Chapter XXXX

(In which freedom is sought)

It was Virgil Freedman who chose Tamaulipas as a haven for the group of people he and Lafitte had rescued. Mexico had declared slavery illegal less than a decade before. They would be safe there. They would not have to live in fear. They would not spend their lives in hiding. There would be others like them there. Most runaway slaves sought the northern route to freedom, but some others had taken the southern route once slavery was declared illegal in Mexico. The northern route was long and arduous for people as far south as Louisiana. It was much easier to flee to Mexico. Easier if one had access to a ship and the expertise to sail it, of course, which Lafitte did.

The land in Tamaulipas was fertile. They could cultivate any number of crops, from sorghum to corn or wheat. They could raise cattle, goats, pigs, and sheep. If they preferred water to land, they could settle by the shore and fish or harvest shrimp, oysters, or crabs. They would have all these options before them and the means to explore them. Captain Lafitte did not have an unlimited treasure hidden away in Barataria, but he had enough. He had enough to buy the *Freedman* and outfit it with proper weaponry, ensuring they could make it safely to Mexico. He had enough to give those aboard a start in their new home.

What else was he to do with it? His brother would never take money from him; such a proud man he was. Virgil was the same. Lafitte knew this because he had tried back in Barataria, when they were making plans to ambush Grambo.

"What's this?" Virgil had asked when Lafitte handed him a bag of coins.

"Recompense for future services rendered."

"The hell it is. I ain't takin' your money." Virgil had pushed the bag away.

"Why not? You know I've got plenty. Can't think of a better use for it."

"Because we're friends, that's why. Friends help each other. Don't expect nothin' in return."

Lafitte could see he'd touched a nerve. Virgil's arms were crossed, his brow furrowed like a storm was setting in.

"I apologize," Lafitte said quietly.

They'd spent countless hours side by side, casting lines or rocking on Lafitte's porch, wrapped in the silence only true friends could share. But this silence was different—tight, cold. Like a stranger had wedged himself between them.

Virgil finally broke it. "You know I feel this mission deep in my bones. I'm doin' it for nothin'. Cuz that's the way it oughta be. Use your pirate gold for somethin' else. Somethin' that needs buyin' more'n I do."

Lafitte nodded. He'd think about what to do with the remainder of the treasure he'd amassed over the years. Time was running out. That's when he'd decided it could be used for the people they were saving. And so Lafitte and Virgil settled the little group in

Mexico and saw they had all they needed.

Before long, it was time for Captain Lafitte and Virgil to depart. Lafitte had hired a small crew to assist them in sailing the *Freedman* back to Louisiana. Where Lafitte planned to go after depositing Virgil back home was a mystery to him. Try as he might, Virgil had not been able to pry the information from the man. Little did he know, he was about to receive an answer, though indirectly.

As the group of former slaves, now settlers, bid them farewell warmly, Louisa, who had served brilliantly as the group's interpreter, approached Lafitte.

"Captain," she and the others always addressed him as such, since he had not revealed any other information about his identity. "We would like to know your name."

The group had never asked Lafitte for anything. He therefore knew this request was an important one to them. Lafitte decided to oblige them. "It is Lafitte, Jean Lafitte."

Virgil looked at him with wide eyes. He had never heard Lafitte speak his real name to anyone. He knew then that Lafitte would not be returning to Louisiana. Though he did not want to admit it, even to himself, he also knew that Lafitte was not long for this world. Virgil now understood why Lafitte had displayed such reticence regarding his plans for the future. If he was sharing his name and his treasure with others, he no longer had use of either for himself.

* * *

Dominique You was a worried man. This was unusual for him, as he was generally not one to fret about life. He had always been easygoing. During his privateering days, his mates knew he had a temper, but more often than not, he was joking around, guffawing, and generally having a grand time at whatever he was doing. He had a reputation among the patrons at his tavern as a stand-up sort, the kind you could trust. His demeanor may appear gruff, but he was quick with a smile for his friends. His Freemason brothers knew him as the most loyal of men, steadfast to a fault when it came to his friends and family.

Lately, those who knew him well would say he did not seem like himself. Most knew his health had been declining. Although Dominique You was never one to complain, his stiff movements and winces betrayed him to anyone who took the time to notice. But they did not know that in addition to his physical ailments, Dominique You was beside himself with concern for his brother.

As each day passed, Dominique You grew increasingly anxious. He knew if Grambo wanted to find out where Lafitte had taken the stolen slaves, he would be able to do so. There were still those in Barataria who would talk to him. They would no doubt inform him of the *Freedman*'s unusual journey. It was why Dominique You had been so skeptical of his brother's plan. Grambo would undoubtedly find out where Lafitte had gone, and Grambo would certainly make chase. Dominique knew Lafitte better than anyone else, and though his brother had never disclosed his intentions to him, he suspected that was precisely what Lafitte wanted. All Dominique You could do was wait in New Orleans for word from his brother.

* * *

Lafitte was a man who did not care to share his thoughts with others. Olivia had been the person he confided in the most, and even she did not know all that was in his head. The people he cared about each knew a piece of him, but none knew the whole,

199

not Dominique You, not Virgil Freedman, not even Olivia. He had lived like this for so much of his life that he knew no other way. He wondered whether he should feel sad about that or have some regrets. He decided it was too late to be concerned about such things now.

He found himself pondering thoughts like these on the journey back to Louisiana. He had noticed that he had become increasingly retrospective, even before Olivia's murder. Spending time in the bayou, contemplating his next move, had given him time to think. It had provided him the space to consider what he wished to do with the remainder of his life.

When he had finally decided not to let his grief drown him and to take revenge on Grambo instead, he had expected fury to take hold of him. He thought it would eclipse all else. He was surprised to find that it did not. He certainly wanted Grambo dead, but that was not all he wanted. Lafitte had decided he wished to be the man Olivia thought he was and the man his grandmother always knew he could be.

Lately, he'd been thinking about his beloved grandmother. She had always known him so well. The Jewish woman of Spanish descent who had adopted French culture, whose husband had suffered at the hands of the Inquisition, had raised her grandson to be a champion of egalitarianism. She boasted that her grandson would stomach no injustice to others.

She had told him time and again, "You have been bestowed with special gifts, Jean. You must use these gifts in the service of your fellow man. I believe you are destined to liberate those who have been brutally exploited. To relieve their suffering."

She thought he would accomplish this through his quill. He knew he would do so with his sword or his pistol. He felt that he had not lived up to his grandmother's expectations. He had cast aside his sense of duty in favor of his desire to chase danger through the deep blue waters. He now realized that sailing the seas, privateering against his enemies, had occupied his efforts for far too much of his life.

"I have had defeats but never illusions," he once told Dominique You. He was not one to lie to himself. Lafitte recognized that he had not lived his life as his grandmother had hoped.

He thought he would have made her proud by fighting for Napoleon as a young man or rescuing the emperor from imprisonment on St. Helena. He never imagined he might make her proud this way, by saving a small group of slaves from Grambo's scheme. He could not free Napoleon, but he could free these people.

Although she had been dead for many years, Lafitte thought that perhaps his recent actions had finally made his grandmother proud. Now that he had done so, there was one more job to do. It was of critical importance. The future of those he held dearest in this world depended upon his accomplishing this task. He had to kill Grambo.

Chapter XXXXI

(In which Captain Lafitte and Grambo clash one final time)

When Captain Lafitte decided to fake his death all those years earlier on the *General Santander,* he chose a battle at sea in which he could fight to the death. It seemed a wise choice because it was how he had envisioned, or perhaps hoped, his life would end. No one lives forever, especially not a pirate. A pirate's life is short but hopefully merry, as the infamous Black Bart said over a hundred years ago. Lafitte did not think past the immediate future in those days and thought of little but himself. He felt that many aspects of his life had changed for the better since then.

Now, as the *Freedman* made its way back to Louisiana, Lafitte found himself looking to do battle on the seas once more. Yet this time, he was searching for only one foe. He did not know what kind of ship to look out for or when he would come across it, but he knew deep in his soul that Grambo would come for him.

Two dead men, yet only one can live. He had left enough clues even for the likes of that buffoon. He knew Grambo would take the bait. He could imagine no scenario where Grambo did not come after him.

Lafitte relished the opportunity to confront his enemy. It had to happen here, on the water. He would not bring that danger back to New Orleans, where it would hang like the Sword of Damocles over the heads of Dominique You and Virgil Freedman. He would have left Virgil in Mexico, but the man turned out to be as stubborn as Lafitte himself. He was determined to see this through and would brook no argument. Lafitte found this simultaneously frustrating and admirable.

It happened early one morning when they were nearing the end of their journey. They avoided the shipping lanes, keeping a low profile. Lafitte did not wish to encounter other vessels, and he knew the routes that offered the best chance of concealment. He also knew Grambo was familiar with these routes from his pirating days. Lafitte felt certain that the two vessels' paths would eventually cross.

As he looked out at the approaching schooner, he knew it was Grambo's craft. This was it. Their battle would soon begin.

The first thing Lafitte ordered was surrender.

Virgil stared at him like he'd lost his mind. "Are you daft? Or just plain mad?"

"No doubt both. Yet I will do this my way, and you must not try to stop me."

"Surrenderin', though? That's your grand idea?"

"We're only *playing* at surrender. Never trust a pirate, my friend. His word's worth less than a clipped coin. You should know that by now."

Virgil cracked a grin. "So we're trickin' 'em."

"Precisely. Now go round up a few hands to lower the jolly boat."

"What for?"

"I'm rowing out to the schooner."

"Not without me, you ain't," Virgil said, stepping forward.

"I have to face Grambo alone. This ends one way."

"And what way is that? You even got a plan, or are you relyin' on wishful thinkin'?"

Lafitte's gaze grew serious. "I do. And you must promise to follow it to the letter." He shared the details with Virgil.

"Suicide! That's what this is! Stay onboard and fight—we're armed and ready. They wouldn't stand a chance if it came to it!"

Lafitte looked him in the eye and shook his head slowly. "I only armed this brig for defense, not war. There'll be no sea battle. The risk is too great."

"What risk compares to gettin' killed out there if you take the jolly boat by yourself?"

"The risk of getting my brother killed."

Virgil's jaw tightened. He swallowed hard, words failing him for a moment.

Lafitte laid a hand on his shoulder. "You are every bit the brother to me as Dominique and Pierre." Lafitte hopped into his tender before Virgil could stop him.

As Lafitte approached the enemy ship, he could see the curious looks from Grambo's crew. "I've come to speak with Grambo! Tell him to show himself!" he yelled out from his tender.

Lafitte was counting on Grambo's ego. He knew Grambo wished to have the pleasure of killing Lafitte himself. Had Lafitte been wrong about that, he would already be dead, struck down by the ship's cannon before he could have made it this far. His instinct proved correct when the man emerged on deck, his arm still bound from the wound Virgil had inflicted.

* * *

Grambo had been searching the waters of the Gulf for Lafitte for several days now. He knew the man's routes and did not think him clever enough to alter them. Lafitte would not know Grambo was chasing him, after all. Dominique You thought he was so smart, fitting out the brig for his brother, so that thief could take Grambo's slaves to market. Grambo was unsure why Lafitte did not simply sell them in New Orleans, but he had not given it much consideration. Grambo's desire for revenge crowded out all other thoughts. It consumed him. He could think only of finally getting his revenge on this man who had stolen from him not once but twice.

Grambo was thrilled to see Lafitte's brig strike its colors. He wanted very much to take the fine ship, and the less damage incurred in the process, the better as far as he was concerned.

"I've come to speak with Grambo! Tell him to show himself!"

Grambo could hardly believe his enemy had spoken these words. It was decidedly odd that Lafitte was approaching his ship. Grambo could not fathom why Lafitte would do such a thing. He was generally not a man to question his good fortune, but the curse was still hanging over him. Could he really be this lucky? He'd had an exceedingly easy time of it up to this point, first finding information about Lafitte's intention with the brig, then spotting him along his usual route, and now having the captain approach him.

Could he be falling for a trap? Possibly. Yet he practically had Lafitte in his grasp. He was so close. He could not resist. Curiosity got the better of him, and he allowed the captain to approach his vessel.

"We have each taken from the other that which we hold dear," Lafitte shouted over the winds that swept through the open water. "This can end only one way. I challenge you to a duel!"

A duel?! As if they were two dandies, setting aside their port to engage in a duel. Grambo had never heard such a ridiculous suggestion in all his days. Yet there was Captain Lafitte, fighting to stay upright in his bobbing jolly boat, demanding satisfaction for the murder of his woman. He looked ludicrous, pathetic.

Then an idea occurred to Grambo. If he played along with the captain's absurd suggestion, he could shoot him before the duel even began. Then he would be free to take his ship. He did not expect Lafitte's crew to offer any resistance.

"All right, Captain," Grambo replied. "If a duel is what you desire, a duel is what you shall get."

Grambo cautioned his crew to hold their fire. He would shoot Lafitte as he attempted to board Grambo's ship. He wanted to be the one to fire the shot. His desire for revenge precluded all other thoughts.

Lafitte rowed his jolly boat alongside the schooner in preparation for boarding the ship. He moved to exit his boat, but at the last second, he removed his pistol in a flash and shot Grambo through the heart.

"Never trust a pirate, Grambo," he managed to say before Grambo's crew fired on Lafitte.

Two dead men, and neither one can live.

As these events transpired, Virgil and the crew of the *Freedman* fired their cannon upon Grambo's ship in a stunningly swift display of violence. Grambo's crew was forced to surrender. No one aboard the *Freedman* was injured.

Captain Lafitte fell out of the tender and into the waters of the Gulf of Mexico, mortally wounded, as he knew he would be after taking his lethal shot at Grambo. There was no gris-gris bag to protect him this time. There was only the one that had saved him from Grambo's blade, just as there had been only one Olivia. And so his life ended just as he always knew it would, in a battle on the open water, fighting his fiercest foe. He would not have wanted it any other way. At long last, the sea had come to claim our intrepid Captain Lafitte, the Terror of the Gulf.

Chapter Nineteen

New Orleans

April 1833

Tobias Whitney felt like a man who knew how his story would end, only to have a plot twist turn everything upside down. Since he had always been a cautious man who enjoyed following a well-thought-out plan, he found such twists and turns unsettling. Indeed, this had been his feeling in the past. His life had not turned out the way he had planned it as a young man. Growing up in his father's bookshop, he thought he knew his future. He would one day manage the bookshop and live in the cottage his father had built. He would marry and start a family of his own. These were his decisions to make, of course, but they were the result of choices made by those who came before him. Tobias did not mind this. He appreciated the simplicity of needing only to follow the path laid out before him. While there was little excitement, there was also little risk. And Tobias was not a man who required excitement. Or so he told himself.

He was too grateful to feel anything but contentment regarding his life plan. Tobias appreciated that his parents had settled here a generation before, opening Chapter and Verse and building the lovely cottage he now enjoyed with his family. He thought about how much better off his family was than the Irish immigrants who were currently streaming into New Orleans.

Many of them had found work digging the new Basin Street Canal, a waterway that, when completed, would stretch from Lake Pontchartrain to the American sector of the city. It was to be six miles long. Construction had begun only a year or so ago, and already, casualties among the mainly Irish-immigrant workforce were concerning. Tobias knew about the deplorable conditions under which they and their families lived because Mary Catherine accompanied the Ursuline nuns in doing charitable works in the Back of Town neighborhood, an area of New Orleans inhabited by the poorest of society—slaves, some free people of color, and immigrants like those digging the canal and their families.

"Those men are digging a canal sixty feet wide, seven feet deep with only picks and shovels," she'd told him just last week after returning home from her visit to Back of Town. She'd been riled up about the injustice of it all. "Their women are barely scraping by, looking after their children while their men are away, sleeping in shanties next to the canal. They come home with their backs broken from exhaustion. That's if they come home. All that bad miasma in the swamps out there—they bring home more Yellow Jack than money, most of the time."

Yet no one seemed to care enough to improve their conditions. The seemingly endless wave of Irish immigrants entering the city provided a cheap, expendable labor force. These yellow fever fatalities, along with the dreadful number of cholera victims from the outbreak of the previous autumn, combined to ensure that many of the Irish immigrants did not live long once they arrived in New Orleans.

The cholera deaths of this past fall had not just targeted the poor. Many people in the city had fallen victim to the epidemic. Enduring another outbreak of disease exacerbated Tobias's old fears of losing the rest of his family. He'd even tried to dissuade his wife from her weekly outings to the Back of Town for fear of her health.

"Tobias Whitney, the Lord didn't put breath in my lungs so that I'd waste it trembling. I've two hands and a heart for helping, and I'll not stand by while others suffer," she had told him.

He knew better than to argue with her. He'd had to decide if he could overcome the terrible fear of disease taking his family from him. Illness was all around them. It would forever be a threat. Could he go on living and not allow the worry and anxiety to rob him of the joy in his life? He was not certain, but he knew he must try.

Losing his children had been the plot twist Tobias had never imagined. It was a pain he would wish on no one. Yet he now understood that it was not an insurmountable pain. He had figured out how to survive it, and he felt stronger for having done so.

The second plot twist of his life was finding Dominique You's journal. It had been Captain Lafitte, of all people, who had made Tobias realize he possessed the strength to attempt to live without focusing on death. For years, Tobias had felt isolated in his grief, though he could not say exactly why this was. Plenty of people around him had lost loved ones. But Yellow Fever was especially cruel in that it elicited fear and repulsion from those it spared. When his children died, their tiny bodies had been whisked away for a quick burial to avoid contagion. He'd yearned to accompany them to the cemetery, but he had not been permitted to do so. He had never gotten to say goodbye to them properly, and consequently, he'd struggled to move on with his life.

Tobias sensed a similar yearning to say goodbye in the captain's story. Lafitte had been forced to grieve his brother Pierre from afar, and he'd blamed himself for Olivia's death. The losses the captain had endured, and his journey to overcome them, had intrinsically changed the way Tobias viewed his own life and loss. Tobias felt a kinship with the man, although they had never met. However, unlike Lafitte, who had been separated from his home and family, Tobias had the blessings of both. In helping him recognize this, the journal had proven more valuable than any hidden treasure.

It compelled him to get his life back on track, even if it was not the track he had initially envisioned. Writing the adventure novel had been a departure from his prescribed life course, and he was glad he had taken the chance. And though it had not yielded a treasure map, it had undoubtedly paid dividends. With the advance he'd received, he was able to purchase the shop in full from Mssr. Loutrel. The Whitney family once again owned Chapter and Verse.

Tobias now realized that he had just experienced the third plot twist of his life. It had occurred only a few moments before, in fact, in Chapter and Verse. This twist began several weeks ago, when a customer entered the shop and engaged him in conversation. Tobias enjoyed interacting with customers, so much so that Mary Catherine had recently described him as a dog with two tails. While not as outgoing as Mary Catherine, he was pleased to discover he could be gregarious enough to put people at ease as they browsed.

He was also finding that he was becoming adept at selling his wares. Instead of merely placing quills about the shop and waiting for people to purchase them, he would wander around, offering to answer any questions they had. He would engage them in conversation about the merits of steel pens versus quill pens. His ability to repair and maintain quill pens was an additional bonus, as people came in to have their quills sharpened and often walked away with additional purchases they may not have intended to make. In short, Tobias was making a great success of Chapter and Verse, and he was enjoying it immensely.

He was not surprised, therefore, when a man looking to purchase some writing paper and ink entered and began conversing with him about his book. This was not in the least bit unusual, as such conversations were a regular occurrence. After all, it was not every day that the proprietor of a bookshop was also the author of one of the most popular books of the year. The book proved to be a particularly rousing success in New Orleans, where people were still very much interested in the legend of the infamous Jean Lafitte. Tobias displayed *The Amazing Adventures of the Life and Death of the Pirate Jean Lafitte, Terror of the Gulf* in his shop window and on a table near the entrance. At first, he felt self-conscious about placing his book in such a prominent location, but it was his shop, after all, and people often came in expressly to purchase the book their friends and neighbors were talking about.

This discussion, however, was different. The man was of short stature, with an impressive girth. Judging by his rheumy features and the telltale red and purple veins that ran along his nose and cheeks, he was fond of visiting the many taverns around the city. However, he was friendly and good-natured, so Tobias was happy to oblige and answer his questions about the book.

"I hear it's a corker of a story!" exclaimed the man.

Tobias did not have an opportunity to respond before the man continued.

"A real live pirate adventure! I used to keep up with Captain Lafitte's antics when he was alive, you know. Never was a man more audacious nor more daring! Don't you think?"

Tobias had thoughts on the subject, but no time to interject them.

"I recall once when he had a bounty on his head, and he went about holding a market in Pirate's Alley. Just as if it were any other day. You'd never have known he was a wanted man, I can tell you that much! Can you imagine? I could not think of staying in a place where I was a wanted man, that's for certain. Can you? Much less put on a market for anyone to attend!"

The pace of this one-sided conversation was reminiscent of many Tobias had with Mary Catherine, so he was quite comfortable listening and nodding his head occasionally while the man chattered away.

"And I'll tell you another thing. It wasn't just Captain Lafitte who had that kind of bravery. No indeed! His brother Pierre was cut from the same cloth, I can tell you!"

Now Tobias's interest was piqued. He always enjoyed hearing stories about the Lafitte brothers from people who had known them. "You knew the Lafittes, did you?" inquired Tobias.

"That I did! Knew them both. Had some business dealings with them, if you understand my meaning." The man punctuated this remark with a wink and a nudge of Tobias's arm. "Back in the embargo days, buying from the Lafittes was the only way we could get what we needed, especially when trade was shut down, and prices went sky-high. Real heroes they were, if you ask me! Captain Lafitte would have been an honest businessman if those customs crooks had let him! Our very own Robin Hood, he was!"

Tobias had heard this sentiment expressed many times before by his customers when discussing the markets. The man's next comment, however, commanded his attention.

"I knew his half-brother, too, Dominique You."

Tobias felt a closeness with Dominique You that he found difficult to put into words, but he suspected it stemmed from discovering his journal. He was always glad to talk to someone who knew him. "Tell me about Dominique You. When did you know him?"

"He owned a tavern, he did. I went there often."

Tobias was not surprised to hear this. It was evident that the man enjoyed tippling.

"We became chums, we did. He was generous with his pours, and I helped him with his books. That's my profession, you know. I'm a bookkeeper." He gestured to the paper and ink he was about to purchase to emphasize his point. "Needed my help, he did. He was not good at all with numbers," he chuckled and added, "and he was even worse with his letters!"

This remark caught Tobias off guard. "Do you mean to say that his penmanship was deplorable?"

"Penmanship?!" The man let out a full-bellied laugh. "Dominique You had no penmanship! The man could not sign his own name, let alone read or write!"

The look on Tobias's face caused the man to compose himself. He sheepishly continued, "I mean no disrespect to the dead, mind you. Dominique You was a hero to this city and a fine man. Some of the finest men I know don't have their letters, and I'm not telling you anything Dominique would not have told you himself. He wasn't ashamed. No, sir, not him. He was proud of what he had done and rightfully so. He lived a good life, that one, at least at the end. I was sorry to hear he passed."

The man concluded his business at Chapter and Verse and left. In a state of shock, Tobias had forgotten to ask his name. He had been too occupied with struggling to decipher the meaning of this revelation. Could this man be mistaken? Was it possible that Dominique had concealed his literacy when he had settled into his life in New Orleans? Why would he do such a thing? What was Tobias to think of all the letters Dominique had received from Jean Lafitte? Were those real? If Dominique could not read or write, his half-brother would have known this and would not have corresponded with him. Could it be that someone else was reading the letters to him?

Was it possible that Dominique was the narrator of the journal but not the author? If this were the case, who wrote it? Pierre? Indeed, he must have been literate. He had handled the business dealings of their enterprises. However, he died in 1821 and thus could not have been the one to write the journal, as the events within its pages occurred as late as 1830. No, that was impossible. If Dominique had not written the journal, who was the author?

Tobias had read through Mary Catherine's translations several times in the weeks since his bizarre encounter with the bookkeeper. He kept the volume in his pocket, alongside *The Last of the Mohicans.* Whenever he had a moment to spare, he pored over the pages, trying to make sense of the man's claims. He'd told Mary Catherine, of course, and she had considered the possible scenarios, yet she confessed she was as flummoxed by this new mystery as Tobias was. At least, she professed to be. Tobias could not help but think that she didn't seem as shocked by the news as he had expected.

How many mysteries could one book hold? Just when he thought he had unlocked its secrets, more bubbled up to the surface. Amazing. Tobias wondered if perhaps this was a secret the journal would never reveal.

Tobias had resigned himself to this conclusion when another customer had entered his store this very morning. A tall man with dark features, he was nondescript, though not unpleasant-looking. Tobias could tell by the way he carried himself and by his clothing that he was a gentleman. He wore a navy blue tailcoat, light-colored cotton twill trousers, and a matching navy blue cravat. Tobias greeted the man and asked if he could be of any assistance. The man politely declined, indicating that he would prefer to browse. When he spoke, Tobias recognized the accent as American and assumed his visitor was one of the many who had come to New Orleans after Louisiana entered the union.

The man walked about the shop for a bit, wandering around and pulling a book from the shelf every so often. He dallied over the array of writing paper and marveled at the steel pens on offer. He appeared to Tobias to be a man who enjoyed much leisure time, if his unhurried perusal was any indication. So long did the man linger in the store that Tobias had nearly forgotten all about him. He had been attending to other customers and tidying up his displays.

Eventually, the man walked up to Tobias and inquired about the book he had written. He had been told it was a book he might enjoy and was interested in purchasing it, which pleased Tobias.

"I hear it is an exciting tale indeed," said the man.

"Well, I certainly like to think it is," replied Tobias modestly. Then, remembering his manners, he reached a hand out to the stranger. "Forgive me for not introducing myself sooner. My name is Tobias Whitney, and I am the proprietor of this shop."

"It is nice to make your acquaintance, Mr. Whitney. My name is Robert Huntington."

"Huntington…Huntington," mused Tobias. "That name seems familiar to me."

"It is an Anglo-Saxon surname. I am originally from Philadelphia, but came to New Orleans a few years back. My family hails from England, the East Midlands, as a matter of fact. But you must forgive me for prattling on. We Americans and our family trees! So enamored of our heritage. But from your accent, I would say I am speaking to an Irishman, am I not?"

Mr. Huntington's conversation was forcing Tobias's mind to turn away from the nagging suspicion that he knew this man. Propriety demanded he engage in the conversation and ponder why he seemed so familiar later. "Yes, my parents came here from Ireland some time ago. I suppose I retained some of their accent, though I thought I had lost it."

"Well, many would not detect it, but I confess I am a keen observer of accents. I understand you are the author of this book," Mr. Huntington continued, indicating Tobias's Jean Lafitte tale on the display table before him.

Tobias answered in the affirmative.

"A pirate book, eh? Not the usual literature I am accustomed to reading, but why not indulge in a fanciful tale once in a while?"

Mr. Huntington appeared to be talking himself into the purchase, so Tobias remained silent. "Say, I don't suppose there would be any clues to

Lafitte's buried treasure in here, would there?" the man asked with a grin.

Tobias gave his usual noncommittal answer to this inquiry. "I suppose you'll have to read and find out." He had found this response quite helpful in selling his book.

Mr. Huntington laughed good-naturedly and said, "Yes, I suppose I will." A moment of pensive silence followed before he asked, "Is there truth to the tale? Did the infamous Captain Lafitte really survive the battle at sea only to meet his death some years later in the same waters?"

Tobias was taken aback by the man's knowledge of the plot until Mr. Huntington explained himself. "I am afraid I have a loquacious friend who has told me more than I would have liked about the book."

Again, Tobias answered with the pat response he had used many times before. "I suppose you shall have to judge for yourself."

"Yes," agreed Mr. Huntington. "I suppose I shall." He handed Tobias some coins for payment and added, "Although I imagine we shall never know the real truth. One can never trust a pirate."

Tobias packaged up the book with a trembling hand. *What was happening?* The tips of Tobias's ears were feeling warm, and his heart was thumping in his chest. Something odd was afoot. Tobias managed to master himself long enough to hand the wrapped book to the man and thank him for his purchase.

Mr. Huntington extended his hand. As Tobias shook it, the man looked at Tobias steadily and unnervingly and said, "Thank you, Mr. Whitney. You have been helpful. Most helpful indeed."

This was a polite, if odd, thing for the man to say, considering all Tobias had done was sell him a book. No, Tobias was certain there was more to this statement.

As Mr. Huntington exited the shop, Tobias called after him with the statement he often made to someone about to begin his book, having found that his customers loved the suspense such a pronouncement brought: "Read the pages, and all shall be revealed!"

Mr. Huntington tipped his hat to Tobias, bid him farewell, and turned to leave. Over his shoulder, as he walked through the shop door, he replied,

"Well, 'tis for the best, I suppose. Secrets can't stay buried forever."

Nor should they, thought Tobias, utterly spooked now.

Tobias stared after the man as the shop door closed. The encounter left Tobias unsettled. It was not a feeling of foreboding, quite the opposite. It was a sense of anticipation, as if he were about to solve a mystery. It was reminiscent of the feeling he got when he knew there was a clue right in front of him, yet he could not recognize its significance. It was not unlike the moment Mary Catherine threw the journal at him in frustration when he failed to understand that the treasure was the book. At that moment, everything had become clear.

Why was he thinking about that now? This was just an ordinary encounter with a customer about his book. He had them several times each day. There was nothing special about the man. He seemed a friendly enough gentleman. He was well-dressed and well-mannered, but otherwise, he was perfectly average.

Tobias perused his beloved Chapter and Verse, lost in thought. His gaze fell upon his favorite section of the shop—the part he enjoyed even more than the new steel nibs and other writing accouterments. It was the action-adventure section. His eyes alighted on the selection of Robin Hood books, including *The Rhymes of Robin Hood* and Joseph Ritson's *Robin Hood and the Stranger*, a chapbook he had been enjoying reading to his sons as of late. They were captivated by the tale.

He thought about the stranger he had just talked to. *That story about his name.* He had been so eager to share the details with Tobias. *Robert Huntington.* There was that nagging feeling again in the back of Tobias's mind and that heat creeping up his ears. It all clicked into one shocking moment of clarity. Robert Huntington. Robert, Earl of Huntington, who, legend says, was Robin Hood.

The final secret of Dominique's journal had just revealed itself to Tobias in that strange encounter with "Mr. Huntington." Tobias knew his secret. What next? What should he do? He thought of the man described in the journal, a document that had brought Tobias back to life. He thought of the man at the center of the Whitneys' adventure tale, an endeavor that had given the family a project to share when they most needed it. He thought of the man who had just left this shop, a shop that belonged to Tobias again, in part due to the success of his book. Tobias knew his secret. *Secrets cannot stay buried forever.* With a determined shake of his head, Tobias thought: *Not all secrets. Some secrets need never be revealed.*

Chapter Twenty

New Orleans

April 1833

The man who called himself Robert Huntington strolled noncha-
lantly down Chartres Street, appearing to all the world as a
gentleman with an abundance of leisure time and a dearth of cares.
Yet his casual demeanor was deceiving. One had only to study his eyes to
know the truth. They were not the eyes of a man unconcerned with his
surroundings, who walked these familiar streets regularly, on an afternoon
stroll back home. These eyes never rested. They continually scanned their
surroundings, as if assessing threats from those all around. Yet most people
do not look closely enough to notice such things, or so Robert Huntington
had found. No, people were often content to accept what was presented
at face value and believe what they were told. They asked few questions.
Perhaps they should ask more.

Robert Huntington found this facet of human nature to be beneficial. He
understood that it was a product of people's busyness and self-absorption.
Most were consumed with their own lives and made little time to concern
themselves with others. If he failed to call attention to himself, no one
noticed him, and if they did, he did not linger long in their conscious brains.
His disguises were designed to make him nondescript, to disappear from
people's thoughts as soon as he was no longer in front of them. This was

why they were so effective.

Mr. Huntington took a moment to ensure no one was following him or paying the slightest bit of attention to his movements. Only then did he walk into his single shotgun home, so named because the rooms connected one into the next with no hallways, on so straight a path that one could fire a shotgun through the front door and have the shot exit the back door, hitting nothing along the way. Huntington had not tried this, of course, but he was certain he could have made the shot if need be. He was rather handy with a firearm.

His home was comfortable, if modest. There was nothing on the exterior to call attention to it. It was simply one of many in his neighborhood, painted a nondescript ivory color that blended in with those around it. As an American new to the city, Mr. Huntington would naturally have chosen to reside in the area known as the American Sector. This neighborhood was newer than the original French Quarter. It was separated from the Creole population by Canal Street, which some had begun calling the neutral ground, as it physically divided the two groups. This was helpful, given that Creoles and Americans were not particularly fond of one another.

Inside, the space was sparsely furnished, yet the few pieces Mr. Huntington had acquired were of first-rate quality. His home was inviting yet devoid of any personal touches. In fact, upon moving in, he had brought only a single satchel. Huntington's mementos were not lockets or portraits of loved ones, however. The items he brought with him included a few precious stones and some gold coins. He kept enough of these in his home to live comfortably but not extravagantly.

The man calling himself Mr. Huntington had found that people imagined pirates having chests overflowing with treasure. Yet pirates, and even privateers, did not tend to be stellar savers. They did not bury their fortunes to dig up later. They tended to live for the moment, and to do so extravagantly, because tomorrow was not promised to them. *A short and a merry life* was the best they could hope for. Most, but not all pirates. Some were savvy. Some knew how to bide their time. Some knew how to hide treasure in plain sight.

He parted the chintz curtains, a feminine pattern he would not have chosen but that provided the necessary privacy, and peeked outside the window to make sure there was no one suspicious about. He was a very suspicious man. Satisfied that he had made it home without anyone following him, he closed the curtains, and Robert Huntington was no longer Robert Huntington. His posture changed abruptly. He threw his shoulders back, pulling himself up to his natural height, and stretched his muscles. Mr. Huntington held himself less upright, with shoulders hunched a bit, making him seem shorter, more like the height of an average man. Even as he walked about his house, his gait changed from the smaller, slightly more tentative steps of Mr. Huntington to his naturally bolder, more commanding ones. His facial features altered from the somewhat bored, nonchalant expression Mr. Huntington generally wore to his more intense countenance, with ever-furrowed brows over piercing eyes. These measures made the man a less imposing and less noticeable figure. That is precisely as Jean Lafitte wanted it.

Assuming this second alias had been at the same time easier and more difficult than becoming Mssr. Robin du Bois. Du Bois was a Frenchman, after all, so he had found it unnecessary to disguise his accent. As an American, Mr. Huntington had a completely different manner of speech. However, Lafitte spoke several languages and had become accustomed to adapting his accent, inflection, speech patterns, and accompanying hand gestures to suit his needs. He had practiced aloud until he learned to modulate his tone and lose all traces of his French accent. He had always been adept at blending in with those around him, whether they were rogues or gentlemen. It was how he had survived as long as he had.

He'd had to change the manner of his clothing, as well, since his current alias was that of an American gentleman, not a Frenchman living in the bayous of Louisiana. That part had been quite satisfactory to Lafitte since he enjoyed the trappings of elegant society. He had spent far too much of his life living in bayous, which prompted his decision to hide in plain sight. Plus, he had missed New Orleans.

He was excellent at disguising himself. He had been living in the American Sector for six months, and no one seemed unduly suspicious that their neighbor was not the man he pretended to be. He knew he might not fool everyone. It was impossible to completely disguise oneself. At times, he had been the object of a glance more lingering and curious than he would have liked, and once or twice, he'd detected a flicker of recognition in someone's eye. He hoped anyone who suspected his true identity might still keep his secret. Most thought of Jean Lafitte as a hero in New Orleans. Most, but not all.

Now that he was ensconced in the safety of his home, Lafitte took a few moments to reflect upon his encounter with Tobias Whitney. Going to Chapter and Verse, yielding clues to his true identity, had been a monumental risk. Even Lafitte himself could not elucidate why he had decided to take it, except that he felt he owed Mr. Whitney for the service the man had done for him, unwittingly though it may have been. Captain Lafitte had been watching Mr. Whitney for some time now, the better part of two and a half years, to be precise. He had chosen him to do this most essential work, and Mr. Whitney had performed his job to perfection.

Since Lafitte found himself in a pensive mood that evening and had little else to occupy his thoughts or time, he settled into his favorite parlor chair, poured a glass of excellent Bordeaux vintage, and considered all that had brought him to his present state. When he was Robin du Bois, he had been careful to avoid New Orleans. Living in the bayou meant interacting with fewer people and, therefore, undergoing less scrutiny. It was unwise to return to New Orleans. He knew he could have chosen any number of locations in the Caribbean or elsewhere in the United States to make his home. He might even have gone back to France. He certainly could have easily blended in there. But his heart was in New Orleans, and he felt he had been denied the comforts of the city for far too long. Living the remainder of his life in the closest place he had to a home was worth taking the chance.

He acknowledged that the increased risk he was taking necessitated increased precautions. He was therefore exceedingly careful. He was ever aware of those around him and left his home as little as possible. He had neither the hubris nor the naivety to believe he could mix with society as he once did. No, those days were in his past. He was content to play the recluse, venturing out only when necessary. It had been an easy compromise, as those he cared for most were no longer here.

Those he cared for most were no longer here. He gave a silent toast to the handful of people who had genuinely mattered in his life. One he did not care to ponder, even now. Some scabs were best left closed. Others he thought about in these contemplative moments, especially Pierre and Dominique. He had lost Pierre first, in 1821. Those events had been depicted relatively accurately in Dominique's journal, or so Lafitte supposed. He had not been there when Pierre took his last breath. He'd had to wait for news from the handful of his men who had been with Pierre in Santa Cruz.

After the world thought Lafitte was dead, he found it increasingly difficult to keep up communication with Dominique. Lafitte was not in New Orleans, and Dominique had settled here, determined to live out the rest of his life as an honest citizen. Yet Dominique had never been good at handling his wealth, and being honest severely limited his ability to acquire more. His tavern was not profitable, and Dominique had found himself in dire financial straits at the end of his life. Lafitte recalled that fateful night he had come to visit Dominique. He had not heard from him in years, and some sixth sense alerted Lafitte that he needed to see how the man was faring.

Under the cover of darkness and employing one of his many disguises, he entered New Orleans not as Mssr. Du Bois, but as a nameless vagabond roaming the city streets. No one paid any attention to him. He smiled at the memory of how easy it had been to set foot back in New Orleans, finally. If he had approached the well-heeled set, perhaps begging for coins, they would surely not have even looked his way.

He had surreptitiously let himself into Dominique's house on the corner of Love and Mandeville streets in the Faubourg Marigny neighborhood and had been horrified at the sight before him. Dominique was living in squalor. His home had not been cleaned in some time, and there was no food to be found. Dominique lay asleep on his cot. When Lafitte approached him, he was shocked at the sight of the once robust man's shrunken frame. His skin looked gray, his facial features stretched taut. He was a man near death. Lafitte was furious with Dominique for not sending word to him about his state of penury, even though he knew Dominique was a proud man and would not ask his friends for help, no matter how badly he required it. As much as Lafitte wanted to wake him and visit with him for the first time in years, he could not bring himself to do it. Dominique would not want Lafitte to see him in this pitiable condition. As he turned to leave, Lafitte knew that he would never see Dominique again. The man would not live much longer. The hero of the Battle of New Orleans, friend of President Andrew Jackson, was dying alone in filth and poverty.

His plan to visit Dominique now derailed, he devised a new scheme. The next day, he arrived at La Concorde No. 3, the Masonic lodge to which Dominique belonged, and was welcomed as a brother after identifying himself. He had no fear of the Freemasons. They knew how to keep secrets. He told them of Dominique's plight, and they were appalled, just as he knew they would be. Dominique had told no one about his physical or financial woes. In the following weeks, his Masonic brothers did their best to care for Dominique. He was too far gone to recover his health, but at least he was given proper nourishment and died not wanting for companionship. The Freemasons also agreed to pay for a tomb for Dominique when his end came. Upon Lafitte's suggestion, it was decided that it should be constructed in St. Louis Cemetery No. 2.

Lafitte offered to choose the spot for the tomb. Unbeknownst to his brethren, he had an ulterior motive for this. He began visiting the cemetery daily that fall, identifying the perfect spot for Dominique's tomb. He had to wait longer than he would have liked, as October is traditionally a dry month in New Orleans. His patience was eventually rewarded with a soaking rain that caused some minor flooding. The rainstorm had not been especially troublesome. It was not nearly as intense as the heavy summer rains, but he could already tell that water was collecting in some spots. There was one place in particular that seemed especially suitable. Here, the puddle was the widest and stayed full, while those around it drained. He had found the low spot in the cemetery. He had found the perfect place for Dominique's tomb.

He had chosen St. Louis Cemetery No. 2 specifically because of the sexton. The man was conscientious. Most conscientious, indeed. Lafitte had been surreptitiously observing him for weeks. All day long, he puttered about, caring for the tombs as if they housed his own loved ones. He was a man who would notice the most minor aberration. He was precisely the man Lafitte needed if his plan were to work.

The man allowed himself only one break in his workday, and during this time, he engaged in the oddest behavior. He would sit on a bench in the middle of the cemetery, not far from where Dominique's tomb would be built, and read aloud from a book. Lafitte noticed it was always the same book. The sexton would read a chapter or two each day, then rise from the bench and continue his duties. It took Lafitte some time to discern which book the man was reading. Lafitte was careful to conceal himself so that the sexton never saw him hanging about the cemetery, but one day he ventured a bit closer and peered over the man's shoulder. He could see the title of the volume he held, *The Last of the Mohicans. Here is a man who is ripe for an adventure,* he had thought. *Here is the man to tell my story.*

It was not long after the tomb was completed that Dominique died. Lafitte was proud and touched that the citizens of New Orleans honored Dominique with a grand funeral. No one deserved it more. Lafitte had been there on that day, disguised again, of course. He could not miss seeing Dominique one last time.

Once Dominique was buried, Lafitte and one of his most trusted Freemason brothers entered the cemetery at night, wrenches and chisels in hand, and removed the nameplate from Dominique's tomb. Lafitte would have found the work exceedingly difficult by himself, but with the strength of two men, they accomplished the task. They removed more marble from the back of the nameplate than was necessary, but this was by design. By the time they were finished, the marble nameplate was little more than a thin veneer. Lafitte slipped the book into the crevice they had carved for that purpose and returned the now-compromised nameplate to the tomb, taking great care to bolt it into place without cracking it. That would come later, or so Lafitte hoped. Lafitte and his accomplice hauled off their tools and the excess marble and left the cemetery. The man with Lafitte never asked why they were engaging in such peculiar work so late at night, and Lafitte did not tell him. Lafitte had chosen him for his ability to keep quiet and his remarkable lack of curiosity. Such friends had been useful to Lafitte in the past and continued to prove their worth.

Once that task was complete, Lafitte had nothing more to do but bide his time and wait for the inevitable summer rains and oppressive heat to put his plan in motion. He hoped that the spring rains would set up a pattern for the sexton to keep an eye on Dominique's tomb, located in that troublesome low spot, as it was. He hoped that over time, the cold winter and scorching summer would wreak havoc on the thinned-out marble and bow or crack it. He did not know it would do both. He hoped he'd gauged the sexton correctly, as a man who would take pride in the cemetery and keep the areas around the tombs clear of dirt and debris as best as he could. He hoped the sexton would notice the defective nameplate and be curious enough to investigate. He hoped the man would find the journal and tell the story. Jean Lafitte did not generally rely on hope, but sometimes hope was all a man had.

He had been growing exceedingly tired of his life in Barataria by then. Hiding out in the bayous was not the life he had envisioned. He was older now. Past injuries were returning to taunt him, the pain a constant reminder that he was no longer in his prime. He wished to spend what time he had left in New Orleans. It was a risk, certainly, but one he was willing to take. People, by and large, believed him to be dead, whether as a casualty of the naval battle he had engaged in while captaining the *General Santander* or through any number of other rumors that flew about the city and beyond regarding the death of the notorious pirate. He knew he could disguise himself, and he felt reasonably certain that most would not reveal his identity even if they could somehow guess it, but he could not be sure. And there were others from his past who would reveal his identity if given the opportunity. He needed an extra layer of protection. He needed people to think he was dead. Again. What man would fake his death not once but twice? What man would go to such great lengths and then hide in plain sight? Lafitte could think of such a man.

Just as in the battle aboard the *General Santander,* another regrettable situation provided an ideal opportunity if one was shrewd enough to recognize it and bold enough to seize it. After he realized the dire state of Dominique's health, his plan had shifted. He once again used less-than-ideal circumstances as the impetus to remake himself. He had taken the utmost care in writing the journal, even though he knew he must complete it quickly. Dominique would not live long. In those chaotic weeks before Dominique died, Lafitte had tirelessly written an account of his own life and "death." He had to be cautious in writing it. The journal needed to walk a fine line. The story itself must be exciting, but it must be a pirate's tale without treasure. Otherwise, who would share it? And Lafitte needed the story to be shared.

He had assumed that the sexton would approach one of the broadsheets or newspapers in New Orleans with the journal. Perhaps the *Louisiana Chronicle* or the *New Orleans Bee*. He could sell the story and make a tidy profit. Lafitte would have been quite happy with that outcome. He did not need everyone to believe he was dead, but he did need to plant a seed of doubt, to make those who would search for him less aggressive in their efforts, to allow enough time to pass for his hunters to move on to other, more pressing matters.

The sexton's decision to turn the journal's account into an adventure novel exceeded Lafitte's expectations. He was enjoying the fame and notoriety, albeit from afar. It was the best possible outcome, as far as he was concerned. Captain Jean Lafitte's name was on everyone's lips, yet no one was looking for him. He had heard people discussing the book as he went about his business in the city, a rare occurrence, which spoke even more to its popularity. And he was right here to witness it all. He was very pleased indeed. And exceptionally curious. He wanted to read the book for himself. He felt enough time had passed that it would be safe to enter Chapter and Verse and purchase a copy of Mr. Whitney's book.

Additionally, he acknowledged to himself that he wished to meet Mr. Whitney. He had spent time observing him in the cemetery and felt an odd kinship with the man who brought his tale to the world. Mr. Whitney had performed a valuable service for Lafitte, and he owed the former cemetery sexton a debt of gratitude that he wished to repay in some small way, even if it was a foolish risk. He needed to shake the man's hand and thank him. That is what he had done this afternoon.

Lafitte's thoughts drifted back to Tobias's parting words: *All shall be revealed.* Such an honest man, Mr. Whitney. He believed he knew the truth behind the journal. He was probably reassessing what that truth was after today, since Lafitte had given him the clues necessary to discover that Lafitte had written the journal. He had no doubt Mr. Whitney had arrived at that conclusion. He was too bright a man not to do so. Mr. Whitney must feel a sense of satisfaction, believing that he had finally solved all the journal's mysteries. Lafitte was glad that the man who had given him protection and the freedom to live out the remainder of his life in his home would sleep better knowing there was nothing further to puzzle over. How wrong he was.

All shall be revealed. Mr. Whitney was partially correct. All that Lafitte wanted to be revealed had been revealed. Nothing more. Revealed as Lafitte intended it to be. So many believed the Whitneys' version to be true. Lafitte suspected the Whitneys themselves believed it. They seemed an honest, trusting sort. It was for the best. They would sell many books with this version of Lafitte's tale. People love a good story and are keen to believe what is presented to them. But perhaps the Whitneys should have been more cautious. Perhaps they should have asked more questions. Lafitte wondered if Mr. Whitney might have harbored some slight doubt about the journal's authenticity. He was smart. He should know better than to trust a pirate. Well, after today, he knew, or at least he knew more than most.

He picked up the package from the table beside him and unwrapped the book—*The Amazing Adventure of the Life and Death of the Pirate Jean Laffite, Terror of the Gulf.* The title made him chuckle. *Jean Lafitte, Terror of the Gulf. Jean Lafitte.* What a dashing name for a pirate. He had called himself Lafitte for so long that he almost believed it was his name.

But of course, it was no more his surname than it was Pierre's or Alexandre's. Lafitte was as fine a French name as any, just as Pierre and Alexandre (or Dominique) were as fine a "brother" as any. It was of no consequence now, regardless. They had been brothers in all the ways that truly mattered.

A strange realization settled upon the man who called himself Lafitte, Du Bois, and Huntington. No one still walking this earth knew his real name. *Some secrets shall never be revealed.* A pirate must protect his identity at all costs. He truly had learned that from Dominique. *My name is my treasure. I do not care to share it.* He had kept that treasure safely buried. It was a treasure no one would find.

Chapter Twenty-One

New Orleans

October 1833

Tobias walked from his shop on Chartres Street toward St. Louis Cemetery No. 2 for his daily visit. He had continued to sit on his bench and read, even though he no longer worked there. The routine made him feel grounded, and the stroll gave him some time to himself. Lately, his thoughts had been cheerful, although it was difficult to feel maudlin on such a pleasant day. He felt a bit guilty for leaving Chapter and Verse to go to the cemetery, but Mssr. Loutrel had taken to minding the shop while Tobias was away, so that he could leave without worry. He seemed to understand that Tobias needed this, particularly today.

Mssr. Loutrel was a wise man. Tobias truly did require quiet time. Mary Catherine had increased her yelling to a level Tobias had to admit was impressive, although if her pitch rose any higher, only the street dogs would be able to hear her. Not one to do things by half measures, Mary Catherine had also increased the number of tirades, an impressive feat to Tobias's mind, considering her normal frequency. Everyone seemed to "work her last nerve," as she often announced. He could hardly blame her, considering she was not sleeping well as of late. The baby seemed to become active at night when she tried to recline. Tobias had not slept well either, as Mary Catherine felt he should be awake along with her, and to that end, elbowed him painfully in the ribs whenever she was unable to rest. She found it necessary in these sleepless moments to inform him for the thousandth time that this child must have longer legs than the boys, for all the kicking he was doing.

Tobias suspected that the activity level keeping Mary Catherine awake at night indicated she was carrying more than one child. The amount of movement, coupled with his wife's impressive proportions, reminded him of when she'd carried their twins, Riley and Imogen. He had not mentioned his suspicions to her, but he figured she was far enough along that they would find out soon enough. That was for the best because, in addition to her incandescent mood, Mary Catherine's abdomen was, at present, protruding at an alarming angle. Her slight build and short stature allowed little room for the child, so she seemed to grow forever outward. Tobias was more than slightly concerned she might topple over forward if she did not give birth soon.

Despite the challenges for Mary Catherine and, by extension, Tobias, he was thrilled to have another child and felt exorbitantly grateful. His sons were thriving, he had Chapter and Verse back, and he had the promise of new life on the horizon. All the pain he had gone through made this present moment that much sweeter. He was thankful for the sense of belonging in a place where his memories lived, both happy and sad.

He entered St. Louis No. 2 and made his way to his usual bench. Tobias felt eyes on him, but it was no longer unsettling. He was just another visitor to the cemetery, and the sexton would be about, glancing his way from time to time. Besides, he'd finally solved the mystery of who had been watching him, or more accurately, Mary Catherine had solved it. Looking back on it, he wondered how he had not put the clues together sooner. In fact, her reaction to his news that he suspected Jean Lafitte was still alive and had assumed the alias of an American living in New Orleans had struck him as one of the most curious aspects of a very curious series of events.

"Ah, so it was Lafitte who wrote the journal after all," she'd said when he told her, not even bothering to take her eyes off the pot of chicken stew she was cooking.

"Kitten, why don't you seem surprised? This is remarkable news!"

"It never made a bit of sense to me that Dominique You wrote it," she'd said.

"What do you mean?"

"Ask yourself—what had he to gain by setting down the tale? No pirate, reformed or not, would disclose the whereabouts of his treasure. I thought from the start that wasn't the purpose at all. So why did he write the journal?"

"To tell the world Lafitte's story, of course," said Tobias.

"Aye, that's what the journal claims, but why?" pressed Mary Catherine.

Tobias had considered this for a moment before replying. "I thought it was so Dominique You could salvage his brother's good name and tell his true story. But even if Lafitte wrote it, the purpose could remain the same—he wanted history to view him favorably."

"That may have been a pleasant extra, but I'd say the real reason was practical. It's always struck me as strange that the author would go to such pains to hide it, knowing it'd be found soon enough when the tomb changed hands."

Tobias said, "But fifty years would have passed before then. Enough time would have gone by that no one could be hurt by the story coming to light."

"But think about it—the writer was careful, even vague about who was involved. Who'd have been hurt if the journal were found the moment it was written? No—I've long thought you were the one it was meant for, though someone wished to make you believe you'd happened upon it by chance."

"You think Captain Lafitte meant for me to find it sooner rather than later?"

"Aye, that was my conclusion."

"And he was watching, waiting to see when I would?"

"And no doubt after, to see what you'd do with it," Mary Catherine added.

"That's why you weren't concerned when I told you I felt eyes upon me that day in the cemetery."

"I couldn't know for certain it was him, of course, but it made sense. I asked myself who had the most to gain from you finding the journal, and every time, I came back to Lafitte. After all, the man had already feigned his death once, and how many times did he warn us in the journal that we shouldn't trust a pirate? He never wanted his secrets to stay buried. He needed you to tell them. He gambled his freedom on it. And he won."

Tobias had felt a most uncharacteristic anger welling up. "You deduced all of this, yet you said nothing to me? Why would you keep me in the dark?"

She'd matched his sharp tone without flinching. "You needed the adventure that journal gave you. You never questioned a thing because you didn't care to. The answers didn't matter half as much as the chase." She'd placed a hand on his arm, in an uncharacteristically gentle gesture. "I once told you the book was the treasure. What do you think I meant by that?"

"That we would write an adventure tale, and that was the real treasure the book led us to. And you were right. It's how I bought back Chapter and Verse, after all."

"Aye, and that was the truth. But it was only half of it. The book was the treasure, but the treasure was the book."

Tobias threw up his hands in frustration. "Enough riddles!"

Mary Catherine's lips turned down in displeasure at his outburst, but then she explained her meaning. "The book drew you back into the world, back to the boys and me. From that very first evening you came home and asked me to translate it for you, you were changed for the better. *That* was the real treasure we found within its pages."

"But I was simply a pawn. Lafitte used me to tell his story," he said softly.

"Perhaps. But he gave you a gift as well. I could see the power in it, but I had to let the book work its magic on you. Don't you understand—I'd have done anything to bring you back to us, Tobias. Even if it meant keeping my suspicions from you."

When Tobias looked into her green eyes, he saw that they were misty.

She turned back to her simmering pot with a sniff. "Now off with you if you ever want supper on the table. And tell those boys to wash up good this time. Did you even see the dirt beneath Connor's fingernails this morning? That boy looks as though he lives in a barn!"

He'd observed her for a fleeting moment, bustling about the tiny kitchen, her usual choleric temperament restored, and wondered how he'd gotten so lucky.

He smiled now at the memory, then read the tomb in front of him, as was his habit, before reaching into his pocket for his book.

* * *

Jeremiah Wallace was proud of his position as sexton of St. Louis Cemetery No. 2. He had come a long way and worked diligently for this opportunity. As a free man of color, reaching this point had not been easy. He had spent years working below his skill level in maintenance. But now that he was sexton, he was finally earning a decent wage and could support his wife and baby girl. Most would not relish working in a cemetery, and he had been taken aback a bit that the man who had the job before him had been white. Of course, the man was Irish, and Jeremiah figured he was probably thrilled not to be a ditcher living in a shack next to a mucky, mosquito-infested dig site. Jeremiah shuddered at the thought. The cemetery and its unfortunate smells were not so bad, he mused. At least the inhabitants were quiet, a joke he liked to share with folks when they teased him about his job.

Jeremiah was proud of his position. He walked around the cemetery, ensuring everything was in order, as was his routine. He understood Mr. Whitney had been meticulous about fulfilling his responsibilities. Jeremiah was equally diligent in his duties. When he turned the corner to the oldest part of the cemetery, he paused at the familiar sight before him.

Sitting on a bench facing a tomb was Mr. Whitney. Even though he resigned as sexton at St. Louis Cemetery No. 2 almost two years ago, the man came nearly every day. It was always the same routine. He would stay for a short spell, then leave. The man sat on the same bench, pulled a book out of his pocket, and read aloud. At first, Jeremiah had found this behavior perplexing, if not unsettling. He had tried to ignore it for a while, but he could not fathom why a man would come to a cemetery daily to read a book. Out loud. And the oddest part about this behavior is that the book the man read was the same one. He read it all the way through, a few chapters each day, and then started over. At one point, a month or so ago, Jeremiah could no longer stand it and asked the man what he was doing.

Mr. Whitney had responded, "Reading."

Jeremiah shook his head at the memory. You just could never figure people out.

Jeremiah watched as Mr. Whitney flipped the book open and paused before reading, looking at the tomb before him. No man should look so serene in a cemetery, at least not to Jeremiah's way of thinking. Jeremiah himself did not feel entirely comfortable here, if he was being honest. But Jeremiah had to remind himself that the man had once worked here, too. He wondered why the man would keep returning to his former place of employment almost daily. Why had he left the job at all?

Jeremiah studied Mr. Whitney's features from across the path, careful not to let him know he was being observed. Jeremiah did not wish to appear rude. He was simply curious about this odd behavior. A man should be left alone in his grief. He should not be subjected to another person's scrutiny, Jeremiah reminded himself. But it was strange that for someone who spent so much time voluntarily at a cemetery, Mr. Whitney did not seem grief-stricken or even sad. He appeared to genuinely enjoy sitting on the bench, watching the tomb, and reading.

He assumed Mr. Whitney was coming to pay his respects to his loved ones, although not many visited so regularly. Jeremiah suspected the man had grown accustomed to being near their final resting place while working in the cemetery, and that perhaps he missed seeing the tomb each day. He had worked here for three years, after all. Mr. Whitney had taken the job in 1828. That made sense. The names carved on the tomb's faceplate, which the man sat directly in front of and read aloud to, had the same date, 1828. Jeremiah's curiosity became a more compelling force than his mother's carefully instilled good manners and got the better of him. He hazarded a closer look at the tomb before which Mr. Whitney sat.

Kathleen Whitney b. 3 September 1825, d. 18 October 1828
Riley Whitney b. 18 January 1828, d. 27 October 1828

Imogen Whitney b. 18 January 1828, d. 29 October 1828
Beloved children of Tobias and Mary Catherine Whitney
God has you in His keeping. We have you in our hearts.

Today was October 18. Jeremiah realized with a shudder that Kathleen Whitney had died on this day five years ago. He wondered for a moment if Mr. Whitney would do anything out of the ordinary to commemorate the day. Jeremiah looked more carefully at the man, and sure enough, he noticed that he had pulled out a new book today. This was highly unusual, as far as Jeremiah knew. Although he was loath to admit it, curiosity had gotten the better of him one day, and he had taken a peek at the book the man was reading. It was *The Last of the Mohicans*. And over the past few months, he had heard dribs and drabs of the story as he walked about the cemetery, attending to his duties. Jeremiah still could not understand reading aloud in a cemetery, never mind reading the same book over and over, but he had to admit that this one seemed exciting and full of action. Apparently, the man had finally grown tired of the book, as he had moved on to a new one.

Jeremiah tried to ignore Mr. Whitney and focus on the glorious weather. It was a picture-perfect day, with hardly a cloud in the sky. The gentle breeze carried the man's words over to Jeremiah, and even though he knew that his mother would disapprove, he could not help but hear, "My name is Dominique You, and I have a tale to tell."

Afterword

The adage that truth is stranger than fiction accurately describes the story behind this novel. Jean Lafitte's life reads like an adventure tale that is too unbelievable to possibly be true. The story of how this book came to be is equally incredible.

The idea was right in front of me throughout my childhood. My parents had some framed papers hanging on the wall in our dining room. They were oversized, browned with age, and written in flowing script. They were also in French and, therefore, incomprehensible to me. I only had a smattering of French that the Ursulines taught me, and the early nineteenth-century handwriting, with its flourishes and scratch-outs, was too much of a challenge. I remember lying on the floor with my feet propped up against the wall when my parents weren't looking, gazing up at the parchment within the frame, attempting to decipher the words.

When I asked about them, my parents told me they were "a legal contract to do something illegal." The papers were written by Jean Lafitte and delineated the terms and conditions for one of his privateering captains to commandeer ships. They outlined in meticulous detail what was to happen and how the spoils were to be divided, leaving nothing to chance. Here was a man who ran a well-organized business. However, the nature of that business was shady at best, depending on whether you believe he was acting as a government-sanctioned privateer or as a pirate.

Those papers were a fascinating mystery to me—one I very much wanted to solve. Yet, try as I might, I could recognize only the last two words in the document. They were the man's signature, *Jn Laffite*, spelled with two f's and one t, as he had done all his life (contrary to the Americanized spelling of his name, with one f and two t's, which is more often used, even in Louisiana).

Underneath his signature was the date, 1805. As a child, I thought the year written across the final page of the contract seemed so impossibly long ago. Yet there it was, in my dining room, a tangible connection to some shadowy past version of our city, New Orleans. I used to daydream about what it was like to live here that long ago.

Those papers were in the background of my life growing up. They bore witness to all our major life events as celebrated in a formal dining room: holidays, parties, just-because family dinners. Enigmatic and inscrutable, they came to symbolize mystery and adventure for me. They were written by a pirate, after all, and one that, according to family lore, was a distant relative, though we could never prove it. My mother's grandmother was a Saint Amant and owned land in Barataria, supposedly land inherited from Captain Jean Lafitte, through an illegitimate branch of the family. There are many such stories around this part of the world, given that Jean Lafitte was a popular guy in his time. Regardless, my paternal grandfather had done some business in London and was repaid with these papers, which he gave to his daughter-in-law (my mother) because of her supposed connection to the man.

During Hurricane Katrina, my parents' home suffered extensive damage. It is an antebellum beauty that has seen her fair share of hurricanes, but this one was different. My parents knew it was time to store these papers in a place where they would be properly cared for and made accessible to scholars. They decided to place them with the Historic New Orleans Collection. As a result, researchers and scholars gained access to these papers, and my mother would occasionally receive calls about them, inquiring about how she had acquired them, what she knew about them, and so forth. As a thank you for her help, these scholars would often mail her copies of their books, which she shared with me.

I wonder if growing up with those papers sparked my interest in history. If it did, I was not consciously aware of it. I went on to earn a PhD in history, but I never studied Jean Lafitte. He was too familiar to consider a subject for scholarly research.

That changed in the spring of 2023, when my mother and I had lunch with a pair of Lafitte scholars, also a mother-daughter pair, coincidentally. I was fascinated by their theory that Jean Lafitte had faked his death and ended up in Lincolnton, North Carolina, where he lived to a ripe old age. The historian in me was intrigued at this point, and I began researching Lafitte, merely to satisfy my curiosity. I began to imagine what Lafitte might have done with the second half of his life had he managed to fake his death. What would he have wanted his legacy to be? How would he have wanted his story told? The result of my musings is *Lafitte Lives*. It is a combination of a child's daydreams about the past and an adult's curiosity about a man whose life was too incredible to be believed.

Jean Lafitte's life events read like an adventure novel, which is why he has been the subject of extensive historical study. However, there is little consensus about his life or identity. Lafitte scholars disagree on even the most basic details, such as when he was born, where he was born, and when he died. If there is one thing I can state with certainty regarding Jean Lafitte, it's that very little is certain. While frustrating for historians, those gray areas yield endless possibilities for a novel.

Here is where I should confess that when faced with differing versions of a life event, I chose the version that best fit the story I wanted to tell. Allowing myself the creative freedom to pick and choose from various sources while attempting to adhere to the historical record as much as possible helped me craft (what I hope is) an engaging and satisfying story. After all, I was not just trying to tell the story of his life and what he might have done afterward if he staged his death. I had to think about what Lafitte would want people to believe about his life. And like any good sailor, I would imagine he could spin a yarn. Therefore, the challenge I faced when writing Dominique You's journal was that I had to write only what I imagined Jean Lafitte would want revealed about himself. As the reader now knows, he is the true author. This informed which parts of his life I included, which I merely alluded to, and which I left out altogether. I will try to indicate where I strayed most egregiously from the historical record, but generally speaking, the events up to his staged death (the first, in 1823) are supported by historical fact, albeit his version of the facts, spun to show him in the best light.

Now onto the "what's true" part. That depends on which sources are considered trustworthy: case in point, Jean Lafitte's journal, *The Memoirs of Jean Lafitte*. I drew a considerable amount of material from this source about his early life, and, as I will mention later, his change of heart regarding slavery. The dilemma is that the journal's authenticity is a hotly contested topic among Lafitte scholars. For example, two scholars who have studied my family's Lafitte papers have reached two different conclusions regarding the memoirs. One firmly believes it to be authentic (Francisco Forrest Martin's *Pirates, Puns, and Prizes on the Peace River*), while the other considers it spurious (Ashley Oliphant and Beth Yarbrough's *Jean Laffite Revealed*).

It might be helpful for me to delineate which aspects of his life, as portrayed in this novel, are true, or at least those I believe to be true, based on my research, and which are products of my imagination.

Jean Lafitte's birthdate and place of birth: I chose to use the location and date as depicted in his memoirs, but there are divergent opinions on this. Most seem to think he was born in the early 1780s.

Dominique You: There was a man who went by the name Dominique You (sometimes spelled Youx). Some scholars believe he was Alexandre Lafitte, half-brother of Jean Lafitte. Lafitte claims this is the case in his memoirs. However, no journal written by Dominique You has ever surfaced, and it is possible he was illiterate, though I cannot confirm this. I used Lafitte's memoirs as the basis for the journal's description of Jean's life events up to his staged death, including the influence of his brother, Alexandre (Dominique You), on his and Pierre's desire to become privateers. However, I took some creative liberties with the information.

Dominique You's tomb: His actual tomb is in St. Louis Cemetery No. 2 in New Orleans. The description of the tomb, as well as the engraving on the nameplate, both the epitaph and the Freemasonry symbol, are all accurate. Its deliberate positioning in a low spot in the cemetery and Jean Lafitte's tampering with the marble nameplate and placing the journal inside are fiction.

Pierre Lafitte: According to Lafitte's memoirs, he is Jean's brother. He handled the business side of the brothers' enterprises in Barataria and

Galveston. He probably did own a blacksmith shop in the French Quarter, and most scholars believe he died in Mexico in 1821.

Grambo: He is an amalgamation of two different pirates. In *New Orleans: The Place and the People*, Grace King recounts a story told by an old Baratarian about a pirate named Grambo. The story of one of his men opposing Lafitte and Lafitte's response of drawing his pistol and shooting the man comes from this account. The description of his physical appearance and temperament is based on another pirate, William Mitchell, who was a pirate in the Gulf. Mitchell really did fake his death through a newspaper obituary. I took some creative license, combining the two pirates to create the Grambo character.

The Whitneys: Tobias, Mary Catherine, and their children are all fictitious. They represent the experience of Irish settlers in New Orleans. Those who came to New Orleans in the late eighteenth century and the early years of the nineteenth century generally fared better than the droves of Irish Immigrants arriving in the 1820s and 1830s. The conditions surrounding the "ditchers" excavating the Basin Street Canal are factual.

Barataria and Galveston: The general events described are based on the Lafitte brothers' work as privateers. They had a fleet of ships in both places, and they sold goods (illegally) from the privateering done by those ships.

W.C.C. Claiborne: He was the first governor of Louisiana, and he had a contentious relationship with the Lafittes. The raids on Barataria are true, as was the reward he offered for Jean Lafitte's capture and the retaliatory award for Claiborne's capture. The letter Jean Lafitte wrote to him about being a sheep wanting to return to the fold is factual.

The Battle of New Orleans: Most of this is historically accurate. Dominique You led a band of pirates in an artillery unit. The comments by Andrew Jackson regarding his skill and bravery are historically accurate, as is the participation of the Lafitte brothers in the celebrations following the battle. Another historically accurate component is the Ursuline nuns leading the city in prayer the night before the battle. They prayed to Our Lady of Prompt Succor. The national shrine to her is now at the school's State Street campus. It is a stunning historic church.

Freemasons: The journal hints at Freemasonry throughout, but it does not go into detail, mainly because I did not think Jean Lafitte would reveal much about them, particularly since he hoped the journal would be discovered sooner rather than later. It is true that Dominique You was a Freemason; in fact, there is a lodge named after him in the area. There is no evidence that Jean was one, but some scholars believe he may have been.

Plans for the rescue of Napoleon and the Bonapartists: Here we enter the shadowy realm of Lafitte folklore. The Bonapartists in Alabama (the Vine and Olive Colony) and Galveston (Champ d'Asile) are historically accurate. Scholars believe that Nicolas Girod (who really was the mayor of New Orleans and spoke only French) devised a plan to rescue the emperor and constructed (or remodeled) the building now known as the Napoleon House to serve as Napoleon's residence when he was brought to New Orleans. New Orleans folklore holds that Girod enlisted the Lafittes' help in the rescue attempt and that Dominique You oversaw the planning. They were set to go when word came, just before their departure, of the emperor's death. The submarine part of the plan is not mentioned in this legend. However, there were many plots to rescue Napoleon, including using a submarine like the one I described.

Robert Fulton invented a submarine as early as 1806. A man named Tom Johnson was a smuggler and builder of submarines. He claimed to have been enlisted by Bonapartists to rescue Napoleon. I derived parts of the plan depicted in the novel, specifically the bosun's chair, from his account. Some scholars believe the Freemasons may have been involved in plans to rescue the emperor, but there is no evidence to support this claim. There are even legends that Jean Lafitte rescued Napoleon, but that he died at sea before he could bring him back to New Orleans. There is no proof to support this claim either, though the story seems more believable after a few drinks at the Napoleon House.

Le Brave and Captain Desfarges: The account of his hanging is historically accurate, including his attempt to shoot himself or drown himself rather than face the humiliation of the gallows. Some of the documents my family was given include this captain's privateering activities aboard the *Le Brave*, so, of course, I had to include his story.

Lafitte and the slave trade: The Lafitte brothers were involved in the slave trade, specifically in the buying and selling of human beings. If Jean's memoirs are to be believed, he came to regret his actions deeply and became an abolitionist in later life. I chose to use that theme in this book, assuming shame and regret might have kept him from going into too much detail about his activities in that realm. Therefore, he alludes to the slave trade but does not elucidate. One further note: the scheme to turn in enslaved people to authorities, collect the reward, then repurchase them at auction was employed by the Bowie brothers, as outlined in William C. Davis's *The Pirates Lafitte*.

The Lafitte brothers' time as spies: When it came to spying, I felt Jean Lafitte would mention it because others were aware of it, and he would therefore feel the need to address it and defend his actions. It does appear that he spied for Spain, although it is unclear whether he acted as a double agent for the United States. He was most likely in cahoots with Mexico, further complicating the situation. I imagine he felt trapped after leaving Barataria and wanted to make a new start in Galveston, which required a great deal of capital to get the place up and running.

Faking his death: In *Memoirs* and sources such as Ashley Oliphant and Beth Yarbrough's *Jean Lafitte Revealed*, Jean fakes his death. There are multiple accounts of his death, and while most have him "dying" in the early 1820s, there is no real consensus. I chose to use Davis's account of his death, although he does not argue that Jean Lafitte faked his death. I wanted a sea battle for my purposes, as I imagined Lafitte would want people to think he died that way. Of course, the second staged death is entirely fictitious.

This leads me to the part of the novel following his faked death. Here is where my imagination completely took over the story. Because there is no documented history of his life after the 1820s, I could speculate about what I thought might have happened or what Jean Lafitte would have wanted people to believe he did. Therefore, the short answer to what is true about that part of the book is absolutely nothing.

Olivia: She is a fictitious character, although her fellow Voodoo practitioners (Dr. John, Marie Laveau, etc.) were actual people.

Southern Underground Railroad: Although there is no proof that Jean Lafitte assisted in bringing enslaved individuals to freedom, I very much wanted to tell the story of the Southern Underground Railroad, which has not received the historical research it deserves. Learning about the perilous journey of enslaved people as they crossed the Sabine River into freedom was fascinating. I hope more scholars will study it and bring to light the stories of those involved. If you would like to learn more, see Alice L. Baumgartner's *South to Freedom: Runaway Slaves to Mexico and the Road to the Civil War.*

I would like to apologize for using terms in the novel that may be offensive to contemporary readers. "Octoroon, mulattoes, slaves, [and] free people of color" were the categories and verbiage people used in the South in the early nineteenth century for legal purposes. Similarly, the term "Indians" was in use during that time. I used these terms for historical accuracy.

A note on Lafitte's legacy in New Orleans: There are remembrances of Jean Lafitte throughout New Orleans and southeast Louisiana, including a town in Barataria and a National Park, both named after him. There are streets that bear his name, and Lafitte's Blacksmith Shop Bar in the French Quarter, which purports to be the oldest structure in the United States used as a bar. If legend is to be believed, the building served as the base of operations for the Lafitte brothers' smuggling operations. Patrons and employees alike claim Lafitte still haunts the place. There is also the Jean Lafitte House on Esplanade Avenue, where legend has it he once lived and where hidden tunnels have been unearthed below the premises, possibly constructed for smuggling goods. And, of course, it's said to be haunted.

Although Jean Lafitte had a complicated relationship with the city of New Orleans, his ghost apparently does not. According to local legends, he is everywhere. He can occasionally be spotted making plans with the ghost of General Jackson in a room on the second floor of the Old Absinthe House, where their historic meeting took place before the Battle of New Orleans (and where his ghost is said to hang out with his entire crew and sometimes with Marie Laveau's ghost because the more the merrier). He is also said to haunt Pirate's Alley, near St. Louis Cathedral, where black markets took place.

I had the best time researching Lafitte, imagining what he would say, and what he might have gone on to do if he did fake his death. It was all great fun. I hope you enjoyed the story.

Finally, I would like to mention that I firmly believe Jean Lafitte was not his real name. I am convinced this is why there is such a discrepancy about where and when he was born. My takeaway is that Jean Lafitte did not want anyone to know his true identity. He was adept at hiding that information, as a skilled pirate should be. (I don't buy the "privateer" claim.) Well done, Captain Lafitte. Your name is your treasure; you did not care to share it with us.

A Note from the Author

Jean Lafitte spelled his own name *Laffite*. I use the Americanized spelling in this novel, as this is more common, even throughout Louisiana. There's a town named after Jean Lafitte, along with a national park, streets, and bars, most notably the one still operating in the blacksmith shop owned by the Lafitte brothers. All of these use the Americanized spelling (Lafitte), so that's the spelling I chose. I suspect Jean Laffite wouldn't approve.

Acknowledgments

This book would not have been possible without the help of so many.

A heartfelt thank you to everyone at Level Best Books for helping bring my vision to life! Special thanks to Verena Rose for seeing the potential in my book, to Deborah Well for her patient answers to my endless questions, and to Shawn Reilly Simmons for her excellent editing and stunning cover design.

I am grateful to my friends and family for reading early drafts of *Lafitte Lives* and providing feedback. Your suggestions have made it a much better book.

Thank you to my husband, Leni, who has been my biggest cheerleader throughout this adventure. Thanks to my son Jason and daughter-in-law Katie for getting married the day before my youngest daughter Winky went off to college—that swift kick into empty-nesthood sparked my writing journey. And thank you to Hayley for being my only child who actually reads my books!

Finally, I want to thank my parents for instilling in me a love of history. If you hadn't hung Lafitte's papers in our dining room for all those years, this book wouldn't exist.

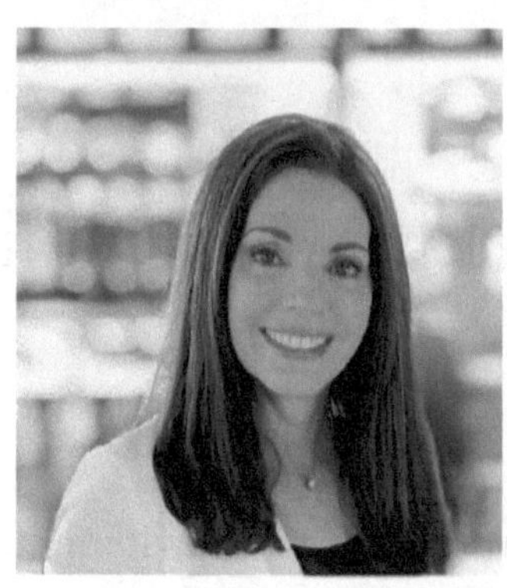

About the Author

Christi Keating Sumich is a lifelong resident of New Orleans. She is married to her high school sweetheart and is the mother of three grown children (plus a daughter-in-law). She has a soft spot for "unconventionally attractive" animals who need homes. Her claim to fame is being the winningest contestant on Hollywood Squares.

She holds a PhD in history from Tulane University and a master's degree in English. She has taught history classes at Tulane University and Loyola University New Orleans.

Christi's writing combines her fascination with history with her love of the mystery genre. Her debut novel is *Lafitte Lives* (Level Best Books, February 2026), a historical mystery centered around her ancestor, the notorious pirate Jean Lafitte. She is also the author of the Old New Orleans Bookshop Mysteries, featuring characters from *Lafitte Lives*. *The Swamp Ghost* is the first book in the series (Level Best Books, September 2026).

Christi and her mom, Sharon Keating, are the co-authors of *Hauntingly Good Spirits: New Orleans Cocktails to Die For* (Wellfleet Press, August 2024) and *The Brandy Milk Punch* (Louisiana State University Press, March 2025), part of the Iconic New Orleans Cocktail Series.

AUTHOR WEBSITE:
   https://christisumich.com/

SOCIAL MEDIA HANDLES (live links):
   https://www.facebook.com/christi.keating.sumich.author/about?sectio
n=contact-info
   https://www.instagram.com/christisumich/

Also by Christi Keating Sumich

The Brandy Milk Punch (Louisiana State University Press, March 2025), part of the Iconic New Orleans Cocktail Series (with Sharon Keating)

Hauntingly Good Spirits: New Orleans Cocktails to Die For (Wellfleet Press, August 2024) (with Sharon Keating)

Divine Doctors and Dreadful Distempers: How Practicing Medicine Became a Respectable Profession (Brill 2013)

Don't miss the Whitneys' next adventure! Sign up for my newsletter to receive the first chapter of *The Swamp Ghost* and publication updates delivered straight to you at https://christisumich.com/

The Swamp Ghost

In 1833, Irish immigrants are hard at work digging the New Basin Canal, a waterway that will connect New Orleans to Lake Pontchartrain. When one of the workers sees a strange blue orb glowing in the swamp at night, he fears it is a Fifolet (fee-foo-lay) guarding Jean Lafitte's buried treasure. Legend has it that pirates killed a crewman and buried his body with their loot, dooming his ghost to stand guard forever. When the worker turns up dead the next morning, the men believe the site is cursed, and Aiden Doyle, the crew's leader, must uncover the truth or risk losing his job. When the newly formed police force refuses to investigate, Aiden seeks help from Mary Catherine Whitney, now renowned throughout New Orleans for her mystery-solving skills after she and her husband, Tobias, unraveled the secrets of the notorious pirate Jean Lafitte and wrote a popular adventure story about it. She'll need all her cleverness and wit to unlock the secrets of the Fifolet, and she may even need a little help from Captain Lafitte himself.

Continuing characters from *Lafitte Lives*, *The Swamp Ghost* is the first in the Old New Orleans Bookshop Mysteries, featuring Mary Catherine

Whitney, irascible wife, mother, and amateur sleuth in this charming series set in nineteenth-century New Orleans.

Coming September 2026 from Level Best Books

 **The Swamp Ghost**